Double Masquerade

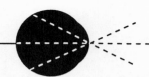

**This Large Print Book carries the
Seal of Approval of N.A.V.H.**

Double Masquerade

Martha Powers

Thorndike Press • Thorndike, Maine

Library of Congress Cataloging in Publication Data:

Powers, Martha.
    Double masquerade / Martha Powers.
       p. cm.
    ISBN 1-56054-146-6 (alk. paper : lg. print)
    1. Large type books. I. Title.
[PS3566.O888D68   1991]   90-28491
813'.54—dc20   CIP

Thorndike Press Large Print edition published in 1991
by arrangement with Berkley Publishing Group.

Cover photo by Alan J. LaVallee.

The tree indicium is a trademark of Thorndike Press.

This book is printed on acid-free, high opacity paper. ∞

To Kathryn Hills —
More and more I'm impressed by the
person you have become

To Paul Hills —
For eighteen years of great bridge
and an introduction to the
"treasure of my life"

prologue

1807

"An actress, my dear," Lady Yates said, "is merely a slut who can sing."

"Aunt Haydie!"

Lady Haydie Yates sniffed at the shocked expression on her niece's face. "This is no time for missish airs, gel. Might as well know what you're getting into before you make the first misstep."

Blaine Margaret Meriweather shifted uncomfortably on the satin settee and tried to face the older woman with a worldly air she was far from feeling. Smoothing the skirt of her black mourning gown, Blaine looked warily at the upright figure in the wing chair and tried not to flinch under the steely glance of the gold-hazel eyes so like her own.

"I realize, Aunt Haydie, what I propose would be considered outrageous by some, but I thought you, of all people, might have more sympathy with my idea. After all, you have always told me a woman should not be held

7

back by the conventions of society."

"No need to quote me, Blaine. I am well aware of all my tiresome preaching." The sixty-year-old Haydie waved her blue-veined hand in a dismissing gesture. "I am not unalterably opposed to the plan but I must be sure you are aware of all the pitfalls to this freakish start. A young gentlewoman does not become an actress without losing a great deal."

"It seems to me, Aunt, that there is little left to lose." Sadness tinged Blaine's voice and she swallowed back the rising lump in her throat.

"Thus speaks youth," Haydie said. "Believe me, child, there are things more important than money and land in the balance here. I cannot imagine what your father would think of such a decision."

"I can." A sad smile tugged at the edge of Blaine's generous mouth. "He would shout down the house while my stepmother Juliette would sniffle into a lacy handkerchief, her violet eyes awash with tears. Ah, Aunt Haydie, I miss them so."

"It was blessedly quick, child," the older woman said in bracing tones, then she snorted in annoyance. "A lot of trumpery, that kind of statement, but one must hold on to something. In all truth, I cannot believe that either your father or your stepmother suffered long after the carriage left the road. Your father was not one who would have been a cheerful invalid and Juliette was already terrified of growing old. She would have been devastated over any form of disfigurement. Perhaps my words are harsh, Blaine, but one can only deal with the present. They were a charming, improvident pair. And my brother's inability to think beyond today has landed us all in the soup."

Blaine sighed and leaned wearily against the back of the settee, noticing the worn spots on the satin upholstery. As her eyes roamed around the drawing room, she was aware that all of the furnishings needed attention. The room was clean enough. She had seen to that herself, but she ought to have considered redoing some of the coverings and adding new draperies. Now it was too late.

She had been in charge of the household, since she was fifteen, the year Valerian was born. Then her stepmother, having finally presented a male heir to her husband, demanded that they remove to London for the season. Blaine had been delighted with the responsibility of the estate and equally pleased to be with her half sister, Fleur, and the new baby, who were also left behind at Weathers, the family estate. For six years, the three children had seen little of their parents except for at Christmas and the occasional house party. They had been happy years but now, with the death of her father and stepmother, Blaine could see that their comfortable way of life was truly threatened.

"Now, child, tell me about this cork-brained scheme."

Haydie's voice interrupted Blaine's musings and she tried to gather her thoughts. Without hesitation, she declared, "I would like to go to London and become an actress."

"I heard that part of the plan," Haydie said dryly. "It's the rest that I'm waiting to hear."

"Well, to be perfectly honest, I haven't worked out any of the details." A puckish grin widened her mouth and she peered through a cloud of dark lashes at her formidable relative. "I have given our difficulties a great deal of thought and I truly believe that this might be the answer to our present situation. You must admit, Aunt Haydie, that if we are not in the River Tick, our ship of state is sinking fast."

"Cheeky gel!" The old woman's words were snapped but there was a twinkle in the wise, old eyes that did not go unnoticed.

Blaine's face sobered as she continued. "According to the lawyer, everything has been left in trust for Valerian until he is twenty-one. Val is only five now. For the

10

most part the estate is self-supporting. I have gone over the books very carefully with Higgins, the estate manager. With stringent economies, we should all be able to survive but, in actual fact, we will live no better than our tenants for the next sixteen years. Worse, we will have nothing in reserve in case of some unlooked-for casualty."

"I cannot believe Cedric arranged things so poorly!" Haydie reached out for the glass of sherry on the table beside her. She took a bracing sip, then cocked her steel-gray head to the side as she stared at the portrait of her brother that hung above the fireplace. "On second thought, I can well believe it. At times, my dear, your father was a thundering lackwit. He assumed, like most of us, that he would live to his dotage."

Blaine's eyes rose to the portrait and she smiled. Her father was dressed in his hunting pinks, seated on a low stone wall, his hand on the head of his favorite hunting dog, Knolly. In the background was Weathers, the country home of generations of Meriweathers. The warm golden tones of the Cotswold stones shone like a beacon at the end of the narrow, tree-shaded lane. The land around the house was flat, perched as it was on the edge of Salisbury Plain in Wiltshire. Tears sheened Blaine's eyes at the thought that they might eventually be forced to sell the house that was Val's patrimony. Never! she vowed silently, and pulled herself erect to face her aunt with determination.

"We need money, Aunt Haydie," she announced. "Our tenants depend on us to help them in an emergency. There are no dowries for either Fleur or myself and there is nothing for Val's schooling. Papa wanted him to go to Cambridge and for that he will need tutors. Our governess can hardly prepare him."

"You're right, my dear. Frau Puffentraub has been fine for you and now Fleur, but Val must go off to school," Lady Yates agreed. "I have wondered in the last few days if it might not be a kindness to release the good frau to find another position."

"Let Puff go? Oh, Aunt Haydie," Blaine cried, a stricken look on her face as she thought of the sturdy little governess who for so many years had stood as mentor and friend.

"Buck up, child," Haydie said bracingly. "We'll manage. After all, I have my money."

"Oh, no! Papa left that allowance to you and you mustn't even consider spending it on us."

"Save it for my golden years? A thoroughly lowering thought." Haydie snorted and took another hearty sip of the sherry. "Wish Ceddie had thought to leave you girls a dowry.

That would be more to the point. Despite my allowance, there's not enough to scrape together to interest even a London Cit."

"For myself, I don't mind," Blaine said. "It's Fleur I worry about. She's going to be so beautiful, Aunt Haydie. Even at eleven, one can see her potential. Hair the color of sunshine and those lovely violet eyes, soft and velvety like pansies. With her beauty she could marry anyone and yet, by the time she's eighteen, we won't have enough for a season, let alone a dowry. It's an almighty shame."

Lady Yates smiled at the protectiveness of her niece for her half sister. Blaine's mother had died when the girl was eight and, a year later, Cedric, anxious for a heir, married Juliette Montclaire, a young French émigrée. The motherless child had welcomed her new stepmother and was overjoyed at the birth of her half sister Fleur. In the six years that followed, Juliette miscarried time after time and Fleur's care and entertainment fell primarily to Blaine. In Haydie's opinion, Blaine rather spoiled the girl but it was easy to do when faced with the angelic face and sweet temper of the child.

It was not that Blaine Margaret was a dowd. At twenty, Blaine was already a beauty. Her loveliness was far more classical, reminding one of an ancient Celtic princess. Her looks were not in fashion but Haydie suspected she would gain the title of "Incomparable" were she to go to London. She was tall with a gracefully rounded figure. Her skin was tanned instead of the sickly white that most debs preferred. She had high cheekbones, a wide mouth, and enormous golden hazel eyes. These attributes alone would have made her quite noticeable but added to this was a thick mane of white-blond hair that flowed down her back like a stream of satin. Once seen, she would not be forgotten.

The problem was that in Wiltshire the girl saw virtually no one. Haydie pursed her lips as she remembered chiding Juliette for not bringing Blaine to town for the season. She suspected the woman was slightly jealous of her stepdaughter, although to give the devil her due, she had never been outwardly unkind to Blaine. Treated her like a housekeeper and nanny, but then the girl herself had accepted the role with joy. Blaine had little idea of her own possibilities in the marriage mart — and now this foolishness.

"Why have you decided to become an actress?" Haydie asked, abruptly returning to the original argument.

"Because I think I would be good at it and I am little fitted for any other sort of work."

"The thought of you working at all does not

14

sit well with me, child."

"I know, Aunt Haydie," Blaine said, her voice soft with understanding. "But it is the only answer. We need money and I am young and healthy enough to try to earn it. I have given this a great deal of thought and I truly believe I have hit upon a solution. With my youth and appearance, I have little chance of a position as a governess or housekeeper. For a while I was considerably angry that my looks should count against me but then I realized that only in one profession would my appearance be a decided advantage."

"In point of fact, I can think of another profession," Haydie drawled, earning a blush from her discomfited niece. "Sorry, Blaine. My sharp tongue got the best of me. I shall try to be more circumspect in my comments. Pray continue."

"When faced with the realities of our situation, it would be truly missish of me not to consider such a step. Even if I could find some more respectable employment it would not improve our finances a great deal. A companion or governess usually receives no more than room and board. There is little employment open to a woman that could result in a good income." Blaine sighed heavily. She had given this a great deal of thought and hoped that her aunt would see the reasonableness of

15

her decision. "The theater seems the answer to my prayers. I think my appearance would gain some attention and I actually do have a talent for acting and singing. It will take some time but I truly believe I have a chance of being successful. Besides, Aunt Haydie, I see few alternatives."

In silence, Haydie raised her silver-rimmed lorgnette to better scrutinize the girl. "Are you fully aware of the kind of life the women of the theater world lead?"

"Yes, ma'am." Blaine raised her chin, her eyes unwavering under the older woman's gaze. "I have heard talk."

"Lord love you, child! Talk indeed. The gentlemen of the town go to the theaters to pick out their latest light o' loves. The women are coarse, loose-moraled, and pass through the men's hands like the cards in a gambling hell. Is this the sort of life you wish?"

"Of course not," Blaine said. "I have heard that some women conduct themselves properly. You told me yourself that Mrs. Siddons was quite acceptable."

"Unfortunately, Sarah Siddons is an exception. She is a woman of strong principles. Unlike most, she has been able to adhere to a strong liaison. She's been married for years and has three children. Of course now she is at least fifty, not a flighty chit of twenty.

16

Temptation is easy to avoid if not offered," Lady Yates intoned ominously. "The moment you set foot onstage, there will be a lineup of gentlemen from Covent Garden to the Haymarket, all quite eager to initiate you in the pleasures of the boudoir."

"Aunt Haydie!" Blaine said, covering her flushed cheeks with her hands.

"Are you objecting to my general statement or to the fact that I label them pleasures?" Haydie asked. "After a week in London, I suspect you'll be hard pressed to force a blush to your cheeks."

"It doesn't have to be that way," Blaine said. "You told me yourself that if a woman behaves in a ladylike manner, then she will be treated as such."

"That is true in a drawing room, but not likely in a theater."

"Aunt Haydie, can't you help me? I can only guess at the kind of situation that exists in the theater. With Papa and Juliette away so often, I have not even been out much in Wiltshire society. I truly believe that my idea is a good one but I am the veriest of babes concerning London."

Blaine rose and paced in front of the older woman, whose face was set in disapproving lines. She was silent for several moments then turned to face her aunt. "When you married

17

Uncle Neddy, he was a soldier and against your family's wishes you followed the drum. I'm sure that army life was far different from the society you had been brought up in, yet you survived. In order for Val and Fleur to survive, I must go to London. Will you help me?"

"And if I refuse?" Lady Yates raised the lorgnette, her hazel eyes unwavering.

Blaine blinked under the harsh gaze but raised her chin in determination. "Much as I would hate to go against your wishes, Aunt Haydie, I am going to London."

There was silence in the room as the old woman attempted to outstare the young girl. Slowly a smile curled the edges of Lady Yates's mouth.

"Good show, my dear." Haydie relaxed in her chair, saluting the startled girl with her glass of sherry. "Come and sit down. And don't look so surprised. I would never condone a whim but, as it seems you are determined to set your feet to the boards, I would be sadly remiss in not giving you all of my assistance."

Blaine crossed the carpet in quick strides, hugging her aunt with enthusiasm. She collapsed on the couch in relief, well aware that, despite her strong words, without the woman's support she never would be able to consider

18

such a venture. Lady Yates was an unconventional woman even in the enlightened year of 1807. With her advice, Blaine felt assured of success.

"It just so happens that I can give you some help," Haydie said, smiling benignly at the girl. "I had an abigail who was quite mad about the theater. Tate is working at Covent Garden as a dresser. I will send you to her and I will also send a letter to Sarah Siddons with whom I have some acquaintance. You could have no finer mentor. The woman is magnificent. Onstage and off, she maintains the highest standards. Her friendship may afford you some protection but, as an additional insurance, I will send Sergeant McCafferty with you."

Sarge had been batman to Lady Yates's husband. He was well above the normal height with a build that would dwarf an elephant. The combination of a lantern-jawed face and heavy-lidded eyes of an indeterminate color tended to be extremely intimidating when set above an enormous bull neck. Blaine had loved the gruff servant since she was a small child. For all his ferocious looks, he was a gentle giant. Although she would feel safe in his care, she hesitated.

"How can I take Sarge?" she asked. "He has always been in your household."

"I have decided to remain here with Fleur and Valerian," Haydie said calmly. "If you go off to London, someone must remain to fortify the battlements. No Friday-face, if you please, miss. This is not self-sacrifice on my part. My days of gallivanting are over. I have little enough to keep me occupied and besides I have found a real enjoyment in the children."

"I hadn't thought of how much I shall miss them," Blaine said, a quiver in her voice that matched the lost look in her golden eyes. "I hate to leave them after such a tragedy, but at least I can feel more at ease, knowing you will be here."

Having a fair knowledge of the risks her favorite niece would be taking, Haydie feared for the girl. Blessedly the young had little conception of the evil that predominated in the world. As she took in the innocent glow that surrounded Blaine, she had little doubt that her beauty would bring her to the notice of the London audiences. However it was this very radiance that would make her the target of the jaded rakes who flocked to the theaters, circling like birds of prey over a downed sheep.

Silence filled the room as the old woman stared thoughtfully up at the picture of her brother. Her mouth was pursed in displeasure and she tried not to show her anger at the realization of how his care-for-nothing attitude had led her niece to such a dramatic pass.

"No time for dark thoughts, child," Haydie said, swallowing a lump in her own throat. "Now is the time for planning. Naturally no one must know of your plans. It would be social disaster for both you and the children. You are too young to appreciate the scandal that would erupt if word of this became known. I cannot stress this enough and hope you will be discreet about your background when you arrive in London."

Blaine's eyes darkened at the thought of such a deception but she was wise enough to take her aunt's words to heart. "I will be careful, ma'am. But what about the children and the neighborhood?"

"It seems to me," Lady Yates continued, "that we shall have to put it about that you have gone to London to care for an aged, and no doubt crotchety, relative. Perhaps a cousin of your father's. The Meriweathers never did anything with any great success, except breed. Always whelped with the steady frequency of rabbits."

At this latest outrageous comment, Blaine fell into whoops of laughter. The amusement did much to encourage her for the coming adventure. Although part of her still feared the unknown, there was a core of excitement that she could not gainsay. There was an air of fantasy to the plan, almost as if she were going to a masquerade ball. She would hold to that thought and then she would not feel so shattered at the thought of parting from her family and all she held dear.

one

1813

"La Solitaire! La Solitaire!" The enthusiastic chant of the audience rose in a mighty roar as Blaine dropped into a deep curtsy. The flowers raining around her gave the appearance of snow until they fell to the stage in a profusion of color. With a graceful sweep of her arm, she shared the applause with the other players and ignored the tokens of affection thrown by the dandies in the pit. As if they expected no less, the cheers increased.

In the rising tide of approval, a single white rose fell at her feet.

Blaine raised her eyes to the private box of Lord Andrew Farrington. Even at a distance, she was able to see the sparkle of his green eyes as he raised his quizzing glass and kissed the rim in a sardonic salute. Her eyes swept him coolly before returning to the audience and she favored them with a smile of warmth that she denied her single admirer. Again, she dropped into a graceful curtsy, holding the pose for a moment and then rising to move away from "the rose," the bright spot of clustered footlights. She turned her back slightly, to indicate that the play was continuing, and the audience, used to this gesture by the popular actress, immediately quieted.

Blaine was enjoying the performance since it was the last one of this production. The pantomime was entitled *Love's Peril or the Wicked Captain of the Guard* and her part was Theodosia, Princess of Egypt, the frequently kidnapped heroine of the piece. The story was full of breathtaking escapes, sword fights, jugglers and, most fascinating of all, a performer who walked a rope that was suspended above the stage.

The audience always appreciated the light antics of the pantomimes after a tragedy. *Hamlet* had been the early bill, and since the Green Mews Theater had no license for spoken drama, a chorus had warbled incongruously throughout the play much to everyone's amusement.

As the green-liveried stage attendants moved furniture on the stage for the final scene, Blaine found her eyes drawn to the private boxes at the sides of the theater. Lord Farrington's box was the closest to the proscenium arch but she suspected the man would be equally as visible were he in the upper

24

gallery. There was no question that Andrew Farrington was an exceedingly handsome man with his wavy brown hair and flashing green eyes. Keeping well in the shadows of the side curtains, she stared up at him, wondering why she should find him so fascinating.

For the past three months, the infuriating man had been waging a campaign to gain an introduction. She had heard that he had kept various opera dancers as his mistresses and she suspected his intentions toward her were along the same lines. The mere fact that he would assume she was open to such an arrangement incensed her. Despite the fact that his approach to her had been respectful, she was hard pressed to forgive his arrogant belief that she would not be insulted by such an offer.

Lord Farrington sat alone in his private box, his pose exceedingly relaxed on the velvet-covered gilt chair. He was dressed in black, in sharp contrast to the red velvet hangings in the box. His face, above the whiteness of his linen, was tanned and patrician. At this distance Blaine could make out the movements of his hands, which were thin, almost graceful, and, like his body, only hinted at an underlying strength.

The audience roared at the antics of the

Clown, and Blaine returned her attention to the stage. Ever since Joseph Grimaldi had introduced the stylized makeup of his character to the pantomime, the public had taken the buffoonlike Clown to heart. Even at the Green Mews, they were beginning to refer to the character as Joey, and sometimes, as tonight, the audience picked up the chant as an additional accolade.

Hearing her cue, Blaine moved toward the center of the stage, reunited at last with Prince Tatum, the hero of the piece. She ignored the sweaty odor of the actor, gingerly accepted his embrace, and chimed her voice with his in a sweet duet. As the curtain began to fall, the door in the proscenium arch opened and the Clown staggered out, dragging the subdued Captain of the Guard on a rope. Blaine dipped into a curtsy as the audience howled its approval of the performance. After numerous bows, the green stage curtain came to rest and the players relaxed.

"Well done, my dears," John Tibbles said, bearing down on the performers from the wings. "A fitting end to this production."

As the short wiry manager bustled about the stage congratulating the players, Blaine chatted with the other actors. They were all rather tired but, as always, buoyed up at the end of a performance. John approached her and she smiled, bracing herself for his enthusiastic embrace.

"My dearest Maggie," he said, using her stage name. "You were truly magnificent this evening. Four reprises on that last solo and 'fore God, the boys in the pit would have quite torn up the scenery if you'd done any less."

Blaine linked her arm with John as he led her toward her dressing room. In the year that she had been associated with the Green Mews Theater, the energetic manager had stood as her friend and she enjoyed his company.

"It was the coup of the decade when I managed to lure you away from Covent Garden to join my troupe. The name of the Green Mews Theater owes much of the reputation it enjoys to the luster of your performances," he said with enthusiasm.

"You are entirely too kind, John," Blaine said, wondering why he should be more effusive than usual. She kept her pace even as she waited for his next words.

"And now, my pet, after praising you to the skies, is there any possibility I can inveigle you to make an appearance in the Green Room this evening?" he asked. Feeling the immediate tension in her arm, he sighed heavily and patted her hand. "Needn't bristle, darling girl. It was only in light of a question."

27

"John, you know Tate would never permit it," she answered.

"Seems to me that hatchet-faced dresser treats you as though you were all of two and ten," he grumbled.

Blaine chuckled, as she had often had the same feeling, but now she used it as a convenient excuse since it coincided with her own desires. From the time she had arrived in London to try to become an actress, she had never gone to the green-walled room to mingle with the upper-class men who came to ogle the actresses and in some cases to choose a new mistress.

"I would not normally ask but two of your admirers have been most persistent," John continued as they approached the door of her dressing room. "They seek only an introduction."

"You have been so good to me, John, that it is difficult to refuse you anything but in this I remain adamant." Although she spoke lightly, there was a stubborn edge to her words. Since Blaine was tall, her eyes were on a level with his and she held his gaze for a brief moment before her mouth stretched into a grin. "Will you be joining me for a dish of tea before you race off to receive the congratulations from your clamoring public? Tate will be much put out if you refuse. She has such a soft spot for you, you know."

"Hmmph," he mumbled. "Soft spot, me maiden aunt! The biddy fair terrifies me."

Blaine's dressing-room door was snatched open from the inside and the dour Tate stood framed in the doorway. For all her ferocity of face she was a tiny, thin woman of some sixty years. She wore severe black bombazine covered by an ample apron, and her gray hair was neatly covered by a white mobcap devoid of lace or ribbons.

"Well, Tibbles, don't you be nattering me poor lamb's ear off," Tate snapped. "If you're coming in, kindly do so. The air in this noisome theater is ne'er good for Maggie's throat."

Blaine and John meekly entered under Tate's eagle eye and with a shared grin moved to the seats indicated. With another admonishing look, the old woman bustled over to the tea tray and carried it to the table in front of Blaine's chaise longue. The porcelain tea set had been a present from Aunt Haydie, and since her early days in the theater, Blaine had relied on the ritual to remind her of home and to cast away the feelings of loneliness that frequently assailed her.

Tate poured the tea into the handpainted, handleless cups set in deep, matching saucers. She handed one to the discomfited manager, placing the small glass cup plate on the table beside his chair with a thump. Instantly she turned with concern to Blaine.

"You're looking plain peaky," she announced. "You're sorely in need of a holiday. It's glad I am that we'll be out of London for a few weeks. Now put your feet up and drink your tea."

Obediently Blaine swung her feet up on the chaise longue and winked at John as she raised her tea and sipped the pungent brew directly from the cup. Preferring the old way, the manager poured his tea into the saucer, then with a quick glance at Tate's back, placed his cup in the exact center of the glass plate on the side table. It always amused Blaine that John should be so terrified of her dresser's censure.

The warmth of the tea filled Blaine with a sense of well-being. She knew in part that it was the fact that she had satisfactorily completed her month's engagement and would be free to return home for several weeks. It was a far cry from her beginnings in the theater, when she had gone for more than two years with only a few days at Weathers at Christmas. Looking around the dressing room, she realized how far she had come in six years and was grateful.

The room was small but at least she was no

longer forced to share the communal dressing room with the other bit players. She could still recall her horrified shock at the casual nudity displayed by the women of the chorus. Her painful modesty and strong sense of privacy made her the natural butt of the coarse humor of the other girls. Had it not been for the presence of Tate, who shielded her from much of the abuse, Blaine doubted if she would have survived even a day.

From her first days in the theater, she had worked to gain the additional privileges that stardom could provide. To her, privacy was all-important. For the last several years at Covent Garden, she had had her own dressing room and it was one of the requirements she had demanded of Tibbles when he'd hired her away. As the premier star of the Green Mews Theater, her dressing room was fitted with some comfort. There was a chaise longue, tables, and two upholstered chairs to indicate her status in the troop. The triple-mirrored dressing table was old and scarred but the beauty of the intricately carved walnut front was a pleasure to her eyes. Her own addition had been a four-paneled screen of Oriental design. The dark wood moldings were in sharp contrast to the ivory parchment and added dimension to the barbaric red dragons painted on the panels.

A small stove and a cot were in an alcove that Tate had taken over, where she might brew tea and rest while Blaine was onstage. The addition of a wardrobe and bookcases gave a more personal touch to the room and filled Blaine with a sense of belonging.

Tibbles cleared his throat to remind Blaine of his presence and took several satisfying sips from the saucer before setting it on the table. "You'll be back in time for the start of rehearsals on the new burletta, won't you?" he asked, his wide brow furrowed with worry.

"Never fear, old friend," Blaine assured him. "You know I always come to rehearsal."

"Not like some I could mention." Tate sniffed, sitting down and reaching into her mending basket for something to occupy her hands.

"Which reminds me," John said. "Richard Petersham will no longer be a part of our troupe. I warned him about speaking to friends in the audience but tonight his actions were outrageous. Even for him. Not only did he wave and call to various friends but he threw a billet-doux to that redheaded piece of goods in one of the boxes."

Blaine giggled despite her own disapproval. In most theaters such behavior was considered quite acceptable but she liked Tibbles for trying to raise the standards in his own productions. Even the great John Philip Kemble, actor-manager of the New Covent Garden Theater, was known to make a sign to a friend while carrying on with the action of the play. Most were less skilled and delighted in the attention of the audience, much to the detriment of their performances.

"Poor Richard," Blaine said. "You will have to admit, John, that the man does have some talent. He played Prince Tatum quite well, although I would wish he took more care in his personal habits. The audience assumed I was shrinking away from him in maidenly fear but, if the truth were told, Richard smells rather like a wet goat."

"I gave him a note to Kemble at Covent Garden that said Richard 'ranked' with the best."

"Oh, John, you didn't!" Blaine gasped in amusement.

"No, I'll admit it only just occurred to me." John retrieved his saucer and sipped thoughtfully for several minutes before he looked up. "I'm hoping to do Sheridan's *School for Scandal* later in the year."

"Really, John. If you push too hard the Lord Chamberlain is bound to close down the theater." Blaine's face was full of concern. "You've only a license for music and dancing."

Tibbles sighed, finished his tea, and set the porcelain saucer on the table. "One must challenge the patent theaters, my dear. I long to do *Othello* but I cannot bear the thought of playing music throughout the performance in order to stay within the letter of my license. Drury, Covent Garden, and the Haymarket have the Lord Chamberlain's blessing to put on any drama they wish. Mark my words, there will come a time when all the theaters will be able to do spoken dramas, not just the lighter fare."

Blaine was reluctant to encourage Tibbles in his usual hobbyhorse but willingly listened to his grievances against the so-called legitimate theaters. She knew that with the inconsistent licensing, the newer theaters were forced to extravagant excesses to attract an audience. Sadler's Wells had installed a water tank so that they could do aquatic plays which involved sea battles and water rescues. Astley's had an equestrian circle and specialized in daring feats of acrobatic prowess. Since some of the theaters were so large, there was little subtlety to the acting. The emphasis was much more on visual effects, and the public clamored for bridges spanning gorges, mounted cavalry, and even elephants. The small intimacy of the Green Mews Theater prohibited such spectacles and was one of the reasons

Blaine had chosen to become a member of John Tibbles's troupe.

"Well, my dear, enough," John said, pushing himself to his feet. "I shall not bore you with further animadversions. I shall adjourn to the Green Room to accept the accolades of my adoring public."

Blaine waved Tate to remain seated and swung her feet off the chaise. She accepted John's hand as she rose and walked him to the door. "Try and stay out of trouble with the law while I am gone."

"It is an actor's burden, my pet. In the words of the Lord Chamberlain, 'Actors performing without a license are vagrants and sturdy beggars.' A trumpery charge at best!" John announced, leaning over to kiss her on the cheek. "Have a lovely holiday and hurry back."

"I shall," Blaine said. She opened the door into the hallway, then froze, blinking in stupefaction at the figure standing outside.

Lord Andrew Farrington made an exaggerated leg, although there was a hint of amusement in his eyes before he bowed his dark head. Blaine swung her head toward the stage manager, who was looking slightly abashed at the glare of accusation in her eyes.

"Forgive me, my dear," John mumbled. "I had quite forgot I told Lord Farrington to await me here and we would go on to the Green Room together."

Blaine pulled herself upright, her face set in icy dignity as she started to close the door. Lord Farrington was too quick for her and his hand shot out, holding the door open by main force. His tanned fingers were so close to Blaine's face that she could feel the heat from his body. Her heart lurched, unconsciously her eyes rose, and she felt impaled by the sharp green gaze he bent on her. Her mouth was dry and she swallowed convulsively but was unable to break contact with his searching glance.

John Tibbles's voice sounded unnatural to her ears and seemed to come from a great distance. "My dear Maggie, may I present Lord Andrew Farrington. Lord Farrington, Maggie Mason."

"It is my greatest pleasure, Miss Mason, to finally meet La Solitaire. Your performance this evening was flawless."

Blaine let the sound of his words wash over her, annoyed that, despite her antipathy toward the man, she liked the deep timbre of his voice. She would have thought she would be disappointed with a closer inspection of Lord Farrington but his actual presence was almost overwhelming. If possible, he was more handsome than she had suspected, with none of the

36

lines of dissipation so prevalent in most of the gentlemen who frequented the theater. There was authority in his bearing and a character etched into the lines of his fine-featured face. She was annoyed with herself for staring at the handsome nobleman, but at his nearness, she had dissolved into the veriest ninny-hammer.

"Thank you," she said, finding her tongue at last. She took a step backward and prepared to close the dressing-room door but his words held her in place.

"Since you have failed to respond to any of my notes, I hoped to impress you with my earnest desire to make your acquaintance by presenting myself at your door with great humility."

Blaine narrowed her eyes at the contrast between his meekly spoken words and the gleam of arrogance in his eyes. "Your humility is totally apparent, my lord."

Lord Farrington's gaze sharpened at the sarcasm in her voice and one dark eyebrow raised in decided interest. "I am prepared to lay the world at your feet for merely a sign that you do not find my presence repugnant."

A wave of color flashed across Blaine's cheeks at the none-too-subtle proposition. Better men than he had offered her a slip of the shoulder and she longed to slap the lazy grin off Lord Farrington's face. Instead, she controlled her emotions and favored him with a smile of angelic sweetness.

"I could never find your presence repugnant," she said, and she gritted her teeth at the self-satisfied look that transformed his expression. "For the simple reason that I do not acknowledge your presence."

With dainty fingers, she detached his hand from the door, as though she were loath to contact any part of his body. She smiled in satisfaction at his thunderous expression from her sharp set-down, and with a final glacial stare at the thoroughly chagrined John Tibbles, she slammed the door.

"The nerve of the man!" Tate snapped, rising with the look of a warrior about to charge the enemy.

Blaine moved across the room to Tate, who was glaring at the door in high dudgeon. She patted the arm of her dresser. "Give over, Tate. The man is not worth your anger."

"I cannot believe that Tibbles would do you such a turn," the feisty little woman muttered as she put away her sewing.

"John told me that Lord Farrington was one of the shareholders of the Green Mews." Blaine sighed heavily as she sat at the vanity and began to undo her elaborate hairstyle. Most assumed that her hair was powdered but the white-blond color was natural, and she pulled at the pins, eager to brush out the curls. "I assume he pressured John for an introduction. John's defection does not surprise me. I have few illusions about men."

"So young and so jaded." Tate's voice was disapproving as she picked up the brush to untangle Blaine's hair. " 'Tis not a fit life for you, lamby."

With the wisdom of experience, Blaine winced, remembering her naïveté when she had first arrived in London. It was only in blessed ignorance that she ever could have decided to pursue a career as an actress. She had known little of the petty jealousies of the other players, the lustful glaces of the men who hoped to bed her, or the dogged hard work involved in reaching the top of her craft. She was a star now, for as long as the public chose to lionize her. It was exhausting work to walk the line between keeping the audience at a distance and beguiling them into the belief she was worthy of their adoration. She was on guard every minute, fully aware of how quickly her popularity could fade. She admitted she had been lucky to have survived with so few scars other than exhaustion, loneliness, and a total disillusionment with the company of men.

It did not take her long to learn that she

could not associate with any of the gentlemen who besieged her with flowers and notes. After the novelty of her innocence wore off, the girls in the dressing room spoke freely in front of her, candid discussions that she would as soon have forgone. From them, she learned the shallowness of the men who showered them with attention. For some of the girls, the life of an actress was no better than being on the streets.

Despite Tate's protection, Blaine learned the crude facts of life in her new world and painfully acknowledged what she had given up by joining the ranks of actresses, opera dancers, and theatrical courtesans. No man of good family would ever look on her as anything other than a woman of easy virtue. Any relationship she entered into would be one solely for the accommodation of some rake's physical pleasure. When not actually performing as an actress, for men of the ton, her only value was her facial beauty and her bodily attractions.

Blaine had realized several years ago that she would never marry. She had seen too much of the lustful and depraved side of men to convince her that she would not be giving up much. She had cried for the children she would never have but, in her usual common-sense way, she had accepted the fact. Through

Val and Fleur, she would enjoy a family and, in the rare times she could visit, she would delight in their antics and store them up for the long years ahead.

"A holiday will refresh us both," Blaine said dreamily, relaxing under the rhythm of the efficiently wielded brush. Her eyes were drawn to the single rose in the vase on the dressing table. The opaque green of the Bristol glass accentuated the pure whiteness of the rose. She guiltily raised her eyes to Tate's face in the mirror but the dresser's attention was centered on her hair.

Blaine had taken one bud out of the basket of white roses that had been delivered to her dressing room. Without question, Tate would be furious if she knew that the flowers had come from Lord Farrington. There had been no card with the flowers but Blaine had guessed they were from the arrogant man. He had been inundating her with flowers and gifts for several months.

Since first coming to the notice of the dandies, Blaine had received notes and presents that the senders hoped might predispose her to favor their attentions. The notes went unanswered and the gifts she returned unopened. The baskets of flowers she generously distributed among the bit players. According to theater gossip, she had never accepted any-

41

thing from any of her admirers. As her popularity grew, one disappointed gentleman threw flowers at her feet during the performance. She had been so embarrassed that she had not even acknowledged the tokens. The next night, others in the audience threw flowers, and once more she ignored them. It was this supposed hauteur that earned her the sobriquet, La Solitaire.

The nickname might not have stuck if she had not been solitary indeed. In her six years in the theater, she had never accepted an invitation from any of the gentlemen who clamored for her attention. In a world where morals were as loose as an old crone's teeth, Blaine's eccentric behavior was noticed. In the beginning it was supposed that she was merely holding out for a better offer. Now most assumed she had some mysterious private protector and was discreet in her affair. In general, her admirers accepted and prized the elegant dismissal of La Solitaire. All except the persistent Lord Andrew Farrington.

"I've laid out your traveling dress and I'll pack the gown you've got on with the rest of the things here," Tate said, finished at last with plaiting Blaine's hair into a heavy braid. "All of your costumes have been packed and are already in the carriage."

Actors and actresses were generally required to provide their own costumes, and a varied wardrobe was a valuable asset for any player. Blaine could recall how Sarah Siddons had wept after the fire that had demolished the Covent Garden Theater five years earlier. Her tears had not been for the gutting of the historic building but for the loss of her immense wardrobe of costumes and jewelry. In the beginning of her career, Blaine had worn the stock costumes from the theater wardrobe like the other bit players. As her parts increased, she had used her precious salary to buy materials that Tate magically sewed into clothing appropriate to her roles. Reminded of all that she owed the little woman, Blaine rose and hugged her.

"No time for your nonsense," said the flustered dresser as she pushed Blaine away, turning her around to unfasten her gown. "The carriage will be here any second now."

As though she had conjured up the devil, there was a blistering knock on the door and Blaine dashed behind the screen as Tate bustled to the door. She listened to the low-voiced exchange between her dresser and Sarge, her other guardian, as she hurried into her traveling clothes. Her dress was a dark green mousseline de soie, embroidered with a delicate line of small white satin roses at the neckline and around the edge of the puffed sleeves and the hem. The crisp fabric held its shape while traveling, and yet was light and cool in the early spring weather. Clasping her cloak around her neck, she bundled up her discarded clothing and stepped from behind the screen.

"Evening, Sarge, I'm almost ready."

"It's about bloody time, miss. She says" — Sarge jerked his head in Tate's direction — "we still have to stop at the 'ouse and pick up the rest of your folderol."

"Stubble it, you old sot," the dresser snapped. "I've enough on my plate to get ready for a stint in the country wi'out your bellyaching."

Since Blaine, in the company of her late uncle's batman, Sarge, had arrived on Tate's doorstep, there had been hostility between the old soldier and the London dresser. Sarge had not approved of Blaine's decision to become an actress and he had originally viewed Tate, who worked in the theater, with the contempt reserved for fallen women, Frenchmen, and cats. The two old servants scrapped like bee-stung bulldogs, united only in the protection of their charge, Blaine. Over the years a mutual respect and affection had grown up between the two but the old habits were comfortable and it seemed to Blaine that they generally enjoyed their brangling.

44

"Enough, you two, or I shall refuse to leave," she said, teasing. "I know you're anxious to be off, Sarge, but we'll still be making a stop at the Silver Stallion and that little barmaid will be waiting for you."

"Miss Blaine!" the red-faced man lamented. "You'd think Tate and I hadn't done our very best to keep that sort of sordid business from your eyes."

"As if you could," Blaine said under her breath. Aloud she said, "I'm ready."

Tate took the bundle of clothes and placed them in the top of the portmanteau along with the last of Blaine's theatrical makeup and the precious tea set. Closing it, she handed it to Sarge and crossed to fuss over Blaine.

"Pull the hood up snug around your face, and once we're outside stay close to Sarge."

Blaine smiled at the oft-repeated cautions but she obediently raised her hood, feeling stifled in the stuffy air of the theater. She followed Sarge along the hallway back toward the stage, walking carefully in the dim light of the wings. The huge man outstripped her as they crossed the stage and Blaine stopped in the center, looking in bemusement at the tiers of seats. The vast emptiness always awed her with its blandness; under the stage lights there was such an aura of mystery about the unseen audience. At Tate's hiss, she turned away and continued across the stage, plunging into the darkness of the wings.

"Careful, my pet, there is danger in the dark," came a voice at her side and Blaine gasped in fear as a hand clamped around her wrist.

"Where are you, lamby?" Tate called, her voice tight with worry.

Fighting the pressure on her arm, Blaine batted away the drapery hangings until light filtered into the wings and she was able to see who had accosted her.

"Unhand me at once, milord," she snapped.

At the barely concealed contempt in her voice, Lord Talbott Stoddard's blue eyes narrowed for a moment before his mouth flashed into a white-toothed grin of apparent amusement. He released his grip on her wrist and held the curtains graciously for her just as Tate descended on them.

"What's all this, then?" the dresser shrilled, pulling Blaine away from the hovering figure.

"It is nothing, Tate. Only Lord Stoddard." Blaine could hear the hiss of Stoddard's breath at the implied insult. She felt justified in giving him such a set-down because in defiance of her refusal to acknowledge him, he had become increasingly persistent in his attentions over the last several months. He was tall, with the body of an athlete and the face of a Greek

Adonis. She could not like the man despite his cherubic face and head of curly blond hair. There was something about his pale blue eyes that chilled her.

"Miss Mason was lost in the wings," Stoddard explained to the angry dresser. To Blaine, he said, "If you were mine, goddess, you would not need to find your way alone."

Instead of a blush of embarrassment at his plain speaking, Blaine felt a rush of anger flood her cheeks. After years of brushing off the blatant advances of eager dandies, she found herself unable to dismiss this man lightly. Beneath the softly spoken words there was a hint of menace that she could not deny and, notwithstanding her bravado, she felt a frisson of fear in Stoddard's presence. She moved a step closer to Tate and then turned, her face lighting up at Sarge's welcome appearance.

The enormous man said nothing, only glared at Lord Stoddard through slitted eyes until, with a graceful bow, the nobleman turned and crossed to the far side of the stage: Tate and Sarge closed in around Blaine and hurried her through the labyrinthine halls until finally they exited the building onto a dark side street. The carriage was waiting and after bundling the women inside, Sarge leapt to the driver's seat and they were off.

Inside, Blaine was treated to a blistering of her ears by Tate but she barely acknowledged the woman's words. She had been badly shaken by the brief encounter with Stoddard. From the first time that she had seen him, she knew he was dangerous and in the ensuing months there had been nothing to change her opinion. She shrugged away her uneasiness, determined to think only about the joyful re-union with Fleur and Val and her two-week holiday at Weathers.

two

Lord Andrew Farrington elected to walk home rather than endure the confinement of his carriage. The late March weather was warmer than usual, although there was a bite to the air that indicated spring was still only a promise, not a reality. Drew walked with head bent, a look of discontent playing around his normally smiling lips. He strode along the cobblestones, his cloak bellying out in the wind and his stick swinging loosely at his side. After only one glance the denizens of the night shied away from accosting the young gentleman. There was an assurance in the man's bearing that suggested he would not be an easy mark.

"Damn!" He spat out the word and slashed impotently at the night air. He had rarely experienced such a frustrating evening. He obviously had been wasting his time in pursuing La Solitaire. The much-sought-after Maggie Mason had stared at the rose he had thrown at her feet as if it were the most contemptible of objects. She had glanced at him coldly with her golden eyes and then, as if to indicate how little she cared for his interest, had bestowed a breathtaking smile on the audience.

Another slash of his walking stick emphasized the anger he had bottled up since his abortive introduction to the tantalizing woman. Despite John Tibbles's assurances, Drew realized he had done further damage to his suit by approaching her directly.

Drew did not understand what there was about the celebrated Maggie Mason that he found so compelling. Over the years he had been aware of the rising popularity of the actress. Several times he had seen her onstage and thought she was beautiful, with her patrician features and her powdered white hair, but he was not one of her slavish followers. At least not until four months ago.

Just before Christmas, he had gone to the Green Mews Theater with a party and for the most part had been bored by the company. He had sat apart from the rest, his mind more involved with the play in progress than was usual. His eyes had been drawn to the white curls of La Solitaire and for once he focused his attention solely on her. During the first act, as a connoisseur of female beauty, he watched her with pleasure, admiring her exquisite features and lush body. By the second act, he had fallen under the spell of the woman. There was something in her voice and actions that suggested a depth of character that he had not expected. By the end of the third act, he was impatient for the next evening to begin so he might see her again.

Night after night, he returned to the Green Mews. Eventually he grew accustomed to her breathtaking beauty and began to observe the woman behind the characters she played. Watching La Solitaire, he caught hints of humor, intelligence, and sensitivity that was in total contrast to the shallowness he had expected. She was not jaded or blowsy. She exuded an elegance and a curious innocence that intrigued him. As he sat in the comfortable darkness of the theater, he became obsessed with the need to know more about the singular Maggie Mason.

To his chagrin, he discovered that there was little known about the woman outside of the theater. No one of his acquaintances knew where she came from or where she lived now. It was said that she was being kept by an incredibly wealthy nobleman; in fact, due to the mystery behind his identity, some had hinted that the man in question might even be Prinny himself. The latter, at least, Drew discounted since he knew the man's tastes did not run to such youthful actresses.

The more elusive the woman became, the

more she interested Drew. He did not really think beyond a light flirtation and he chafed at the continued thwarting of his plans. He questioned his companions for someone who could introduce him but all to no avail. According to his friends, no one had gotten close enough to Maggie Mason to form an acquaintance.

Thus he began a campaign of his own. He sent an enormous basket of flowers only to discover that it had been distributed among the women in the chorus. He sent notes backstage but they were never acknowledged. He was amused by the standoffish behavior of the actress, but as she continued to ignore him, his determination grew. In a gesture guaranteed to win her attention, he bribed one of the stage attendants to place a diamond bracelet in her dressing room before the performance. He had arrived at the theater before the raising of the curtain, confident in his ultimate success, only to find, on the seat of his solitary gilt chair, the unopened box.

Since well before he had reached his majority, Drew had become used to instant approval from females of all ages and classes. He knew he was well looking and, with his vast fortune, the majority of women he had met had fawned over his every presence. Why was Miss Maggie Mason so contrary?

Drew flung off his cloak as he took the stairs of his town house two at a time. The door opened under his hand, unlocked since he hated to alert the house of his comings and goings. Frosty's white head appeared like a specter in the semidarkness of the foyer as the impressively bearded butler shuffled forward to take his things.

"I'll be in the library but I shall require nothing further," Drew mumbled as he crossed the marble foyer. "Good night, Frosty."

The old man observed the tightness around his master's mouth and refrained from informing him of the visitor who waited in the library. He would alert Mrs. Gladdie to prepare a room for Drew's brother and then take himself off for a well-earned rest. " 'Night, milord."

Drew opened the door of the library and stopped on the threshold at the awareness of another presence. A figure rose from the chair beside the fireplace and a grin of delight erased the dark expression on his face.

"Robbie! Devil take it, man, but it's good to see you." Drew crossed the Aubusson carpet in long strides to clasp his brother's hand.

The two men exchanged greetings and then Drew pushed Robbie away in order to look more carefully at him. Although only five years separated the two, Drew felt all of his thirty years were evident beside the boyish appearance of his brother. Robbie's straight hair was a light brown and his eyes were the liquid brown of a young puppy. While Drew had the sleek look of a Corinthian, Robbie's shorter and stockier frame had the solid look of the landed gentry. All in all, the lad looked well, Drew thought, indicating a chair.

"Why didn't you tell me you were coming to town? I should have been here to greet you."

"I didn't know; that is, it was sort of a spur-of-the-moment decision," Robbie said, stammering. "I hope you don't mind."

"Mind?" Drew raised one eyebrow as he crossed to the sideboard. "It's about time you left the wilds of the country for a more civilized milieu. Brandy?"

"I've already made inroads on your supply." Robbie raised the snifter on the table beside him. "French?"

"Naturally. And before you lecture me about patriotism, be it known that before one had to revert to smuggled goods I had laid in a particularly heavy supply." Drew lifted his glass and inhaled the full bouquet before continuing. "I will be most grateful when that upstart Corsican is finally confined. The free flow of spirits is essential to the good nature of all citizens."

Drew brought the decanter with him and set it near at hand as he sat down across from his brother. He asked a question or two and listened as Robbie talked enthusiastically about the running of his estate. He took in the nervous gestures and the too-quick speech and wondered what was bothering the boy. He grimaced, realizing Robbie was no longer a young lad to be worried over. At twenty-five, he was a man and well able to manage his life without his older brother's interference.

Habit was hard to break. Drew's mother had died giving birth to Robbie, an unfortunate occurrence for which Drew's father, Henry, had never forgiven him. From the moment of his birth, Henry Farrington had ignored the boy. Robert was a sickly child, prone to frequent congestion of the lungs, which for the most part kept him confined to the nursery. Drew had done his best to make up to his brother for his father's neglect and spent many hours entertaining him. In the instances he was able to lure Robbie out-of-doors, he had watched over him carefully, anxious that no injury or illness should befall him.

Despite his father's rejection, Robbie had developed a sunny disposition and, having seen little cruelty or abuse thanks to his brother's protection, had a thoroughly trusting nature. Drew was the cynical one, made so through bitter experience, while Robbie saw the world through a haze of goodness that endowed everyone with the finest motives and purest intentions.

It was amusing to see how the pale, weak Robbie had grown up to be such a sturdy fellow. He was several inches shorter than Drew but built with the solidity and endurance of a thick oak tree. While Drew chose to travel extensively, Robbie had a real love of the land and preferred to remain at home. At an early age, the lad had shown a preference for Fairhaven, the estate willed to him by his grandmother.

Although periodically Drew had coaxed him up to London with the hope that a little town bronze would toughen him, Robbie remained untouched by the seamier side of life. Noticing the harried look that clung to his brother, Drew wondered what bumblebath the boy had tumbled into. He sipped his brandy, knowing the news would eventually be forthcoming.

Under the steady gaze of his brother, Robbie ground to a halt. "I suppose the idea of crop rotation isn't of much interest."

"Faith, lad, you're well out there," Drew said, his voice a slow drawl. "When next I am asked to a social function, I am sure I shall dazzle my audience to have such gripping details to pass on. Did you come all this distance just to keep me abreast of the newest agricultural advances?"

"Well, no," Robbie said, laughing nervously. "Not that it wouldn't be a bad idea for you to take a greater interest in your land. I have often told you, Drew, that your estate managers are not making decisions in either your best interests or the best interests of the land."

"Cut line, shaveling. As much as I am delighted with your precipitous visit, I suspect there is some purpose to your arrival on my doorstep. Out with it, lad, so I can seek my bed."

Robbie's mouth opened but no words issued forth. Drew found himself leaning forward in anticipation as his brother struggled to find his voice.

"I want to get married," he finally blurted out.

Drew did not even blink at the words that seemed to hang in the air between them but his eyes took on a frosty color. Robbie shifted uncomfortably under the fixated stare but, pluck to the bone, he held his ground.

"Perhaps you'd like to enlighten me on this matter," Drew said. "I was not aware that you had formed a tendresse with any of the bucolic beauties in your vicinity."

Robbie winced under the sarcastic tone but refused to cry craven. "I'm sorry to spring this on you this way, Drew. It's not that I've been holding out on you. It's just that I wanted to be sure of my own feelings before I got your hopes up."

Since Drew had few hopes, he sighed. He heard the appeal in his brother's voice and could not doubt the sincerity of Robbie's affection. Perhaps it was not as bad as he suspected.

"Forgive me my jaded humor," Drew said by way of apology. "Why don't you tell me about the young lady. And then tell me what I may do to be of service since I assume that is why you have come up to London."

"You've caught me out there." Robbie laughed, much relieved at the softening of his brother's tone. "I do have a favor to ask but first let me tell you about Fleur."

"Fleur? French?"

"Her mother was french but Fleur was born here in England. And you will never believe my good fortune, for she lives not twenty minutes from my estate," Robbie enthused. "I can't wait for you to meet her. She is unbelievably lovely. Tiny, blond, and she has the most exquisite violet-colored eyes."

Drew groaned inwardly at the fatuous look on his brother's face. It was apparent that

Robbie had seen little beyond the blond hair and violet eyes. He only hoped the chit was not some milkmaid. Or worse. "Has she family?"

"Yes. No."

"Well? Which is it?"

"Her parents are dead. Fleur told me it was a carriage accident six or seven years ago. Not titled but landed gentry. Fleur is being raised by her aunt, who I gather is in rather ill health. I've met her brother and there's also a half sister who is older and lives outside London taking care of an ailing relative."

"Sounds like the health of the family is rather precarious," Drew intoned.

"Not Fleur," Robbie defended. "She's in the very pink of health. We take long walks and she has excellent wind."

Drew snorted in disgust and took a restorative sip of brandy. "And what does her aunt think of your suit? Does she find it acceptable?"

"Well, there is a bit of a problem," Robbie began. "I have not had the opportunity to make my suit known."

Drew's brows lowered over his eyes at the hesitant tone of voice. Something definitely havey-cavey was afoot. "You mean, you have not asked for the girl's hand? Ah, perhaps the aunt is not this Fleur's legal guardian. Is her guardian so intimidating that you wish me to make the offer in your behest?"

"No. Devil take it, Drew! I've never even spoken to the aunt." The words burst from Robbie and he slumped back in his chair under the baleful gaze of his older brother.

"Do you mean to tell me, Robbie, that you have been meeting this young person in some hugger-mugger fashion?"

At the condemnatory tone, Robbie sprang forward in his chair. "She is not a young person! She is a young lady and the woman I love. I know how this must sound but if you would hear me out I think you'll understand."

Drew stared at his brother, who sat with elbows on his knees and hands clenched in a curiously touching manner. He sighed once more and nodded his head obligingly. "Forgive my shortness of temper. Tell me your story and I promise not to interrupt."

Robbie smiled gratefully and then launched into his story. "I first saw Fleur in the village. I cannot tell you how impressed I was with her grace and beauty. She was with her governess and a young boy who I later discovered was her brother. I did not approach her but we did exchange smiles. A week later I saw her on the road to the west of Fairhaven. She had been out riding and was very properly accompanied by a groom. Her horse had taken a stone and I stopped to see if I could be of some assistance. As before, I was much struck by her. She has a sweet innocence and a gentleness of manner."

Robbie paused, and from the glazed look in his eyes Drew could tell that his brother was once more seeing blond curls and violet eyes.

"When I discovered that she lived so near to Fairhaven, I asked if I might call. She hesitated and then explained that her aunt was not well, so they were not receiving. Since, by then, her groom had taken out the stone and the horse did not turn up lame, I had no excuse even to accompany her home. But quite naturally, I could not leave it at that."

Robbie finished his brandy and placed the glass carefully back on the table. He looked across at Drew and was relieved to find his brother's austere features set in an encouraging expression.

"I asked various people in the county if they had acquaintance with the Meriweathers but no one did. It seems that when the aunt first had come to the area she had been less than sociable, so the family is little known. Fleur is only just eighteen and is not out in society. At any rate, I did understand the general vicinity of her daily rides and so over the next several weeks I was able to run into her quite by accident. Sometimes she was able to get away without her groom and we were able to meet in the old mill on the edge of the village, which was a decided improvement since it has been extremely cold this winter."

The conniving chit had set her trap well to enmesh the trusting Robbie, first refusing to allow him to meet her obviously disreputable family and then by letting him know how he could find her. And finally meeting with him secretly. Was there ever such an innocent? Drew muttered. "How long has this been going on?"

"Three months."

"Good God, Robbie! Have you compromised the wench? Is that what this is all leading up to?"

"Devil take it, Drew!" Robbie rose to his feet with a roar. "Fleur is not that kind of a woman!"

"They are all that kind of woman," Drew answered cynically. Then he waved a hand at the red-faced man across from him. "Sitdown. Sit down. If I have misread this situation, my apologies. But get to the point, lad, before I succumb from apoplexy. I will take your word for it that Fleur Meriweather is an innocent maiden. What, then, is the problem?"

Robbie resettled himself after refilling his

snifter from the cut-glass decanter. Color rode high on his cheeks but he was back in control as he continued. "We were forced to these clandestine meetings because the aunt was never well enough to receive guests and would not approve of Fleur having callers. The old woman keeps her close and does not permit her to go out in company. Neither one of us liked the idea of meeting secretly but we did enjoy each other's company. I will admit, to my shame, that at first I was only interested in a light flirtation but I soon realized that she was too fine a person for me to offer her such an insult. Little by little I discovered that I had quite lost my heart."

Drew suspected that unless he took a hand in the discussion he would be regaled once more with the wondrous charms of the lovely Fleur. Clearing his throat to gain his brother's attention, he asked, "And Fleur? Is her heart also engaged?"

For the second time in their unusual interview, Drew saw a wave of distress cross his brother's features. When Robbie raised his eyes, he could see the uncertainty and confusion in his mind.

"No," Robbie finally answered. "I do not think that Fleur is in love with me."

"Good Lord, what have you two been doing for the last three months?" Drew hoped his horrified tone might lighten his brother's mood, but the man was oblivious to anything but the gravity of his situation.

"Talking."

"Talking?" Drew asked in disbelief.

"On my honor, that was all we did. I confess that at times I contemplated less innocent pursuits."

"Well, I should hope so!"

"It is very difficult to explain but I was afraid of frightening Fleur. She has never really met any other men and at this point I think she looks on me as just a good and kind friend. I have wanted to declare my feelings but I did not wish to take advantage of her youth and inexperience. Am I making myself clear?"

Drew was hard pressed not to shake his head in exasperation but instead just nodded encouragement for Robbie to continue.

"Well, once I had come to understand the strength of my feelings for Fleur, I felt it would be logical for me to make the acquaintance of her aunt. I would be able to ask her permission to call on her niece. It is my belief that, when I can call on her formally, Fleur will then begin to look on me in the role of both a friend and a suitor."

"I see," Drew said, although in many respects he was sure he would never understand. He waited for his brother to continue but when he didn't, Drew prodded gently. "Now, Robbie, where exactly do I come into this affair?"

"Well, it occurred to me that if you came for a visit I would have an excuse to have some sort of a party. When I mentioned my idea and the possibility of your visiting quite soon, Fleur became quite excited. It seems that her aunt has been getting steadily better and she might be strong enough to receive visitors. Fleur has high hopes that if we ask her she might accept an invitation to the party."

"An invitation is always a singular restorative to women," Drew stated, aware that his sarcasm was wasted on his besotted brother. "I suppose I could arrange my schedule to afford myself the dubious opportunity to visit Fairhaven. How long would I be required to rusticate?"

"A month?" At the raised eyebrows, Robbie improvised quickly. "Perhaps a week or two would do the trick. You always had a way of charming the old tabbies. I'm counting on you to convince Fleur's aunt that I would make an admirable match for her niece. Then all I need do is convince Fleur."

"All right, puppy," Drew agreed. "I may assume you will be leaving in the morning, which if I recall correctly is Monday. I will

65

follow in a more leisurely fashion, if that is suitable."

"Thank you, Drew."

There was such a wealth of honest feeling in the words that Drew felt slightly guilty at his own subterfuge. Although he fully intended to go to Fairhaven, it was not part of his plan to aid Robbie in his affair with the lovely Fleur. Quite to the contrary.

"Seek your bed, Robbie. You've a long ride tomorrow."

After an incoherent babble of appreciation, his brother left and Drew sank back down into the chair and stared glumly at the pattern on the carpet. He could see little hope of extracting Robbie from the relationship heart-whole. He was not looking forward to the trip to Fairhaven, since he could already imagine what he would find.

Fleur Meriweather was no doubt a scheming minx with some beauty and no fortune. It would not have been difficult to discover that Robbie was an extremely wealthy man with a prosperous estate. He was also Drew's heir, which was common knowledge. No matter the story she had spun for Robbie's benefit, no young lady of good reputation would agree to secret meetings with a man she considered merely a friend. She sounded like some clever adventuress set to dig her claws into his brother. Thank God that Robbie was gentleman enough not to have compromised the girl or there might be no way to free him from the chit's clutches.

He supposed there would be trouble with the girl's aunt. There was a bad odor to the story of the sickly woman. The sudden recovery at the word of a possible invitation sounded both miraculous and highly suspect. He had sensed some hesitation on Robbie's part at the mention of the old lady and he wondered what rumors were rampant in the neighborhood. He suspected that it would cost a pretty penny to convince the girl and her unhealthy aunt to look elsewhere for prey.

He stretched his legs out and yawned. He hated the thought of removing to Wiltshire. A more godforsaken place he had never seen and it was a constant amazement to him that Robbie seemed to thrive there. He supposed he might as well leave London. His pursuit of La Solitaire was hardly flourishing. The Green Mews Theater would be closed for a month while they prepared to mount a new production. With luck he would return refreshed from the country and then he could apply all his energies to gaining the affection of the fair Maggie Mason. He could only hope she would miss his attention and soften her attitude by the time he sought her out again.

★

In the windowless room of a gaming hell in another part of town, the air was heavy and the candles flickered in the wall sconces. Talbott Stoddard glowered across the table at his companions. His long white fingers played with a pile of chips, clicking them together with annoying repetition. His pale blue eyes reflected his impatience at the continued conversation.

"Then after Tattersall's, I took him round to Whites," Sir Edgar Willoughby concluded, his voice a monotone of boredom as befitted those aspiring to the dandy set. The fact that he was well under the hatches contributed to a slight slurring of his words.

"Your hospitality has been superb, cuz, but I much preferred yesterday. Spent the evening at a private establishment," James Chittenden announced, snickering at the remembrance.

"You old dog, Willoughby," Chester Morrison cried. "Don't tell me you went off to Madame Farrageau's."

"Well, rather," Sir Edgar said in a drawl. "The madame has a magnificent little blonde who looks all of ten and three but has the ingenuity of a much traveled wench. Startling cornflower eyes."

"Devil take it, Willoughby, are we here to play cards or to discuss the attributes of every tart in the vicinity of London?" Stoddard snarled.

"I say, old chap, no need to go all toffy-nosed, just because you've had little success with the entrancing Maggie Mason," Willoughby said with a smirk. Drink had made him brave and he was unmindful of the deadly coldness that entered Stoddard's eyes.

Chittenden and Morrison eyed each other in dismay but made no attempt to turn the conversation. For all their apprehension, there was an edge of enjoyment in watching the rising anger of the blond nobleman. Over the years, Stoddard had made many enemies by his unwarranted arrogance and vicious competitiveness. Now the men waited to see if he would rise to the bait.

"I do not recall that I intimated my intentions to acquire La Solitaire. If I had, I assure you, even now she would be panting beneath me and you, sir, would be grinding your teeth in envy." Stoddard flicked a hair from his dark blue sleeve of Bath superfine in a patent show of disinterest.

The youthful Willoughby was too deep in his cups to perceive the danger of twitting the man. "The betting book indicates that Lord Farrington will mount her before you ever leave the stalls," he said.

Stoddard slapped his beringed hand on the

table. His pile of chips scattered with a tinkling sound that was loud in the silence that followed. "Perhaps you would care to test your knowledge against mine?" he said, his husky whisper more menacing than a shout.

Chittenden rushed into the conversation, knowing full well that, in his present ugly mood, the nobleman was looking for a fight. "Willoughby's foxed, milord. Just running off at the mouth. No reason the rest of us fellows need take offense." He kicked his cousin brutally beneath the table and vowed he would trounce the doltish youngster for daring to risk angering Stoddard to the point of a duel. "Do apologize, Edgar, so that we might get on with our game," he ground out between clenched teeth.

An awareness of the danger in which he stood seeped through to Sir Edgar and fear sobered him amazingly fast. He blinked owlishly at the malevolence visible beneath the angelic features of the furious nobleman. His body was bathed in sweat as he cravenly apologized for the stupidity of his words.

Stoddard was cognizant of the pulsing tension of the men at the table and the awareness of their alarm went a long way to lighten his mood. Fear in others excited him. He could smell it and the scent heightened his own pleasure. The remembrance of golden-hazel eyes flashed before his mind. La Solitaire feared him despite her sharp words. He had felt the jump of her pulse when he grasped her wrist. Her eyes had flashed with contempt, but before he possessed her those golden eyes would respond as he wished.

Fingers steady, Stoddard gathered his chips into a pile. He smiled at the sigh of relief from his companions as the card game resumed, but beneath the cold mask of disdain, he was still filled with an angry core of determination. Drew Farrington would never win La Solitaire.

Drew had been his nemesis for many years. Since their school days, Stoddard had forever been in the shadow of the man. The pampered only son of a widowed mother, Talbott had learned at an early age that his angelic looks could be used to advantage. For the most part, he had only to ask for something and it had been given to him. The first time that he had wanted a woman and she did not fall into his lap had been a bitter experience for him. It was Drew Farrington that the woman had chosen and, for that insult, Stoddard never had forgiven the man.

A thin smile etched Stoddard's mouth as he remembered the revenge he had exacted. Drew's best friend was Jason Barringer, a man more comfortable with books than with the more manly pursuits. Stoddard had gone out of his way to antagonize Jason until the man had finally insulted him. With steady purpose, Stoddard had demanded satisfaction and met Jason on the field of honor one cold winter dawn.

He could still recall the helplessness in Drew's eyes as he acted as Barringer's second for the duel. Stoddard had taken deadly aim after Jason had fumbled his shot, and it was with great satisfaction that he fired his pistol, killing his man. Granted, he had been forced to leave the country for a short period, but it was worth it to see the agony on Farrington's face as he held the body of his friend.

It rankled that Farrington did not know that his friend's death was a well-planned revenge. Stoddard never baited Jason Barringer in Drew's presence and he was careful to have witnesses that would swear Jason had instigated the final argument that led to the challenge. Stoddard knew Farrington's proficiency with both swords and pistols and he would give him no provocation, gloating in the impotent hate he saw reflected in Drew's eyes.

Farrington did, however, try to thwart Stoddard whenever possible. It still set his teeth on edge when he recalled the set of chestnuts for which Drew outbid him. Later, he had entered a curricle race to Bath, and the damnable Farrington had entered as well, beating him soundly, much to the amusement of the other men involved. The few times they had sat in on a card game together, Drew had stripped him of his winnings with a smile of derision that induced a deep loathing in Stoddard.

He had known of Drew's interest in La Solitaire. It was that which first drew his attention to the actress. Since she was acknowledged to be unattainable, he wanted the status that would accrue in winning the prize, with the additional fillip that he would have beaten out Farrington. However, once he had seen Maggie Mason, he was consumed by desire and the overpowering need to possess her. He pursued her with the single-minded fervor reserved for the Holy Grail. He would risk all to obtain La Solitaire.

three

The carriage rolled from side to side on the bumpy road, nearly knocking Blaine off the seat. She was always amazed that Tate managed to sleep no matter the traveling conditions. By the simple expedient of wedging herself into the corner and pillowing her head on the bundle of her cloak, she had been snoring steadily since their stop for food at the Silver Stallion.

Blaine had dozed on and off during the journey but the excitement of returning home always kept her awake. She wished she were able to stay at Weathers instead of having to return to the smog and confinement of her life in London. Soon that would be possible, but for now she would have to be content with her two-week holiday. It was only in the last few years, owing to the fact she had become a reigning star, that she had been able to take time off from the theater. She remembered all too clearly how much she had missed home but at least she could actually see an end in sight and that made it all worthwhile.

Luck and hard work had been the keys to her success. Aunt Haydie had given her a letter to her friend Sarah Siddons, who was the sister of Kemble, the famous actor/manager of the Covent Garden Theater. At the time, Blaine was not aware of what a stroke of fortune this introduction was. Mrs. Siddons was at the height of her popularity, which at age fifty-two did not depend on her beauty but the talent that made her an outstanding tragic actress.

Sarah had taken immediately to the incredibly naïve Blaine and had become her mentor in the theater as well as her protector from the cruder elements of an actress's life. Mrs. Siddons was a lady in the grand manner and, despite the fact she inhabited a world renowned for its moral depravity, lived a respectable life. She was a wife and the mother of three children and firmly believed in the sanctity of marriage. Blaine could have had no finer sponsor.

Although Mrs. Siddons had been helpful on her arrival, perhaps she would not have been so thorough in her guidance if it hadn't been for a bizarre coincidence. The troupe was doing *The Merchant of Venice* when the actress playing Portia was taken ill. Blaine was her understudy and was forced to go on in her place. Although she was well schooled in the part, the precipitateness of her debut in a major role threw her badly off-stride. When she arrived onstage her voice shook, her lines died off in a whisper, and she totally forgot her stage directions. By the end of the play, she was convinced that her acting career was over and fled the stage in tears. Sarah had been waiting in the wings and, gathering her up, led her to her own sumptuous dressing room.

"I'm so terribly sorry, Sarah," Blaine cried forlornly. "I did so want to prove myself but my vanity is obviously greater than my talent. I am sunk beyond redemption. Better I should return home and never put my slippers on the boards again."

"Oh, la. Such tragedy!" The older woman applauded, smiling at the startled expression on the young girl's face. "I realize that you are feeling great humiliation but I shall tell you, my dear, that it was thus that I myself made my first appearance on the London stage."

"Surely you are only saying that to help me put a good face on my failure."

Sarah patted Blaine's hands, a bemused look in her eyes. "This may be difficult for you to credit but it seems there are similarities in our careers. Not many." She laughed, her face alight with humor. "Before I came to London, I had been playing in the provinces and was considered a remarkable actress. I was twenty, just like you, when I was invited to appear as Portia at the Drury Lane. I was filled with excitement and determined to become a great success. How well I remember that dreadful first night."

Sarah shuddered delicately, more for Blaine's benefit than remembered embarrassment. "I opened the door in the proscenium arch, stepped out on the stage, and froze when confronted by this enormous sea of faces. In those days, the houselights were left on during the performance, so every eye was visible. I reacted exactly as you did tonight, stumbling through my lines and making a perfect cake of myself."

"How horrible for you," Blaine said. Her concern for her friend completely overshadowed her own feeling of humiliation. For the first time she had the thought that perhaps all was not lost. "What did you do?"

"I stumbled my way through the season and then fled to the provinces again. I did not return to London for many years." Sarah reached out a long-fingered hand to wipe the tears from her protégée's face. "You, my dear, shall not be so lily-livered. You shall stand and fight. And I will help you."

In the confines of the carriage, Blaine smiled as she recalled the words of her friend. For Sarah had been a friend indeed and, true to her promise, had been inestimable in the help she provided. Blaine, for her part, had watched every movement the actress made and tried to incorporate her gestures and her stagecraft into her own style. It had paid off, and little by little Blaine became recognized for her talent as well as her beauty. Over the ensuing years, her popularity with theatergoers had increased. She owed a great deal to Sarah and had mourned the woman's retirement from the stage, feeling the loss of an outstanding actress as well as a good friend.

Suddenly the carriage lurched into a deep rut and Blaine was thrown against the side where her head connected painfully with the window. For once, Tate came awake with a snort.

"Are we there?" she asked.

Blaine rubbed her aching head and massaged the stiff muscles in her neck. "Only another bump."

"That fool Sarge will overturn us for sure," the dresser mumbled. "I've told him a hundred times that it is near insanity to push the horses at such a speed."

"We should be home soon," Blaine said. "It's full dark now."

"Arriving home in the dark of night, just like a thief." Tate sniffed. "I can't imagine what Lady Yates would have said if she knew of the straits you had gone to in order to protect the children."

In the light from the outside torches, Blaine could see the expression of disapproval on Tate's face and knew that her own reflected a similar feeling. She hated the life of subterfuge she was forced to live. Sneaking into her own home had never been a part of her original plan.

When she had left Weathers for London, Aunt Haydie had remained to care for the children. Although Blaine had been fearful of the future, she could concentrate on succeeding in the theater, knowing that Val and Fleur were safe in the care of her beloved aunt. All had gone well for two years when, without warning, Lady Yates had gotten an inflammation of the lungs.

Blaine still could not think back on that time without a deep feeling of sadness. She had loved her aunt dearly and still missed her letters of support and her commonsense advice. A messenger had been sent to London when Aunt Haydie had taken ill, and Blaine had raced to Wiltshire, arriving only in time to kiss the old woman good-bye.

As she sat at Lady Yates's bedside, the blue-veined hand pressed between both of her own, she had been filled with a sense of personal loss more severe than she had felt at the death of her parents. Not only had Aunt Haydie been the children's guardian but also Blaine's moral support while she struggled to survive in London. Despite the vast difference in their ages, she and her aunt had had a similarity of spirit and heart. She felt shame that she would not be able to mourn the woman as she deserved. She would have to return almost immediately to London. Knowing her aunt so well, she knew Lady Yates would remind her that her first duty was to safeguard Val and Fleur's futures.

After two years in the theater, Blaine was on the threshold of stardom. If she returned to London, her original plan to supplement their limited finances would come to fruition. She felt guilty at abandoning the children in such a time of grief. Thankfully the household was united in their affection for the family and they would do all they could to help them through such a difficult time.

She arranged her thoughts and called Tate and Frau Puffentraub into the library to discuss her plans for the funeral and her immediate return to London. There was silence when she finished, and then Frau Puffentraub spoke up, her accented voice seeming sharp in Blaine's overwrought state.

"Vell, *liebchen,* of course I vill remain as governess, and all the others vill do their part." Puff's voice was crisply efficient. "However, I do not try to make the problems but I spoke many times to Lady Yates and I do not think this plan will be of sufficiency."

Puff explained that the household itself had been largely maintained with the annual allowance willed to Lady Yates by Blaine's father. According to the will, on the announcement of her death, the allowance would be forfeit. Their finances were in worse shape than Blaine had suspected, and with the small amount she was able to send home, the household could not continue to function. She slumped in her chair and fought back tears as she faced the ruination of all her plans.

The plump governess's voice broke the silence of the room. "Are you a good actress, *liebchen?*" The little woman was unfazed by Blaine's startled expression and cocked her head to the side, waiting for an answer.

"Y-yes," Blaine stammered, confused by the woman's seemingly inconsequential question.

"Could you play the part of Lady Yates?" she asked.

"Of course she could," the ever loyal Tate chimed in.

"What?" Blaine stared into the twinkling eyes of her governess and suddenly realized what the little woman had in mind. "But,

81

Puff, it's not possible. The solicitor knows Aunt Haydie. Porter Upton comes once a year to give her the allowance."

"It is with terrible great sadness that I report the death of your father's solicitor." Although her voice was mournful, there was a wide grin on her plain face. "Your aunt received a letter many months ago detailing Herr Upton's demise. This year his son, Wesley Upton, will be coming to make the acquaintance with your aunt."

A pulsing silence filled the room as Blaine and Tate took in the significance of the governess's words. A low chuckle issued from Tate, which was echoed by the unruffled Puff. Blaine was not as easily convinced.

"We'd never get away with it," she whispered.

Tate stood up and stared at Blaine, her eyes narrowed speculatively. When she spoke, she addressed Puff. "It wouldn't take much. We can use some of Lady Yates's lacy caps and pad her out a bit. She'll look a treat. With the proper makeup, even Fleur wouldn't be able to recognize her."

"I shan't listen to a word of this," Blaine cried. "Tate. Puff. Just think of what you're saying."

Ignoring her totally, Puff spoke over her head. "It vill be her skin that vill give her away. Could she be wearing a veil or something?"

"I assure you, my friend, makeup will do the trick." Tate preened as she pursed her lips in decision. "I do all Miss Blaine's makeup. It will be a simple matter to create a sort of mask that would hide the youthfulness of her skin. Even up close it would pass the test. It's her hands what worry me."

"Mittens!" the governess announced in triumph. "Lady Yates had many pairs of greatest beauty."

"Just the ticket," Tate agreed.

Afraid to listen to the seductive voices of her companions, Blaine jumped to her feet and faced the two women. "We cannot do it. It would not be honest."

"Piffle!" Tate snorted.

"*Gott in Himmel!*" came Puff's more exasperated retort. "The *kinder* must come first."

"Look, Miss Blaine. We've little choice in the matter. Without the money from your father's will, we will have to sell up Weathers and then Val will lose his estate. If your father had known the straits you'd be in, would he have left things as they were?"

"Of course not, Tate," Blaine answered without hesitation. "I cannot like it, though."

"Iffen it will soothe your conscience any, you can pay back the estate when times are better. For now, you've got to think of the children."

The dresser's words were aimed deliberately at Blaine's most vulnerable spot. Deceit did not come easily to her, but fear for the future of Val and Fleur would drive her to take drastic measures. Tate and Puff smiled complacently as Blaine nodded her head in defeat.

And so had begun the Great Deception, as Blaine called it. For her, the saddest part was the feeling that they were not honoring Lady Yates's death as they should. Tate and Puff reasoned with her that her aunt had requested she be buried in the north of England beside her husband. It was easy enough to ignore the neighborhood. Technically the family had been in mourning when Lady Yates arrived, and afterward she had been too involved with the children to feel a need to socialize. Feeling great bitterness that such secrecy was necessary, Blaine sent the faithful Sarge to accompany the body north while the rest of the household hid their grief and tried to carry on as usual. And for four years, she had played the part of Lady Yates for an audience of one, Wesley Upton, the solicitor.

The sudden change in the speed of the horses brought Blaine out of her reverie. The sadness and bitterness eased from her body as she sensed that they had arrived at Weathers. But the tiredness that had plagued her of late did not abate as they approached the house. She sighed and thought of how for the last six years she had been playing a series of roles. In London, she was the celebrated Maggie Mason, La Solitaire, and when she returned home she became Lady Haydie Yates, guardian of Fleur and Val. She would give much to become plain Blaine Margaret Meriweather again.

four

"I want to go to London and have a season," Fleur repeated, her pansy eyes filling and threatening to overflow.

For a moment Blaine was reminded of her stepmother Juliette, who had used the same tearful tactics to get her way. She blinked and the vision was gone and she was faced by the real distress she saw in her sister's eyes. Aware that Fleur had waited up to speak to her, Blaine sighed and tried to ignore her tiredness from the journey and the lateness of the hour.

She was amazed at the transformation of Fleur. At Christmas, the girl had seemed just a child but now she was a woman grown. At eighteen, Fleur had fulfilled all the prophecies of beauty that Blaine had once predicted. She was in every way the epitome of the London debutante most in style. In the golden lights from the candles, she resembled a vision that would set the hearts of the dandy set aflutter. Her hair was the same gold of the sun, naturally curly, falling in ringlets to her shoulders. She was tiny, with fragile bones, and had large violet eyes and the pinkish-white skin of a baby. Her voice was sweet and her laughter held the sound of tinkling bells. In her simple, light green muslin dress, she truly did resemble a flower.

Although Fleur was lovely to look at, there were other things that Blaine noted that did not please her half so well. The girl had a tendency to pout and appeared slightly self-centered but she suspected that much of this was merely a lack of maturity. She assumed her sister would grow out of this stage but she admitted to some worry on this point. She had always cosseted Fleur, feeling guilty that she was not around as much as she ought to be. The young girl needed a strong hand and Blaine suspected that Puff, who adored her charge, was not firm enough.

"You're not even listening," Fleur cried.

"I'm sorry, dear," Blaine said, turning her full attention on her sister. "It was only that I was so surprised at the request. I am gone so much that sometimes I forget you are no longer a child."

"I'm quite grown-up and I think it's time that I enter society." Fleur peered beneath her lashes to see what effect her words had on her sister, and seeing the stiffness of Blaine's face, she immediately launched into speech.

"I'm tired of being stuck here at Weathers. Puff is such an old fusspot, she never lets me do anything."

"It is Puff's job to protect you and see to your welfare. And from the sound of things, I cannot imagine that she has had such an easy time of it." Blaine's voice was soft, but the hard edge warned the girl that she had gone too far in criticizing her governess.

"Puff is wonderful," Fleur said in apology. "But I'm so bored here. I am not allowed to go out in society. All I do is ride around the countryside and go into the village to shop. It's just so unfair! I want to go to balls and the theater. I want to meet other girls my own age and flirt with gentlemen who can talk of something other than their crops. But here I am, kept prisoner in the country, while you're having all the fun in London!"

If Blaine hadn't been so stunned by her sister's accusation, she would have laughed. She stared across at the petulant girl, wondering why it had never occurred to her to expect such a scene. Fleur had been told that Blaine had gone to London as companion to her father's cousin. The fictitious Lavinia Birdwell was said to be old, crotchety, and infirm. Blaine had not realized that her sister would assume she was out in society, going to dances and mingling with titled gentlemen. In horror she wondered how long Fleur had been nursing resentment of her older sister's way of life.

If only she knew, Blaine thought, choking back a sound that was more nearly a sob than a sign of amusement. She was so nonplussed by Fleur's words that she did not know what to say. Finally she blurted out the first thing that came to mind: "We have not enough money to sponsor you for the season."

"That's all I ever hear," Fleur said, stamping her foot before she flounced down on the window seat. "If you had made the slightest push to get married, we would have."

Blaine winced at the girl's words, closing her eyes to combat the pain that suddenly assailed her. As if Fleur realized she had gone much too far, she ran across the room and threw herself into her sister's arms.

"Oh, Blaine, forgive me for being such a beast." There were real tears in the pansy eyes and this time they overflowed, rolling unheeded down the white cheeks of the contrite girl. "I did not mean to hurt you, Blaine. Please forgive me."

Blaine hugged her, knowing that the girl had not intended to be cruel. Calmly analyzing the situation, she could understand the girl's discontent. Her words came from not knowing the true situation of their lives, and Blaine had only herself to blame for such a misunderstanding.

"Come. Come, Fleur. Your tears will only make your eyes red, and then I shall feel twice as guilty at the ruination of your beauty." A damp chuckle followed this sally and Blaine gave the girl a final hug as she pushed her away. "Sit up and dry your eyes while I think."

While Fleur dabbed at her eyes with a scrap of cambric, Blaine examined the girl, trying to view her criticisms objectively. She had to admit her sister did have some justice on her side. Blaine had given strict instructions to Frau Puffentraub that would ensure the safety of the girl. She had wanted to protect the girl from disillusionment by isolating her from society.

After several years of the London scene, Blaine had seen the heartbreak and pain that could result when a young girl was unprepared for the lies and seductions of more experienced men. She had hoped to spare Fleur by keeping her isolated until she was older. As she observed the girl, Blaine realized it was this very isolation that had stunted the growth of sophistication her sister would need to fight off unwanted male advances.

Fleur was eighteen now and should be going about in society. Perhaps it was time that Blaine loosened her restrictions — before, in her discontent, the girl rebelled completely.

"Are there no young men in the neighborhood?" Blaine asked.

"Well, yes." Fleur dropped her eyes to her lap and pleated the muslin of her skirt. "But Puff says I cannot accept any invitations since I am not out yet."

"Puff was merely following my instructions, my dear. Until now I did not feel you were old enough." She raised a hand as Fleur started to interrupt. "However, I can see that I may have been wrong. Depending on the kind of invitation, perhaps you might be able to accept, as long as Puff is included as your chaperone."

"But, Blaine, the trouble is that we never receive any invitations!" Fleur cried.

As tears threatened again, Blaine patted the girl briskly. "Come, Fleur. Don't turn into a watering pot. Tell me what all this nonsense is about."

"It is not nonsense," she answered, her lip jutting out as anger replaced her tears. "When Aunt Haydie first arrived, she refused all invitations since we were in mourning and she had little need to socialize. After she died, in order to keep up the fiction that I still had a proper guardian, we turned everyone away, saying her health was too precarious for visitors. And now the entire county is convinced that there is some dreadful secret that we are trying to hide by our seclusion."

"What kind of secret?" Blaine asked in concern.

"For four years, no one has seen Aunt Haydie. And now it appears that the wildest rumors have been circulating." Fleur raised her eyes to her sister, and Blaine could see the girl was clearly agitated. "So you see, no one will ever invite me anywhere since everyone thinks that Aunt Haydie has gone out of her head and is locked away to keep the secret safe."

"Great Heavenly Day!" Blaine was stunned by the shock of her sister's words. Knowing the country people as well as she did, it amazed her that she had never considered this bizarre possibility.

Their ability to pull off the Great Deception had been possible by the very fact that no one in the neighborhood was acquainted with Aunt Haydie. Although she had impersonated her aunt for the benefit of the family solicitor, it had never occurred to her to continue the fiction for the benefit of the neighborhood. She could understand that the very invisibility of Lady Yates had contributed to wild conjectures about the family.

No wonder Fleur was on the edge of rebellion. Isolated from the Wiltshire society by her sister's orders and ugly rumor, she had some right to her feelings of ill usage. The headache that had been building increased and Blaine raised her hands to her throbbing temples.

"Let me think about all of this, Fleur, and we'll talk tomorrow. It's late and very difficult for me to think. I do not wish to be unfair to you. Between us, sweetheart, we should be able to find a way out of this coil."

Although Fleur's face immediately brightened, Blaine was far from certain that she would find a solution to their problem. She retired to her room and tossed and turned much of the night, but by morning she was little closer to a solution. Dressing quickly, she arrived at the doorway of the breakfast room just as Val skipped down the stairs.

"Oh, Blaine!" The boy hesitated, uncertain how to greet her, then as she opened her arms, he ran across the marble floor to throw his arms around her waist. "I'm glad you're home at last," he said, extricating himself from her embrace.

"So am I, brat," Blaine said, ruffling his hair as she passed into the breakfast room. "And I'm starving."

Mrs. Ames, who doubled as cook and housekeeper, had been waiting for Blaine's arrival and fussed over her as she eyed the service of a freckle-faced maid. "It's glad I am that you've finally come home. With the looks of you, I can see we'll have to fatten you up before we send you back to that heathen city."

"I am only permitted to gorge myself this morning, in honor of my return," Blaine mumbled around a mouthful of steak-and-kidney pie. "I'll burst all the seams in my gowns and then I'll have Tate ranting and raving."

"You can spend the day in the saddle," Val offered, "and then you can eat all you want."

"He's got the right of it, miss. Just look how much he's grown. All of eleven he is, and ever so bright." The housekeeper grinned fondly at the boy as she left the room.

Val, embarrassed to be the focus of his sister's attention, reddened to the tips of his ears and busied himself with his mug of hot chocolate.

"Soon you'll be ready for the hunt, Val. How's Fatima?" Blaine smiled at the elegant name, ludicrous now that the pony had gained so much weight.

"Smashing! I've taught her some new tricks. Would you like to see her after breakfast?" he asked shyly.

"Of course I would, and then perhaps you'll accompany me in a ride."

"Good show!" The boy jumped to his feet,

eager to be off to the stables. At the door, he skidded to a stop and turned back to his sister. "Thanks ever so much for the books. I found them on my nightstand and I only had time for a quick glance. The one about Stonehenge looks to be a proper smasher."

"I thought you might like that one. We all had such a grand time last year when we visited the place." Blaine waved her hand as she picked up her cup of tea. "Run along now and leave me in peace. I'll be along shortly to see the miracle pony."

However, Blaine had only a few minutes before her quiet was interrupted by a sharp wail from the region of the hallway. Before she could rise to investigate, the door was pulled open and Fleur, her face set in a mournful mien, stumbled into the room.

"Oh, la, Blaine," she wailed. "My life is ruined."

Blaine rolled her eyes as her sister sighed melodramatically and threw herself into a chair, staring glumly down at the crumpled note in her hand.

"Perhaps you'd care to share the contents of the missive," Blaine suggested, taking a bracing sip of her tea.

"It's from our near neighbor. His brother has come from London for a visit and he wanted to call this afternoon."

"Are you acquainted with this person?"

"His name is Robbie and I've known him for just ages," Fleur announced breezily, hurrying into speech before Blaine could inquire further. "He owns Fairhaven, which is quite near the village. I have seen him frequently but he has never been to call. Oh, how I wish Aunt Haydie were here!" she wailed.

Suddenly the girl sat up and stared across the table at Blaine. At the look of calculation in her sister's eyes, Blaine narrowed hers, as the realization of Fleur's idea dawned on her. She held up her hand in refusal.

"Don't even consider it, my girl."

"Oh, Blaine, it would be the perfect solution. You will be playing the part of Aunt Haydie for the solicitor, anyway, so why couldn't you do it for your sister."

"Really, Fleur. That is like comparing apples and pears. The only reason I ever agreed to masquerade as Lady Yates was for the sheer necessity of keeping the yearly allowance. You know how I hate the deception."

"My whole life will be ruined." Fleur cried, tears welling up in her violet eyes. "Here is my one chance to stop the talk in the neighborhood and you won't make the slightest push to help me."

Blaine was still feeling guilty over her talk

with Fleur the night before. She hated to see her sister ostracized from the country society because they thought there was something irregular about the family. Perhaps if Aunt Haydie made one appearance, it would give Fleur the entree she needed.

"What time did the gentlemen wish to call?" Blaine asked, defeated by the pitiful expression in the violet eyes across from her.

"Oh, Blaine! You are the very best of sisters!" Fleur squealed as she launched herself out of her chair and danced around the room hugging herself. "I shall send them a note telling them to come after lunch."

Not waiting for a change of heart, the girl dashed from the room. Blaine sighed heavily, suspecting she would live to regret this decision. Although she rode with Val and tried to show the proper enthusiasm for the display of Fatima's talents, her mind continually returned to the problem of Aunt Haydie's appearance. So far the house servants had kept the secret of Lady Yates's death in order to protect Fleur and Val. But would a further deception help or merely add to their difficulties?

"How's Cousin Lavinia?" Val asked as they paused in the woods to rest the horses.

"Poorly," Blaine answered automatically.

"You say that every time I ask," the boy

said, a furrow ruffling the smooth surface of his forehead. "You know, Blaine, you should try to convince her to come here with you on your holiday. I'm sure that the fresh air would do wonders for the old girl's constitution."

Blaine tried not to smile at the gravity of her brother's remarks. "I am sure it would, Val. The problem is that she is really not well enough to travel such a great distance."

"Oh," the boy said wistfully. "I just thought if she could come for a visit you would be able to stay longer. It is such a treat having you at home. Fleur is much too nice to go tramping around the woods. All she does is moan and groan that she will get dirty."

It saddened Blaine to realize what a muddle she had made of things. Val was clearly lonely and she ached that she was forced to neglect him so much.

"Have you any companions to go round about with?" she asked.

"Not so many anymore." He shrugged philosophically, in a gesture far too old for his tender years. At Blaine's questioning look, he continued. "I used to play with some of the tenants' children. Now that I've been able to take over some of the estate affairs, it has become different. It is very difficult to come around inspecting and that sort of thing if the tenants treat me like a baby."

Blaine wanted to hug him for the hurt confusion she heard in his voice. Since the death of the estate manager, Higgins, she had taken over the running of the estate. In the last year or two she had been turning some of the responsibility over to Val so that he would be prepared to handle it when he came of age. She could understand that once he began to show some authority, his relationship with the tenants was bound to change.

"Perhaps it is time that you met other boys in the neighborhood," she said. By the apprehensive look on his face, she realized that he, too was well aware of the gossip. "Never fear, halfling. I have heard what is being said and I think I may have a solution. Come along back to the house and I shall tell you of my plan. Besides, it is still much too cold for Fatima's dainty constitution to be abroad on such a frosty morning."

Val giggled and lay along the fat pony's neck to stroke her velvety ears. "You must not let her hear you talk so, Blaine, or the dear old thing will bolt back to the stable."

"Bolt? It would be more like a slow waddle."

She laughed happily, turning her horse's head to lead the way. In quiet harmony they cooled down and groomed the animals. After a quick wash they met again in the library where Blaine told him of her proposal to masquerade as Aunt Haydie for the benefit of the callers. When she finished, she asked if he would be able to handle one more secret.

"Of course I can, Blaine," he declared staunchly. "After all, it should be no additional strain to have Aunt Haydie return to life since I have not been clap-jawed about her death."

Blaine smiled in remembrance of the boy's words as Tate helped her dress for the reappearance of Lady Yates. The sour face of the old lady indicated her disapproval for this additional impersonation.

"Think of it as a dress rehearsal, Tate," Blaine said. She turned in front of the cheval glass. "You've done a fine job with everything."

"No need to turn me up sweet," the dresser snapped. "I know my job and would never turn you out less than perfect. I cannot like this whole idea and Frau Puffentraub is in agreement. Fleur slumguzzled you if you ask me, which knowing you, I know you won't. You shouldn't give in to the child."

"I'm not really giving in. I just think it might help to allay the talk in the neighborhood. I should have noticed what was happening long before this. It's me own guilt what done me in," she finished cheekily. She threw up her hands as the woman still continued glumly, "My whole life is such a lie that it's monstrously hard to cavil at one more."

One look at her mistress's doleful expression and Tate immediately dropped her air of injury. "Never mind, lamb. I'm sure everything will turn out fine. You've the talent to pull it all off. Don't forget to move slowly and keep your hands still so as not to draw attention to them," she admonished.

Blaine studied herself in the mirror, amazed at the transformation. She wore a stiff bombazine gown, liberally padded so that her figure flowed from neck to waist without a break. A silver-rimmed lorgnette hung from a velvet cord pinned to her imposing bosom. The dress was an unrelieved black so that her skin appeared pale in contrast. To add to the pallor, a white paste, much like the maquillage still worn by some of the old ladies of the court, had been applied to her skin. Rouge stood out starkly on her stiffened cheeks. A fussy lace cap, edged in black, completely covered her hair, and several white ringlets of fake hair hid her ears. All in all she looked a proper old lady, Blaine thought as she pursed her mouth in a prim expression.

"Oh, you look perfect." Fleur clapped her hands in approval as Blaine entered the parlor, leaning heavily on an oak walking stick with an ivory knob. "Just like those high-toned tabbies I see riding through the village."

"Take a damper, Fleur," Blaine snapped. "This is not a game. 'Tis a far riskier venture than fooling an old man like the solicitor. Just try to remember to treat me like an old lady. Forget that I am your sister and think of me only as Aunt Haydie. Then you will be far less likely to make a slip."

Fleur quieted immediately under her sister's uneasy glance. She helped to pull the curtain to darken the room slightly and then scurried to find a lap robe to throw across Blaine's knees to increase the suggestion of Aunt Haydie's invalid status. They had only just finished their preparations when the sounds from the hall indicated the arrival of callers.

Blaine offered up prayers that Fleur would be up to the challenge. She suspected the girl thought the whole idea a bit of a lark and had no conception of the disaster that would result in the event their duplicity was discovered. As the door to the parlor opened, Blaine took in a deep breath and let it out slowly as she prepared to play her part.

A short stocky man with pleasant looks and warm brown eyes entered, beaming foolishly at Fleur. It was immediately apparent to

Blaine that the man and her sister had more than a passing acquaintance and she determined to question Fleur as to the goings-on in her absence. The man appeared to be a gentleman with an air of refinement as he bowed over Fleur's hand. When he moved aside Blaine's eyes widened at the sight of the other man and she caught back a gasp as she recognized the arrogant features of Lord Andrew Farrington.

A wave of blackness assailed her as she stared in horror at the man. She closed her eyes, terrified that the intentness of her gaze would draw his notice. She breathed deeply, trying to control the pounding of her heartbeat. At the sound of approaching footsteps, she opened her eyes and drew herself up haughtily.

"Auntie, dear," Fleur said, her voice a trembling whisper in her nervousness, "I would like to make known to you our neighbor, Lord Robert Farrington, and his brother, Lord Andrew Farrington."

Fingers shaking beneath the lacy mittens, Blaine raised the lorgnette and stared icily at the two men. "Farrington, eh? Any relationship to the Farringtons in Derbyshire?" she asked, hoping the quaver in her throaty voice would be mistaken for age.

"Only distantly, ma'am," the younger man answered.

"A flighty bunch at best. Their pockets have been to let since well before you were born, young man." She hoped neither of the men would notice Fleur, who had the slack-jawed look of a hooked fish. This was the first time that the girl had been privy to Blaine's impersonation and it was clear she was astonished. Under cover of her lap robe, she nudged the girl who snapped her mouth shut, wincing as if she had bitten her tongue. Blaine returned her concentration to the young man. "Can't abide those who play deep and fritter away their inheritances. And you, are you living on your expectations?"

"No, ma'am," Robbie declared immediately. "Fairhaven is a very prosperous estate. It provides a very comfortable living."

"Hmmph" was Blaine's answer. She turned as if to take the measure of Drew Farrington. Her hand shook slightly but she surveyed him from artfully curled head to shining booted feet. She almost sighed at the end of her scrutiny. He was truly a magnificent figure; his tall, lean body beneath his buckskins had the taut muscularity of an athlete. Her gaze returned to his face and she blinked at the sardonically raised eyebrow above his amused green gaze.

"Lady Yates. Delighted to see you in such

fine twig," he drawled, bending his body in a slight obeisance.

"I can see you ain't sickly," Blaine snapped, then noticing her sister's agitation, she turned to the girl. "Stop fluttering, Fleur. Ring for tea."

With an expression of only mild curiosity, Drew took a seat and looked around the drawing room. It was well appointed despite the fact that it was in sad need of refurbishing. The furnishings themselves bespoke of good taste and genteel background, each piece obviously well chosen to suit the room. It was not at all what he had been expecting.

In fact, nothing was quite as he had suspected. He had assumed Fleur Meriweather was a scheming jade of poor, uneducated parentage. Impoverished the girl might be but it was apparent that her antecedents were impeccable. The girl herself, barely a child out of the schoolroom, was a far cry from the cold, calculating chit he had been prepared to write off as an adventuress. Fleur was an innocently wide-eyed child who was trying out her fledgling wings by flirting with him beneath outrageously long eyelashes as she poured tea.

Two things Drew noted immediately. Robbie was truly in love with the golden blond child and Fleur was not in love with Robbie.

Drew's green eyes glittered as he watched his brother. Although Robbie was busy speaking to Lady Yates, his eyes rarely strayed from Fleur for any length of time. His eyes shone with adoration and his color rose and receded at every glance from the object of his affections. On the other hand, Fleur looked at Robbie with the same enthusiasm one might bestow on a younger brother. Drew suspected that she thought of him as a friend but as yet did not consider him in the role of a suitor, let alone a lover. It would be rough times ahead for Robbie before he could hope to win the hand of this pretty child.

"Will you be staying long with Robbie?" Fleur asked, nervous at the steady gaze trained on her.

"I try to keep my country visits to only brief forays, Miss Meriweather."

"But surely you enjoy riding in the woods. There is much to be admired in the beauty of nature," Fleur said.

For a moment Drew wondered if the girl were quite as ingenuous as she appeared but one look at the guileless violet eyes disabused him of such a base notion. "I do find everything in Wiltshire of singular beauty. But that is not solely reserved for the scenery," he answered.

At his words, Fleur blushed, the color rising in an intriguing wave of pink and she dropped her eyes to the hands in her lap, feeling unequal to the sophisticated banter of the man.

Blaine, although she was having a pleasant chat with Robbie, was aware of Drew's every movement. She chided herself for staring at him but found her eyes constantly drawn to his aristocratic features. She was angry at Fleur for making a cake of herself by her attempts to flirt with the man. She had seen the amusement in Drew's eyes at her sister's behavior but she must admit he was being gentle with the girl. Despite his arrogance, he seemed aware that Fleur was not experienced enough to handle even the lightest of flirtations.

"Please say that you and Miss Meriweather will come," Robbie said.

Blaine jumped at the voice beside her. She was embarrassed that she had let her attention wander from the young man at her side. Any more lapses and she would surely give the game away.

"Must have been woolgathering." She snorted, once more firmly back in the role of Aunt Haydie.

"Sorry, Lady Yates, I suspect I did not couch the invitation in clearest terms." Robbie grinned at the raised eyebrow of the old lady. "My brother and I were hoping that you and Miss Meriweather would join us for a small dinner party Friday evening at Fairhaven."

"Oh, Aunt Haydie, may we please?" Fleur chorused with a quick glance at Robbie.

Blaine had seen the shared gaze of the two and suspected that this whole affair had been a well-planned campaign. It was obvious the girl's explanation of a casual acquaintance with Robert Farrington was a clear fabrication. She glared at Fleur, who flushed and dropped her gaze to her lap.

"It is, of course, quite neighborly of you to invite us but unfortunately I do not think I am up to such an adventure," Blaine replied dampeningly.

"I trust you are not unwell, Lady Yates."

Blaine's eyes flashed to Drew's interested face. She wondered what it was about the arrangement of his features that she found so compelling. "Thank you for your concern, but I have been in delicate health this winter."

"One would not think it to see the bloom of color in your cheeks," he drawled.

"Cheeky devil," Blaine said unable to keep the gleam of amusement out of her own eyes at his allusion to her rouged appearance. "More to the point, gentlemen, Fleur is not overused to society."

"It would seem to me, ma'am," Drew offered quietly, "that a family party in the neighborhood might be the very place for a young lady to try out her wings. Unless, of course, you feel that Robbie and myself would be improper influences on your niece."

Drew had to admit the woman intrigued him. She seemed robust enough, although his brother had led him to believe that the woman was prone to ill health. From what little he had observed, the old girl was a real tartar, outspoken and sarcastic. Lord knew there was little enough to amuse him at Fairhaven and in order to push forward Robbie's suit he might as well enjoy himself with the wit and intelligence he saw in Lady Yates's eyes. Nothing in Drew's casual pose indicated that he had thrown down a gauntlet but the keen light in his eyes suggested it as he met the older woman's gaze.

Blaine read the challenge in Drew's eyes and drew herself up straighter in the chair. She wondered if he, too, were involved in this scheme to launch Fleur on society. One look at the ascetic features and she discarded that thought. Knowing him as little as she did, she still thought he would never sink to devious measures. He might be ruthless in battle but his attack would always be made directly, never in an oblique fashion.

"It is not that I mistrust your motives, sirrah," Blaine conceded. "I fear the jouncing of our ancient carriage would be unsettling to my constitution."

"Of course, Lady Yates. At last I understand your quandary." Drew smiled benignly at the old woman. "Naturally, I shall place my carriage at your disposal. It is of the latest design and will transport you as if you were flown on the wings of angels. Shall we say nine o'clock?"

Faced with the amused triumph reflected in Drew's gaze, Blaine could do little more than nod in agreement. Inwardly she raged that she had been placed in such an untenable position. She would comb Fleur's hair with a stool, she thought waspishly at the satisfied look on the girl's face. She might be defeated but she would at least go down fighting.

"Nine o'clock, young man? I am more used to country hours," she said. "However, it will be as you say. Naturally Fleur and I must needs return directly after we eat. Young girls need their proper rest."

Fleur pouted under Blaine's sweetly smiling gaze as the men rose to take their leave. The girl did, however, acquit herself well as she accompanied them to the door. Blaine was finally able to relax in her chair and waited patiently for her sister to return. She would find out just what the girl had been up to and then deal with the dinner party. The thought of making a public appearance as Lady Yates filled her with unease and yet she could see no way out of the predicament. In her attempt to resolve Fleur and Val's isolation from society, she feared she had placed all of them in a very dangerous situation.

five

Despite her misgivings about attending the dinner party at Fairhaven, Blaine discovered that she was enjoying herself immensely. In a way, she felt a reversal of the normal order of her life. As Aunt Haydie, she was relegated to the background, an invisible spectator watching the main players in the drama. Once the fear eased that her disguise might be penetrated, she began to delight in the role she was playing.

Owing to her secluded early life and her self-imposed exile from society, she had never been involved in normal conversation with others of her background. Almost exclusively, she associated with the theater company but even there she had learned quickly that she had to be extremely careful of what she said or the male actors would immediately misinterpret her friendliness. She had adopted a standoffish attitude that many assumed was snobbery but it protected her from undesirable advances.

As Lady Yates, her supposed age gave her a

freedom she had never possessed before. She need not suspect the intentions of anyone who spoke to her, so she was able to enter into the conversation as she chose, asking questions or commenting without fear of creating the wrong impression.

During the dinner party at Fairhaven, the company was small so the conversation encompassed the whole table and, despite the fact that the guests were predominantly youthful, the discussions covered an interesting range of topics. Although much of the conversation revolved around familiar figures of London society, it did not degenerate to the cataloging of scandals and the spicier snippets of gossip. Much to Blaine's surprise, this high tone was owed primarily to the presence of Drew Farrington.

He faced her across the table so that she was aware of his every movement. Dressed in black satin, his linen blindingly white, devoid of jewelry with the exception of a single emerald ring on one tanned hand, Drew dominated the company. It was not that he spoke with any great frequency but he masterfully guided the conversation, choosing topics that would be of general interest to draw out the other guests at table. He had a keen wit, his humor generally directed at himself rather than others. It was a virtuoso performance and one that gave Blaine a more kindly view of the man. He might be arrogant but he was not one to listen for only the sound of his own voice.

Looking down the table, Blaine's mouth formed a thin line of distaste. The only objection she had to the evening was the inclusion of Talbott Stoddard. It had jolted her mightily when the man had entered the salon. He had been visiting one of Robbie's neighbors and as a courtesy was included in the invitation. To Blaine, it seemed inconceivable that the two men who had been pursuing La Solitaire so assiduously were both at the table with her.

Next to Stoddard was Fleur. Blaine's heart swelled with pride at the loveliness of her sister. She wore a puff-sleeved gown of palest pink silk with a wide ruffle at neckline and hem. The color brought out the golden quality of her hair and reflected the pink tones of her complexion. Pearls hung around her neck and dangled from her ears when she moved.

While helping Fleur prepare for the evening, Blaine had noted the glow of excitement that radiated from the girl and felt a keen sense of sadness. She herself had never had the naïve joy of a debutante in her first season. She had gone from a sheltered and isolated home life to the disillusioning experiences of the theatrical world. She prayed that Fleur might never lose the innocence that shone in her violet eyes.

She did not like the fact that Fleur had been placed next to Stoddard. The refreshing innocence of the beautiful girl had immediately drawn the interest of the jaded palate of the nobleman. Blaine could see that her sister was quite taken with the elegant manners of the handsome blond gentleman and she was relieved when the dinner was over, eager to call Fleur away from the dangerous Stoddard.

"Ah, Lady Yates," Drew said, "won't you take my arm?"

Blaine blinked at the speed with which the man had rounded the table. He stood now, blocking her way, and it would only make a scene if she refused him. The footman behind her chair extended her walking stick and she grasped it convulsively as she forced herself to nod graciously at Drew. "Thank you, Lord Farrington."

"Robbie insists I give you a tour of the Long Gallery since this is the first time that you have been at Fairhaven," Drew said, pulling her hand through his arm. Noticing the worried look in the old woman's eye as she looked back at Fleur, he hurried to reassure her. "Robbie will look after your little chick and keep her out of harm's way." He took a step, still sensing her hesitation. "Just lean on me, Lady Yates. I shall walk very slowly, ma'am, and then you will not be inclined to get winded."

"There's nothing wrong with my wind, you rapscallion," Blaine snapped, annoyed at his vision of her as a simpering invalid.

"Excellent. Then we shall move right along." Drew grinned at her as he led her away from the rest of the company.

Once more Blaine realized how quickly he had outmaneuvered her. Instead of objecting to his company she had fallen into the trap of defending her health. *Vanity* she thought to herself, *will be your undoing.*

As they walked through the corridors, Drew treated her to a discussion of the ancestry of many of the pieces on display. He halted before a case of Chinese ivory carvings, while she admired the delicacy of the workmanship. When they arrived at the Long Gallery he led her around the room, stopping at the various pictures, amusing her with scandalous tales of his forebears.

"This is my Great Uncle Danforth. He lived to an amazing age and was the despair of all of our more staid relatives. The man had a penchant for the ladies and was wont to chase the chambermaids through the hallways while shouting 'Tallyho' and blow-ing a hunting bugle."

"Definitely would cut up the peace," Blaine answered, a light chuckle breaking through despite her best efforts. "Had a similar uncle but he had a severe spasm one day and was gone in an instant."

"I suppose the chase was too much for him," Drew said.

"No," she said. "More like the capture."

"Lady Yates!" Drew snorted in amusement. When the old woman raised her lorgnette in question, he threw back his head with a genuine bark of laughter. "I knew when I first met you that I would find enjoyment in your company. Your eyes give you away. They fair sparkle with mischief. And I was afraid that my stay in the country would be deadly dull."

"Why exactly did you come to stay with your brother? A repairing lease?"

"Robbie asked me to come," Drew answered quietly.

"I see. Wants help with his suit, eh?"

"Something like that."

"At least you've not offered me Spanish coin. I like to be dealt with honestly." Being careful to move slowly, Blaine crossed the parquet floor to a grouping of carved walnut benches. She sat down as if stiff with rheumatic pains and crossed her mittened

117

hands over the carved knob of her walking stick. "It's no good, you know," she said, her voice a deep rumble in the quiet room.

"Fleur is very young," Drew said, indicating he understood her perfectly.

"The shameless chit has confessed that she has been meeting with your brother. For her part, it was a harmless lark to relieve her boredom. Luckily for her, Robbie is a gentleman." Blaine met Drew's amused glance with a grimace. "I have seen much of this world and I have tried to make her understand that her behavior might have reaped tragic consequences."

"Did she believe you?" he asked out of curiosity.

"Naturally not!" Blaine shrugged at the uselessness of giving advice. "She sees the world as a place of wonder and purity. Most men would take advantage of such innocence."

Drew's gaze sharpened at the bitterness in the old woman's voice. He knew little of her life and yet he wondered at the jaundiced view of men she held. He waited in silence for her to continue, surprised that he wished to know her perceptions.

"I like your brother, milord. He has a pleasant nature and I sense a stability that would make him an excellent husband. I gather he has no need to make a wealthy marriage, which is just as well, since Fleur has only a small dowry." She paused, looking up into Drew's face. "Is Robbie aware of the fact that Fleur is not in love with him?"

"Yes, he does know that. Unfortunately, he assumed that since she treated him as a friend, all he need do was to declare himself, and she would fall into his arms. Watching him tonight, I would guess he has come to the understanding that it will not be quite so easy." Drew placed one foot on the bench beside Lady Yates and braced his arms on his leg as he pursed his lips in thought. "I think Robbie was not aware of how isolated your niece has been from all society. Tonight, in the presence of the other men at the table, he has received a much different view of her situation."

Blaine nodded in agreement.

"It is my thought that Fleur would be the perfect wife for Robbie," Drew continued. "She looks to him for friendship and generally that is the beginning of love. But she is young and will want to spread her wings a little and try out her powers. If he can be patient, I think he might win her in the end. Would you approve of Robbie's suit?"

Blaine fussed with the silver-rimmed lorgnette but did not raise it to her eyes. She stared across the room, her eyes not really seeing the array of portraits. When she spoke it was as though she were working out the problem in her own mind.

"When Fleur was just a child, I knew she would grow to be an exceptional beauty. I wanted her to go to London so that she might marry a titled gentleman who could give her the world. But in the last several years I have come to the realization that would not guarantee her happiness."

"Is there any guarantee for happiness?" Drew asked quietly.

"Probably not," she admitted. "London is much different than Wiltshire. The so-called gentlemen of the ton are not the kind of men who engender much admiration. Many are morally bankrupt, keeping mistresses or playing fast and loose with other men's wives. Many are on the lookout for rich wives because they have already run through their inheritances. Few have the qualities I would choose for Fleur. In Robbie I find much that is admirable and would accept him as a suitor for her hand."

A low chuckle echoed in the quiet room and Blaine looked up questioningly at her companion. When Drew smiled his face softened, losing the arrogant appearance that she found so annoying. His green eyes sparkled against his tanned face and his teeth flashed whitely.

"It seems our goals for Fleur and Robbie are very similar. I will be frank with you,

Lady Yates. I came to Wiltshire at Robbie's request but my intentions were to save him from the clutches of some scheming jade." He smiled, his eyes crinkling at the corners when she bristled in anger. "Hear me out, ma'am, before you condemn my actions."

Blaine subsided on the bench, caught by the gleam of laughter in his gaze. She wished he would remove his foot. His closeness was having an unsettling effect on her nerves. The material pulled tautly across his leg and she could see the musculature rippling beneath the skin at every movement of his body. She had to keep a tight grip on the top of her walking stick because she was filled with an urge to reach out and touch him. She raised her eyes to his face and forced her mind to focus on his words and not the nearness of his body.

"Robbie, as you perhaps have ascertained, is like Fleur: the trusting type. When he informed me that he had been meeting secretly with a young lady of impoverished circumstances with, if I may be pardoned, an invisible aunt, my suspicions were aroused. I rushed here to save him and, much to my surprise, found the wicked temptress to be nothing more threatening than a well-brought-up babe sprung lately from the nursery."

"Believe me, young man, there is nothing more dangerous," Blaine intoned archly.

"Unless it is her beady-eyed mother," Drew said with a shudder. "However, to return to the subject. Do you think Fleur might come to look on Robbie with some favor?"

"If she has any sense, she will, but one never knows with young girls." Blaine bit her lip, deep in concentration. "Fleur has always had a very sweet nature. Despite her disenchantment of the moment, she loves the country and has a strong feeling for the land. It is just lately that she seems petulant and bored. Perhaps I have been wrong in keeping her so close. In London, with her beauty, she would be sure to take but I do not think she would be happy in that society. The question is, will Robbie be content to stand by while she discovers the joy of being young and a lovely female?"

"I think once he thinks on it, he will. We shall have to do what we can to be of assistance." Drew placed his foot on the floor and held out his hand. "Well, madam, how like you the role of Cupid?"

" 'All the world's a stage,' " Blaine quoted, taking Drew's hand and letting him assist her to her feet. At his touch, she did not need to pretend an aged shakiness as her knees felt decidedly unsteady. "I shall play my part like the veriest trouper."

Drew's brow furrowed at the touch of irony

in her voice but led her back to the main parlor, well pleased with his chat with the old lady. He had not been wrong about the intelligence or the wit of the woman. Her insights were perceptive and he had thoroughly enjoyed himself in her company. Lady Yates would make a formidable coconspirator.

On entering the room, Blaine's eyes immediately found Fleur, seated in a window embrasure, listening raptly to Talbott Stoddard. The girl's cheeks were flushed and occasionally a soft giggle burst from her rosy lips. Blaine's own mouth tightened as she watched the spell being cast by the experienced rake. At her side, Drew nudged her and she followed his gaze to Robbie, who lounged with his back to the mantel.

Despite the casualness of his pose, it was apparent that Robbie was far from relaxed. The expression in his eyes was a mixture of anger, hurt feelings, and admiration for the girl he loved. As though he felt their eyes upon him, Robbie turned and immediately his expression changed to the congeniality expected of a host.

Blaine poked Drew with the knob of her cane. "Tell that flighty chit I would like to go home," Blaine said through gritted teeth.

The carriage ride back to Weathers was made in uncomfortable silence. Fleur pouted at their early departure but Blaine was much too annoyed with the girl to do anything but glower at her. She followed Fleur to her room, determined to lecture her on the inappropriateness of her behavior with Stoddard, but before she could launch into speech, her sister's eager thanks took the wind out of her sails.

"Oh, thank you, Blaine, for making this evening possible." The girl twirled around the room in her exuberance. "I know it must have been horrid for you to tramp around in that fusty gown. Never has a girl had a more unselfish sister."

"I'm glad that you had such a good time." Blaine sighed heavily, loath to cut up the happiness she saw reflected on her sister's face.

"Everything was perfect," Fleur enthused. "I was terrified at first that everyone would think I was gauche but the gentlemen were ever so kind. Talbott — I mean, Lord Stoddard — was most attentive."

"He is not a man to trifle with, Fleur," Blaine warned. "I cannot like the fact that you spent so much time with him. He is far too experienced and sophisticated for you."

"He did not think so."

Blaine groaned as Fleur raised her chin in rebellion. She realized she had handled this poorly and she tried to soften her tone. "It is just that I find Robert Farrington so much more the gentleman," she said. "He is very handsome too."

"Oh, Robbie is aces." Fleur's voice was breezy with disinterest. "He is a good friend but he is hardly a romantic figure. Talb — Lord Stoddard is much more fascinating." She lowered her voice as she stared wide-eyed at Blaine. "When he looks at me, my heart jumps and I do not know whether it is fear or excitement."

"It is probably indigestion," Blaine drawled, hoping her prosaic tone might pierce the bubble of romanticism that surrounded the girl.

"Oh, piffle! How can you be so practical?" Fleur said, stamping her slippered foot in annoyance. "No wonder you're not married if you look at everything that way. You've been too long with Cousin Lavinia. It must be dreadful being at someone's beck and call. You need to think of yourself more. Haven't you found anyone special in London? Someone who would make a loving husband and father?"

"No, dear. I have not come across such a paragon of virtue."

"I noticed that you spent a great deal of time with Lord Farrington. I thought at first I might attempt to attach him but there is an air of amusement about him that I do not fully understand." Fleur looked across at her sister consideringly. "It is a shame that you could not have met him when you were dressed as yourself, not as an old lady. He is a bit intimidating but I do not think that would bother you, since you can be quite bossy when you want. Do you think he is too old for you?"

"Much too old," Blaine answered, moving quickly toward the door before her sister could question her further. "Off to bed now or you will look quite haggard in the morning."

At her words, Fleur raced to the mirror and Blaine made her escape. Back in her room, Tate was waiting to help her off with her makeup and to hear a report of the evening. The dresser reminded her that Wesley Upton would be arriving in the morning to present her with the year's allowance and Blaine groaned that the masquerade would continue for another day.

Climbing into bed, she felt close to tears and put it down to the lateness of the hour. She lay on her back, staring up at the bed hangings, trying to fall asleep. However, Fleur's words kept circling in her mind.

She was glad that her sister did not realize the unintentional cruelty of her questions. How ludicrous that Fleur thought she was

sacrificing her life in the service of the fictitious Cousin Lavinia. In actual fact, the only
men she saw, outside of the actors she per-
formed with, were John Tibbles and Sarge.
As an actress she was not recognized by society. The only relationship she could hope for
was as the mistress of one of the gentlemen
who vied for her attention. Men like Talbott
Stoddard and Drew Farrington.

Her heart jolted at the thought of Drew.
She had to admit that, since her coming to
Wiltshire, she had discovered a different side
to him than she had considered possible. If, as
her sister had so wildly conjectured, she had
met him as Blaine Margaret Meriweather, she
might have fallen in love with him. He surely
had a great many qualities that she could admire. He might even have asked for her hand,
she fantasized.

A silent sob shook her body and a tear
rolled out of the corner of her eye and slid into
the tangle of her hair. She was only castle
building. She could never meet Drew as
herself, the sister of Fleur Meriweather. He
already knew her as Maggie Mason, the notorious La Solitaire. Men of his class thought of
actresses as playthings, and as one, he would
never accept her as anything other than a
woman of easy virtue. Rolling over on her
stomach, Blaine buried her head in her pillow

and cried herself to sleep.

In the morning, her eyes were swollen, but Tate made no comment as she applied the white makeup to her face. The gown was similar to the black dress she had worn to dinner but this time the color was a dark brown, cut in a style long out of fashion. Tate fussed with the cap, until she was satisfied that the fake ringlets covered Blaine's ears, then she handed her a black lace fan and her walking stick.

"Mr. Upton has been cooling his heels in the drawing room this half hour. He brought you roses." Tate snorted at the idiocy of the man.

"Good Lord," Blaine muttered. Shaking out her skirts, she made for the door, already leaning on her stick to get herself into the role of Aunt Haydie. "You'd better come down with me before the flowers wilt. Then if I don't ring for tea in twenty minutes, come in and rescue me."

One of the disadvantages of her perfect acting as Lady Haydie Yates was the fact that Wesley Upton, somewhere in his late sixties, thought of her as his contemporary. He was a sweet man and she hated deceiving him so she had always been especially warm toward him. They had corresponded over the years, concerning the business of the estate, and she thought they had become friends.

The last time she had seen him, she was horrified to discover he had mistaken her warmth for affection and developed a tendresse for her. If she hadn't been so desperate for the yearly allowance, she would have ended the charade in the face of the man's pursuit.

"Ah, my dear Lady Yates," Wesley Upton croaked, rising stiffly to his feet as she entered the room followed by her dresser. His arm was burdened with an enormous bouquet of red roses.

"Mr. Upton," Blaine acknowledged, keeping her voice friendly but impersonal.

"I am delighted to find you well, Lady Yates. I have taken the liberty of bringing you some flowers, which I hope you will accept as a token of my regard." His gold-rimmed spectacles had slid down his nose and in his nervousness as he pushed them back into place, he fumbled the bouquet.

"You are too kind, Mr. Upton. Roses are a favorite of mine." She lowered her head in a regal bow of approval. "Tate, perhaps you would be good enough to put these in water."

The dour-faced dresser took the flowers from Wesley and, with a final sniff, left the room, leaving the door partially open. The solicitor extended his arm and led Blaine to the blue-and-silver-striped sofa. She sat down in the very center, precluding any action of his to seat himself at her side. She grandly waved him to one of the armchairs facing her across a low table of burled walnut. Watching him, she groaned inwardly. The dapper little man was showing all the nervous twitches of an amorous schoolboy.

Blaine had grown quite fond of Wesley Upton over the years. She found his old-fashioned courtly manners quite endearing. He was shorter than she, with skinny legs below a generous paunch. His head was bald, although there was a fringe of soft white hair that made her think of a halo. His plump face did have the look of some benign saint, she decided, studying his blue eyes and pink cheeks.

"I trust your journey from London was uneventful. As I know how busy you are, I think we should conclude our business immediately. I am sure you are in a hurry to shake the dust of Wiltshire from your heels," she suggested.

"Not at all, dear lady. I thought perhaps this visit I might extend my stay to take in some of the beauty of Salisbury Plain."

"Oh." Blaine knew her reply was less than adequate but she did not know what else to say. Without any encouragement, Wesley launched into a lengthy praise of the district, while Blaine kept a stiff smile of interest riveted to her face. She closed her eyes, praying that the little man would not choose this time to make a cake of himself. She was much too tired to cope with any sort of a scene. Waiting only for the man to pause for a breath, she burst into speech.

"This is all quite fascinating, Mr. Upton. Perhaps we should get our business over with so that we might talk more over tea."

"Excellent. Excellent," the solicitor said, fidgeting with his high collar and resettling his treacherous spectacles.

"Have you the papers for me to sign?" Blaine asked. She tried to keep her voice cool although she felt perspiration bead her lip. She flicked open her fan and plied it briskly as she eyed him warily.

"My father always approved of your business acumen, Lady Yates." He waggled his white eyebrows in a roguish manner that sent his glasses lurching down his nose. "It was his opinion that you were the model for the perfect spouse."

"Fustian, Mr. Upton," Blaine said with a snort. "Your father thought I was a stubborn old harridan. And he was right."

Wesley chuckled and reached inside his coat to withdraw a long envelope. Blaine had to restrain herself from snatching it out of his hands. While the little man bustled around to bring the tray of writing materials from the dainty lady's desk at the far side of the room, she clasped her hands tightly, the sticks of her fan crackling ominously at the pressure. He spread the papers on the table, then with great ceremony, he dipped the pen and handed it to her. She clamped her teeth together in annoyance and hastily forged Lady Haydie Yates's signature, feeling like the veriest criminal. She sighed as he rolled the blotter across the wet ink.

"The money will be deposited with your man of business, Lady Yates." He refolded the paper and carefully tucked it inside his coat and patted the pocket lovingly. It was a ritual Blaine had become used to over the years and she smiled, grateful that it was over for another year.

"Perhaps you would care for tea, Mr. Upton."

"I would like that very much, my dear lady," Wesley said, beaming down at her.

She had not realized how close the man had come and now she shifted on the sofa as he made to move toward her. Her eyes squinting with wariness, she swallowed nervously as the little man seemed to marshal his forces. He brushed his hands across his paunch and tugged at the edges of his coat with all of the solemnity of a warrior preparing for battle. Hoping to head him off, she spoke.

"If you would be so kind as to pull the bell cord."

"Before I ring, milady, I would have a word with you."

"Oh, I wish you wouldn't," Blaine blurted out.

"Beg pardon?" Wesley was clearly put off his stride by her outburst. Beads of sweat dotted his forehead and the pink scalp of his bald head. "But, Lady Yates, I have planned everything I wish to say and I know I shall never have the courage again."

"Sometimes, Mr. Upton, it takes more courage to leave a thing unsaid."

Blaine struggled to her feet in agitation, wanting to put as much space as possible between herself and the amorous solicitor. She grasped her fan in one hand and her stick in the other, raising her arms as if to ward off some horrifying specter.

"Oh, Lady Yates, please calm yourself," the little man cried, reaching out as if to take her arm.

Blaine swatted at him with her fan, feeling that the entire scene was degenerating into low comedy. She wanted nothing more than to race from the room before the man could foolishly declare himself. Seeing the determination on his face, she finally decided that nothing would do except to let him have his say. As he reached for her again, she drew herself up, until she towered over him, and raised her stick much like a prophet of old.

"Devil take it, Mr. Upton! There is no need to maul me," Blaine snapped in the imperious tones of a gentlewoman. "I was having a spasm. A slight fit of the vapors, don't you know. It is rather close in here."

She seated herself and permitted him to take the fan from her hand and wave it briskly in front of her face while with the other hand he mopped his streaming forehead. Finally she could stand the suspense no longer and snatched the fan away and waved him back to his seat. She gritted her teeth, waiting for him to declare himself, praying that he would refrain from throwing himself to his knees in an undignified manner.

"Have your say quickly, good sir," she said, finding it increasingly difficult to be gracious. Although the situation was ludicrous, she felt no urge to laugh. She felt sorry for the sweet old man and was annoyed with herself for letting things come to such a pass.

Wesley stood across from her, tugging at the edges of his coat, his mouth partially open although no words issued forth. A tremor shook his body, and his eyes, behind rapidly descending spectacles, were slightly glazed.

"I have always admired you, d-dear lady," he said, stammering. "Over the years I have come to appreciate your fine qualities and I have hinted, on the occasions that we have met, that I was desirous of a warmer relationship. I had no intention of trifling with your affections and hope I have not given you a disgust of me for desiring something that was above my touch."

"Please know, Mr. Upton, that I have always considered you a fine gentleman," Blaine answered kindly. She could feel perspiration soaking through the palms of her mittens and, placing the fan on the table, reached into the voluminous pocket of her skirts to withdraw a black-bordered handkerchief. "I have always thought of you as a friend," she continued, stressing the final word.

"Exactly, Lady Yates." Wesley beamed across at her as if she were an exceptionally bright student. "It was originally my earnest hope that you might consider me more than a business acquaintance. Therefore I know you will understand that I never at any time envisioned that I would dash your hopes for a — shall we say — lasting relationship."

"What?" Blaine goggled up at the man,

wondering if her ears were playing tricks on her. Good Lord! The man was not proposing. He was rejecting her! She pressed the handkerchief to her lips to hold back a cry of relief.

"Please, Lady Yates, do not upset yourself." Wesley was shifting from foot to foot in his agitation. "It was only six months ago that I met a very sweet lady. Euphemia Whiffledon has taken my heart by storm."

For a moment, Blaine thought she might go off in whoops of laughter and she bit the inside of her cheek until tears stood in her eyes. Wesley immediately assumed the tears were signs of her distress.

"I can never forgive myself for giving you a moment of anguish," he said. He tottered around the table and creakily dropped to his knees beside the sofa. "You must think I am a veritable bounder for encouraging you as I have," he muttered brokenly.

Blaine knew she must cut this scene short before she truly hurt the man's feelings by having a fit of hysterics. She drew in a shaky breath and called upon all her ability to play melodrama.

"Dear Mr. Upton, it is only that for a moment I was overcome with guilt." She covered her face with her fan as if in acute embarrassment. "I must admit that I did entertain certain hopes as to your feelings but it has come to me lately that I could not come to you with heart whole. You are too fine a person for me to offer any less than my deepest devotion. Therefore it is with prodigious joy that I wish you happy with Miss Whiffledon."

"Was there ever such a gracious lady as yourself, Lady Yates? I kiss the hem of your gown in homage."

Before Blaine could stop him, the little man lifted the material and touched it to his lips. She raised her eyes in exasperation and then sucked in her breath.

"It wanted only this," Blaine muttered, closing her eyes in agony at the sight of Drew Farrington, lounging against the frame of the doorway.

six

Thankfully, Wesley Upton was so overcome by emotion that he was not aware of another presence in the room. Blaine signaled with a frantic jerk of her head, and Drew, grinning like a baboon, withdrew from the doorway. Bringing her attention back to the solicitor, she reached out and patted him briskly on the shoulder.

"Dear Mr. Upton, please rise. I am appreciative of your feelings but feel it would be best if we cry friends and get on about our lives."

Slowly he struggled to his feet, the joints of his knees popping at the unaccustomed exercise. "You are too kind, Lady Yates," he said.

"To be perfectly honest with you, Mr. Upton, I am a waspish old lady who is particularly fond of you. I wish you happy. Miss Wiffledon will be getting a very fine husband."

It luckily took only a brief time to finally send the man packing, and in the sudden quiet of the room, Blaine covered her face with her hands. In the rising tide of hysteria that threatened to overwhelm her, she leaned forward, elbows on her knees.

Drew stopped in the doorway, touched by the sight of the indomitable old tartar bowed in despair. He had heard enough of the scene to realize what was afoot but he had never suspected that she would be so overcome. He had thought he had seen nothing but relief in her expression. Closing the doors of the parlor, he hurried forward, surprised at his need to offer comfort.

"Dear Lady Yates, the man is surely not worth one moment of your anguish."

At Drew's words a strangled cry burst from the old woman and she rocked back and forth, shoulders heaving with emotion. He stood beside the sofa in an agony of indecision, then seated himself beside her and patted her shoulder awkwardly. This action elicited a sound closely akin to a snort and he narrowed his eyes as he peered at the woman.

From behind the mittened fingers two eyes appeared, tears shimmering on the clumped lashes. In the watery depths, Drew caught the glint of mischief and pushed himself back against the cushions as great rolling waves of laughter convulsed him. As if his laughter had loosed the bonds of restraint, his companion burst into a chorus of throaty chuckles that she tried to smother behind her black-bordered handkerchief. When finally Drew could control his laughter, he shook his head in exasperation.

"I say, Lady Yates," he gasped. "For a moment I was convinced you were in the greatest despair."

"Believe me, Lord Farrington," Blaine answered, dabbing carefully at her streaming eyes. "I was considerably overset. I was so busy thinking of how I might reject the man with gentle graciousness that I almost missed the import of his words. Imagine my consternation when I realized he was not planning to declare himself but to cast me off. Oh la, I was so puffed up with my own conceit, I totally misread the situation."

"From what I heard, madam, you dealt with him more kindly than he deserved."

"He is a sweet little man and I would not hurt his feelings, Drew, uh, Lord Farrington." Blaine was appalled that she would so forget herself in the companionship of shared amusement.

"I would consider it a singular honor if you would call me Drew, Lady Yates."

Blaine's eyes were drawn to his face. The sincerity of his voice was matched by the genuine friendship she saw reflected there. "I would like that," she said.

Reminding herself of her role as an aging matron, she patted his hand in an avuncular manner, unprepared for the shock of feeling at contact with his warm flesh through her loosely knitted mittens. She shifted uneasily and fussed with her heavy skirts in order to reestablish her composure.

"Perhaps you would ring for tea," she said, "since Mr. Upton chose to leave before it was served. Although at this hour, you might prefer something more strengthening."

"If you will promise to keep my secret, Lady Yates," Drew said as he pulled the bell rope, "I have a great penchant for tea. I traveled some little bit in the East in my younger days. The ceremonial drinking of tea seemed to me a most civilized ritual. Perhaps it is that remembrance that seems to imbue each cup with a dose of tranquillity. Devil take it, madam, you are so easy to talk to that I begin to wax lyrical in my enthusiasm."

While they waited for the tea tray, Blaine hastily checked the mirror to be sure her tearful laughter had not dislodged her careful makeup. She needed the reinforcement of seeing the face of an old woman to remind her not to fall into a pattern of friendship with Drew. She, too, was surprised at the ease of their conversation. Since her arrival in Wiltshire, she had discovered a different man than

141

the persistent dilettante who had been pursuing La Solitaire. She liked Drew Farrington and that knowledge was particularly unsettling since any relationship between them was strictly impossible. A wave of tiredness washed over her as she returned to her seat and accepted the cup of tea from Drew.

"Well, young man, what brings you scratching at our door instead of out riding to hounds or some other odious bachelor pursuit? I would not have expected you to appear before me in all your dirt," Blaine snapped, her voice once more the crisp, acerbic tones of Aunt Haydie, as she eyed his riding clothes with disfavor.

Although Drew raised his eyebrow at her tone, he made no comment. "Your pardon, Lady Yates, for my appearance. I was riding and thought I would call as I had an idea I hoped might find favor in your eyes," he said easily. "I talked at length to Robbie and discovered that he is surprisingly perceptive about his relationship with Fleur. It is his belief that once she has the opportunity to see more of society she will be quite content to remain in Wiltshire. He thinks she is only overwhelmed by the novelty of the attention she has received, much like most girls her age."

"Smart lad, your brother," Blaine said. "I think he is correct in his assessment but I must tell you that a season for Fleur is out of the question."

"I do not mean to interfere in your household, ma'am, but I have a suggestion to offer." Drew placed his tea on the table and leaned forward, elbows braced on his knees. "I have a great fondness for Robbie and I would see him happy. In just this short time, it is apparent he feels strongly about your niece and I would do what I could to aid in his pursuit. I have seen far too many marriages founder to be sanguine in the face of such odds. Robbie's deep admiration for Fleur leads me to believe theirs could be a successful match."

"You're doing it too brown, Drew," Blaine said scoffingly. "Would you have me believe love conquers all?"

Drew shifted in his chair as though uncomfortable speaking on such a subject. His voice held a defensive quality when he continued. "One does not often see true love. However, on the occasions that I have, it seems to make of marriage something more than a business arrangement."

"Sometimes that is true. Surely, young man, you have been in love more times than one could count to be aware that that is not always the case." Blaine's voice was sharp and Drew looked up, a grin flashing across his face. She caught her breath at the blaze of warmth that kindled within her.

"Only once have I felt true love," he answered. A soft smile of remembrance flickered across his face. "Her name was Delphine and her eyes were the blue of a Scottish lake and her hair was tumbled curls of shimmering black. I would have given my life for her."

Blaine winced at his tone, not wanting to hear any more of his confidences, but she could not hold back her question. "And did she love you in return?"

"No." Drew shook his head sadly. "When I tried to kiss her, she bit me."

"Bit you?"

"Delphine had little sophistication at seven."

"For shame, sirrah!" Blaine cried, laughing despite the fact she had been taken in by his outrageous story.

Drew chuckled at the flash of fire he saw reflected in the old lady's eyes. "I'll admit I took unfair advantage, but in a way it was an answer to your question. My experience with the toothsome Delphine taught me a lesson and I have never again fallen victim to another pair of *beaux yeux.*"

"Resolved to a solitary life?" Blaine clicked her tongue in mock sadness.

"I never mentioned that my life was solitary." He flashed her a look of pure mischief beneath his lowered brows.

"And what of marriage, Farrington?"

"I assume, eventually I shall become leg-shackled. It is nothing I view with any degree of enthusiasm. If you will pardon my plain speaking, Lady Yates, I will select some light-minded, virginal chit of good family and modest means. She will bear my children, maintain my household, and bore me to death."

"Seems a bleak picture," Blaine responded glumly. "And yet you wish it for Robbie."

"Robbie does not have my abiding need for entertainment. He would thrive in such a situation." Drew got to his feet and wandered lazily around the room, as if inspecting the furniture. "And this, my dear Lady Yates, brings me back full circle to my suggestion. Although I have known you only a short time, I would deal squarely with you, without need to mince words. Have I your permission?"

"Cut line, Farrington," Blaine snapped inelegantly.

Drew turned to face her, running a hand through his thick hair. "I gather your finances are not such that you can consider a season for Fleur. In my opinion, unless the girl has some taste of society she will not settle happily into country life. I would suggest a short spell in

London now before the season begins. The city is light of the majority of the ton and she will not be overwhelmed."

"It sounds a pretty plan indeed, but I do not see how it would be feasible. You are correct in your assessment of our financial condition. Much as I love Fleur, I cannot see how I could manage even a month in London." Blaine's tone was regretful.

"Perhaps I might have the very answer. My Aunt Aurelia Breckenridge has just left town for an extended stay in Scotland. Her house is small but well staffed. Since there is no accounting for tastes, Robbie is her favorite nephew and I think she would approve of anything that might promote his future happiness."

Blaine dropped her eyes to her lap, torn between wanting to help Fleur and the knowledge that she should not listen to the soft words of Drew Farrington. She would be in an impossible situation in London. In a little more than a week, she must return to the theater. Her palms began to sweat at the very thought of masquerading as Lady Yates at the same time as she lived her life as La Solitaire. She pursed her mouth, prepared to turn down Drew's proposition.

"While I am cognizant of your kind suggestion, it would still be an impossibility. The child's wardrobe is insufficient for such a venture."

"It is not as though Fleur would need to be fully outfitted," Drew suggested, his voice agreeable though there was a balky quality to the set of his mouth. "It seems to me, madam, that her gowns are quite up to the mark."

Blaine cursed the fact that she had brought home so many new gowns for the girl. She had purchased the material and over the last several months Tate had sewn the dresses as a surprise for Fleur. She wriggled uncomfortably under Drew's steady gaze, feeling the jaws of the trap closing in. With a wistful sigh, she fluttered her eyes in distress.

"What a shame that it is not possible. I am no longer young and I could not be the sort of chaperone a young girl would need to enter society even on a limited basis."

Blaine folded her hands in her lap as if to call an end to the discussion but did not reckon on the stubbornness of Drew Farrington.

"It was my understanding that Fleur had a governess who might be applied to when your duties as chaperone became too onerous," Drew countered.

"Yes, I suppose Frau Puffentraub would be satisfactory but she would not know how to go on since she has never been much in society herself. Without proper guidance, Fleur would be much like a lamb in the company of wolves," Blaine argued sweetly.

"Then, Lady Yates, both Robbie and myself will volunteer to help navigate the treacherous waters of the ton."

Blaine stared across at the narrowed green gaze and knew he would continue offering solutions as long as she brought up objections. Although she knew the whole thing would be a nightmare, it did coincide with her own wishes for Fleur, and with a brittle nod she admitted her defeat.

"I bow to superior strength," she said.

Despite the fact she had the urge to throw a teacup at his head, Blaine felt the corners of her mouth curl into a small grin. He saluted her with a hand to his forehead and moved to seat himself beside her on the couch. Heads together like conspirators, they planned out the details of the trip to London. They had just finished when the doors of the parlor opened and Fleur, followed by Talbott Stoddard, entered in a flurry of muslin.

"Oh," Fleur cried, stopping abruptly at the sight of her sister and Lord Farrington sitting so cozily together. "I didn't realize you had company."

"Watch your tongue and make your curtsy, child," Blaine warned, fearful the girl would give the game away.

Drew hauled himself to his feet and bowed to the flustered young lady. His smile was less warm for Stoddard since he loathed the man and sensed his interest in Fleur was solely to relieve the boredom of his stay in the country.

"Perhaps you could tell me, Miss Meriweather, where I might find your brother. I met Val in the woods yesterday and promised I would accompany him on a tour of Weathers."

"How kind of you, Lord Farrington. Val will be in high alt. He was just on his way out to the stables when milord came to call." Her voice was breathless and a wave of color flowed up her cheeks as she indicated Lord Stoddard.

"Then if you will excuse me, Lady Yates, I shall take myself off. Your servant, ma'am."

With a brief but elegant bow, Drew left the room and, for Blaine, it was as if the room had suddenly become empty. It was several moments before she could focus on the others in the room. Since she did not wish to put Fleur's acting powers to the test, she asked her sister to help her to a large armchair in the corner where she might rest after her day's exertion. There, under the impression that she was dozing, she was well able to keep an eye on the girl, yet not be involved in further deception. Watching Stoddard from beneath shuttered lids, she could no more like him than she had on first acquaintance. The man flirted outrageously with Fleur and the flighty chit could not see beneath the surface handsomeness of the man to the cold calculation in his eyes. Perhaps in London, she would learn to recognize the real from the counterfeit.

"Fatima is much too old to race, Lord Farrington," Val said, grinning up at his companion. "Even in her salad days, she would not have beaten Corinth."

Drew patted the neck of the black stallion and grinned back at the boy. "You apparently have a good eye for horseflesh. I can imagine your pony gives you a much more comfortable ride than this bony lad."

Val nodded his head in acceptance of the compliment, but the light in his eyes indicated his knowledge that it was a sop. Drew laughed and ruffled the boy's hair as he kneed his horse along the trail. He was enjoying his outing with the youngster. He was surprised at how well run the estate was, despite an apparent lack of funds. At his question, Val smiled gravely.

"It's mostly my sister's doing. She says it's easy enough to manage your land with great heaping piles of the ready. The challenge is managing when you're short."

"I see," Drew replied. He never would have suspected that Fleur would be quite so perceptive. Robbie had found a gem of a girl who was smart enough to cloak her business sense beneath a fluttering exterior. "You seem to have managed quite well."

"Well, sir, it's piecemeal at best. One must keep priorities straight. The tenants come first. We've given them additional land if they'll take care of the repairs on their own holdings. Most have been on the estate for more years than I can remember and so there's a feeling of family here."

Drew was amused at the seriousness of the young boy. At eleven Val was more responsible about his duties than men three times his age. He was a very impressive child. "You have done a fine job, young sir. Despite your limited funds there is no sign of neglect. Everywhere we have been, the estate seems prosperous and well tended. Your estate manager has advised you well."

At this, the boy chuckled. "My sister loves giving advice."

"Your sister runs the estate?" he blurted out in amazement.

At the question the boy clapped his hands over his mouth and the eyes above his fingers were filled with consternation. Drew pulled his horse to a stop and reached over to place a friendly hand on Val's knee.

"Steady on, son," Drew said kindly in the face of the boy's discomfort. "Perhaps we might get down for a bit of a respite."

Dutifully the boy dismounted and, gathering the reins of his pony, looped them over the branch of a nearby tree. Drew busied himself with Corinth, giving the lad a chance to compose himself. The sun was warm and he removed his jacket and, folding it, placed it on a fallen log and sat down beside it. Feet dragging, Val approached. His face was far too grave for a child his age.

"I am a regular loose-lipped Jenny, Lord Farrington," he said. "I shouldn't have told you about not having an estate manager. My sister says that no one is to know. She says people would not approve of a woman making business decisions."

"Unfortunately, Val, she is right. Most men assume that women are too totty-headed."

Val responded to the man-to-man tone of Drew's voice. "Do you think so, sir?"

"Well, in my vast dealing with women, I have found a great many who seem to find difficulty in crossing a room without help." Drew noticed that the strained look had lessened in the boy's face. "However, I have met women with great knowledge and a good head

152

for figures. Just being male does not automatically make one a wizard with finances."

"My father was such a one," Val admitted, then his expression darkened again as he whispered confidingly to Drew. "I worry that I shall grow to be like him."

"What does your sister say?"

"She says I can choose to be whatever I want. If I want to manage the estate well, all I have to do is to grow to understand the land. Knowledge is the key, she tells me."

"Your sister quite amazes me," Drew said, shaking his head at the previous picture he had had of the golden-headed child. "Fleur is indeed a wonder."

"Not Fleur, Lord Farrington. Blaine."

"Who?"

"My other sister, Blaine, is the one who has taught me so much."

"My apologies, Val. I had quite forgotten you had another sister. I was having no end of trouble picturing Fleur as the mastermind of agrarian reform."

It took a moment for Val to catch the humor in Drew's words but when he did, he rolled on the ground in laughter. "Fleur knows only about hair ribbons, curl papers, and needlework."

"A thoroughly male viewpoint, old son." Drew snorted.

"You're right, sir," the boy admitted. "It's that Fleur is just a girl. Blaine is something different. Perhaps because she's older."

"Tell me more of this Amazon."

The boy's face became still, washed of all expression. His blue eyes scrutinized Drew's face and then he nodded his head as if he had made up his mind.

"Sometimes, sir, it's very difficult to know what to do. However, as a gentleman I know you will respect my confidences. While my parents were alive Blaine ran the household but eventually she also became interested in the running of the estate. Old Higgins was our manager and he taught her what he could. When he died, Blaine took over but she was afraid of what the solicitor would think of such an outrageous thing and so she invented a pretend name for the new estate manager."

"Quite an ingenious idea," Drew said. "I trust your sister picked a suitable name."

Val's eyes danced with pleasure as he leaned toward his new friend. "I think you'll appreciate it, sir." He paused to give full significance to his disclosure. "Mr. Inchon Visible."

"Ah. Mr. Invisible, to be sure." Drew chuckled, much to the boy's delight. "Your sister has a devilish sense of humor, lad. I think I would like her very much."

"I know you would, Lord Farrington. Everyone loves Blaine, even though she really makes you to the mark."

"I remember that Robbie mentioned she was away from home. Does she visit frequently?"

"Um, no. Hardly ever, in fact. She lives very far away. Clear to Scotland, I think. She writes letters, though, so I always know what her plans are for the estate."

After this breathtaking burst of words, Val dropped his eyes, his fingers busy pulling up blades of grass. Drew sensed he had once more broached a topic that was clearly off-limits. Evincing disinterest, he changed the subject and soon had the boy talking more naturally on other lines.

After he left the boy, Drew rode slowly back to Fairhaven, his mind uneasy. He felt there was something he didn't understand about the Meriweathers. He had met Val, Fleur, and Aunt Haydie and liked all three. However, he still had a sense that all was not as it should be in the household. He wondered about the other sister, Blaine. It was curious that she was not mentioned in the normal course of conversation. Now that he thought on it, the few times her name had come up there had been an abrupt change of subject.

Val had showed nothing but admiration for his sister and yet he was clearly uncomfortable speaking about her. Even the whereabouts of the girl was questionable. He had heard from Robbie that she lived near London and yet Val had indicated she lived far to the north. Could something be the matter with the sister? His mind spun with various possibilities. Disease? A disfiguring accident?

Perhaps when they arrived in London, he would have an opportunity to find out more about the mysterious Blaine Meriweather. After all, if Robbie planned to marry Fleur, he should investigate the family. It would not do to discover some wretched family secret after the banns had been called. He must assume that the sister was an antidote since she appeared to have such shockingly progressive ideas. Definitely on the shelf, according to the boy. But Drew had to admit to a certain curiosity about the woman Val had so lavishly praised.

A smile touched Drew's face and his expression took on the intent look of the hunter. He would enjoy the challenge of solving the puzzle of the elusive Blaine Meriweather.

seven

"In London two weeks and already you're looking haggard after only three performances," Tate muttered as she brushed out Blaine's hair. "You've circles under your eyes and your color's pasty."

"Remind me not to ask you how I look." Blaine grimaced at her dresser in the mirror.

"Shouldn't ask questions if you don't want answers. I'm plumb worried about you, lamby. You canna keep up the kind of pace you've set for yourself. Chaperoning Fleur in the daytime and then here at the theater to all hours of the night. You'll come down with the influenza and be took off before the cat can lick her ear."

"Surely an exaggeration," Blaine said, her voice reflecting amusement at the woman's words. "I have to make some push to be seen in public to keep up the fiction of Aunt Haydie. Thank goodness Puff has been taking over for the evening parties. As long as Fleur has someone to chaperone her, she won't ask too many questions."

"It's time you told the girl."

"I can't," Blaine said with decision.

Deceit did not come easy to her but now she was living a veritable life of lies. She hated lying to Fleur. She should have told the girl earlier just what kind of life she was leading. Had she told her at a younger age the girl would have been well used to the idea. At eighteen she had heard enough about the theatrical world to view the life of an actress as anything but moral. It did little good to think of what would have happened had she not tried to supplement their income. Fleur in her youth would not see shades of gray. She would feel shame for Blaine and this she could not bear.

She had quieted her sister's questions by telling her that she would not be home in the evening since she had to return to her post as companion to Cousin Lavinia. Too inexperienced to realize the unusual hours Blaine kept, Fleur had accepted the lie with only a momentary pout until she learned that Puff would chaperone her in the evenings.

"Fleur is so young and has such an innocent view of the world," Blaine said. "She would be horrified to discover that her sister was an actress."

"There's worse things." Tate pursed her lips in a thin line of disapproval. "Where will this all end, miss? That's what I'd like to know. You can't play Aunt Haydie for the rest of your life."

Blaine could find no answer to her dresser's comment and she felt her shoulders sag tiredly. It had been a very long two weeks. The house in Portman Square was more than adequate for their small household. Drew's aunt, Aurelia Breckenridge, was a wealthy woman and the rooms were furnished in lavish but comfortable style. With a staff larger than at Weathers, Blaine, if she could have relaxed, would have felt truly cosseted in the new surroundings.

It was not the move to London that had taxed her; it was the confusion of her own life that was taking its toll. By day she chaperoned Fleur to musicales and teas in the guise of Lady Haydie Yates. Then with Tate and Sarge in tow, she left Portman Square for the rooms she had hired in a less fashionable district of London. She had lived on Corridon Place for several years prior to her fateful trip to Wiltshire. There she changed her clothes and her makeup and raced to the Green Mews Theater as Maggie Mason, the celebrated La Solitaire. After her performance, she returned to her old rooms and in the morning began the circle of deception again.

It was hard for Blaine to credit the fact that

she had been able to get away with her disguise as Aunt Haydie. She was an accomplished actress but still she could not believe that she was so readily accepted as the rather eccentric Lady Yates. Granted she took great care with her makeup and her movements but it appeared that most people accepted whatever was before their eyes. Blaine felt twice as guilty, knowing that she was succeeding in fooling so many.

"I'll finish my hair, Tate, if you would find Sarge," Blaine said, anxious to have something to do other than worry over the confusion of her affairs. "Then we can go home and seek our beds."

The dresser handed her the brush and hurried out of the room. Blaine closed her eyes, soothed by the restful brush strokes, but before long the face she had seen so often in her dreams formed in her mind and she jerked her eyes open again. Devil take that blasted man! she fumed as she glared at the single white rose on her dressing table.

The flowers had arrived the first night of her return to the theater. White roses! The card had been signed with a single initial, a flourished *D*. And that evening Drew Farrington had been seated in his private box, his green gaze never leaving her for a moment. In a rage, Blaine had thrown the flowers in the alley behind the theater. The next night flowers had arrived again and she went back to her usual habit of giving them to the girls in the chorus.

Part of her anger was at herself for allowing Drew's personality to charm her into forgetting the kind of man he was. She had actually grown to like and admire the man. Yet at the first opportunity he had returned to the theater to ogle the woman he hoped to make his mistress. She had always known she could not trust men and she was furious that she had ever spoken to the hateful, depraved Lord Farrington.

She banged the brush down on the dressing table and quickly braided her hair and covered it with a close-fitting bonnet. She stood up tiredly and reached for the cloak on the chaise longue. With a flip, she settled it on her shoulders, securing it around her throat.

And to make matters worse, Talbott Stoddard had also returned to plague her. In his case, she had little regret in snubbing him. There was something distasteful about the look in Stoddard's eye. At least within Drew's green gaze she had seen the light of mischief; in Stoddard's there was nothing but cold calculation. The man was definitely to be feared. As if her thoughts had conjured up the devil, her dressing-room door opened and Stoddard walked in.

"How dare you!" Blaine cried, whirling around to face him.

"Softly, goddess," he said. "No need for such temper."

Stoddard closed the door and leaned against the wooden panels, his eyes caressing her body. Blaine pulled the cloak more fully around herself as if in protection from the blatant sensuality of his gaze. She shivered involuntarily as his eyes raised to hers and she saw the blaze of passion within the pale blue depths.

"Get out!" she snapped coldly.

"I think not, my pet. This is the first chance I've had to speak to you without the interference of your two bodyguards and I have no intention of scurrying away at your disdainful command."

Stoddard moved forward, much as a hunter stalks his prey. Although her heart was pounding, Blaine refused to give ground. She locked her knees, determined to face the man in anger, not cowering like some frightened spinster. Instinctively she knew that Stoddard would be pleased by her fear and she would not give him such an easy victory.

"Willing or unwilling, I will have you, goddess."

"I would sooner couple with a filthy dustman," Blaine said, raising an eyebrow, her ex-

162

pression carefully aloof.

She could see by the sudden tightening of his mouth that she had scored a hit but did not relax for a moment. The man was clearly dangerous.

"You will pay for that, my dear." His voice was a thin stream of ice. He moved closer. "I have been extremely patient but I grow weary of the game. I do not understand why you remain so coy. I am sure a woman of the world, such as yourself, is fully aware of my intentions. If you mean to hold out for a better offer, please know that I am prepared to deal well with you. I am an extremely wealthy gentleman."

"Those two words do not naturally follow." Blaine spoke crisply, her cheeks flushing with anger. "A gentleman would not offer a lady such an insult."

"An actress is no lady." Stoddard sneered.

Blaine felt the color drain from her face and caught the smile of satisfaction in the hateful man's eyes. She longed to spit in his face but she reined in her fury, knowing she was far too vulnerable to anger the man.

"Your words bore me, milord. I have nothing further to say."

Ignoring her dismissal, Stoddard stepped forward until they were only a hand's breadth apart. "Your beauty leaves me breathless. Be-

163

neath the makeup, your skin is flawless."

He reached out and ran his finger down her cheek, stopping at the corner of her mouth. The skin burned beneath his touch. Blaine's eyes blazed with fury but she did not move, even when she heard the door open behind Stoddard.

"I cannot believe the lady gave you permission to enter."

At the sound of Drew Farrington's voice, Blaine felt instant relief. She pulled herself away from Stoddard's hand, wanting to scrub the place on her face that he had touched.

"Until later, goddess." Stoddard nodded his head, turned, and passed in front of Drew without acknowledging the man's presence.

As the door closed, there was silence in the room. Blaine looked at the anger on Drew's face and flinched as he approached her.

"Are you all right?"

There was such tender concern in Drew's voice that Blaine felt tears rise in her throat. She blinked her eyes, determined not to cry. He opened his arms, and before Blaine could stop herself, she had stepped into the shelter of his embrace. He held her as a friend, murmuring soothing words into her ears and slowly the tremors that had invaded her body quieted.

Drew closed his arms around the actress as

if his embrace could shield her from all harm. He was surprised at her height; the top of her head came to just below his chin where his lips could kiss the top of her bonnet. Her curves fit the angles and planes of his body as if they were two pieces of a puzzle. He was aware of the scent of her, a fresh gardeny aroma that seemed strangely out of place in the muggy air of the dressing room, redolent with the smell of greasepaint. He was disappointed when she pushed at his chest and he released her slowly, reluctant to lose contact with her.

Blaine could feel the color rise to her cheeks in embarrassment. She could not believe that she had gone so easily into his arms. True, she had been shaken by Stoddard's appearance but to accept Drew's embrace could only lead him to the belief that she was susceptible to his charm and eager for his attention. Granted, his embrace had been one of comfort, not affection; she must keep her dealings with him on an impersonal level. She knew, with most men, one sign of weakness would give them the impetus to continue their pursuit. She hardened her heart to the magnetic force that seemed to emanate from the man.

"Thank you for rescuing me, Lord Farrington," she said, her voice carefully controlled to show nothing but friendly appreciation.

"Delighted to be of service, Miss Mason," Drew responded with a brief nod of his head. "Talbott Stoddard is an evil man. He is the kind of man who will risk much to satisfy his desires. You must beware of him. I have watched him and he is obsessed with you. Determined to have you at all costs."

"I am aware of his interest and in future shall be more on my guard. He is stupid to think he can woo me. I have neither need nor desire for any man's company. Some men find this impossible to understand."

"For myself, I find it impossible to accept," Drew said softly, smiling when she raised her chin in defiance.

"Go away, Lord Farrington. There is nothing for you here."

Blaine found it difficult to concentrate since her whole body seemed to tingle at Drew's nearness. She looked up into his eyes and found she was transfixed by the clarity of their green color. His gaze seemed to pierce her, seeking the secret corners of her mind and her heart. She could feel her heart beating, sounding loud to her ears, but she could not break the power of his glance. Suddenly, his features tightened, taking on a more wolfish gleam and now the green gaze lost its coolness and jolted her with a blaze of passion.

"You are truly a lovely woman," Drew said. His eyes slid over the creamy curves of her face, although he did not touch her. "It pains me not to be able to protect you from men like Stoddard. That he would dare lay hands on you is almost more than I can bear."

Drew's eyes caressed her where the other man's finger had touched. The contact with Stoddard had been repellent, leaving behind only a feeling of distaste. Under Drew's burning gaze, her skin seemed to glow as warmth radiated outward in an ever-widening circle of excitement. Her chest was constricted, her breathing shallow and almost panting. A yearning filled her to be held once more in his arms.

"We belong together," Drew said, his voice a tender whisper as if he did not really want to say the words aloud. "I do not know how I know this but I feel that it is true."

Blaine licked her lips to ease the dryness of her mouth. "It is not possible, Lord Farrington."

"I tried to stay away, but I was drawn here as surely as a moth to a flame. Do you feel nothing?"

She evaded the question. "We belong to two different worlds."

"Perhaps," he answered, his face serious.

"We could combine our worlds."

Blaine blinked, stepping back a pace as if to distance herself from temptation. "A half world is not enough. It would never satisfy either of us."

"A half would be preferable to nothing at all."

"You are wrong, Lord Farrington. Paste jewels have no value."

Blaine kept the expression on her face aloof, her head held regally erect. She focused her eyes on his cravat, not wanting him to see the hurt she felt at his proposition. The anger would come later, she knew. She pulled the cloak more securely around her body.

"Leave me alone, Lord Farrington. I have nothing to give you and you can give me nothing I want."

At her words, there was silence in the room. Drew studied her face and knew he had been dismissed. He stepped back a pace, gave her a curt bow, and opened the door. As he walked down the hallway, his footsteps sounded a hollow beat in the nearly empty theater.

Much later he sat in the quiet of his library and wondered what to do about the intriguing Maggie Mason. He rolled the name on his tongue but he did not like the sound. The name Maggie did not fit the beautiful woman with the golden hazel eyes. When he spoke to her he could not use the name. La Solitaire was a sobriquet and he somehow felt it would be an insult to address her thus. Even in his fantasies, he found no suitable name for her.

She was never out of his mind and had even invaded his dreams. He had hoped his trip to Wiltshire would loosen the strength of his desire for her but his need had not diminished. When he returned to London, he sought her out immediately, wanting to see her, if only from the vantage point of his private box. He did not understand what there was about the woman that so entranced him. He wanted more of her than she exposed on stage. It puzzled him that unlike his other liaisons it was not solely for her physical attributes that he sought to possess her. He had a keen awareness that discovering the mind and soul behind the facade of La Solitaire would be more exciting than anything he had ever experienced.

Drew moved restlessly as his body responded to the thought of the actress. Where she was concerned he was no longer the self-possessed Lord Farrington. She brought out a side of him that he had not known existed. She inspired quick bursts of lust, curiosity, and anger. He had been amazed at the fury that had taken hold of him when he saw Talbott Stoddard enter her dressing room. He had wanted to tear the man limb from limb for daring to touch her.

And yet was he any different from Stoddard? He also wanted La Solitaire for his mistress. But unlike Stoddard, he would care for her, treat her with tenderness, and not merely use her.

This thought drove Drew to his feet. He poured brandy into a snifter and twirled it in his hand, inhaling the bouquet in a slow, even breath. He walked to the window and stared down at the cobblestones in front of his town house. The streets were empty and damp from the brief shower that had passed overhead. He sipped the brandy and wondered why all of a sudden his life seemed filled with contrary women.

He wondered how Lady Yates fared. It was strange to say that he missed her. Although Fleur was much in evidence, he had seen little of the old woman. She had been good company in Wiltshire and he had looked forward to her acerbic assessment of London society. When he questioned Fleur, she had said her aunt was much too infirm to take in the evening affairs. It was strange that everyone talked of Lady Yates's ill health and yet the times that Drew had been with her, she appeared robust and almost youthful.

He had seen a great deal of Val Meriweather. He enjoyed rediscovering London through the eyes of the young boy. It was apparent that Val was in need of male companionship and Drew had asked among his friends to find boys suitable for the lad. He still liked taking the boy about and he smiled, remembering Val's wide-eyed enthusiasm when they went to look at horses at Tattersall's. Yet even with Val, another female of mysterious background intruded on his peace of mind. He was decidedly intrigued by the boy's references to Blaine Margaret Meriweather.

While it was true that Val did not speak of her constantly, it was the occasional mention of her name that piqued Drew's interest. From the small things that the boy had let slip, he had discovered that the girl was a half sister and not as old as Drew had imagined. Blaine could not be more than twenty-five and unmarried, which suggested she might be either an antidote or a bluestocking. By now, he knew enough not to question the boy directly, since at the mention of Blaine's name, Val invariably looked conscious. Drew could not fathom what secret there was about the woman that needed to be so closely held.

Perhaps he should look in on the Meriweathers tomorrow. He could inquire as to Lady Yates's health and perhaps he might be able to find out a little of the family history. They could compare notes as to the state of the romance between Robbie and Fleur. If

Drew was correct, all was not well on that head.

He had watched Fleur as she entered in the whirl of society. After her sheltered life in Wiltshire, even the limited society in London prior to the season appeared to be quite awe-inspiring. Although the girl did not behave in a fashion that could be considered fast, she did revel in the attention that surrounded her. Perhaps if it was the middle of the season and she had been surrounded by other debutantes, she would be less likely to be the center of such a band of admirers. It would give her some perspective at least. As it was, she was a taking little thing and was naïve enough to believe that the flirting of a bevy of gentlemen was of worth.

For the most part Robbie had been patient, but by the increasingly grim expression of his brother's face, Drew wondered how long this state of affairs would continue. Would the girl come to her senses before Robbie lost all patience with her?

He finished off the brandy, wondering if the Farrington men were doomed to solitary lives. Neither he nor Robbie seemed to have much luck in the women they chose to pursue.

eight

Blaine's heart jolted at the sudden appearance of Drew Farrington. She hadn't seen him since the night he had rescued her from Stoddard and hadn't expected him at the Forsythes' musicale. She watched as he bent to speak to his hostess. She liked the tumble of curly brown hair falling on his forehead and the way he brushed it impatiently away from his face. Then she remembered his visit to the theater and she could feel heat rise to her cheeks beneath her makeup.

After he had left her at the theater and she was not so caught up in the spell of enchantment that his nearness spun around her, she had indeed been angry. But more than that, she had been disappointed in him. In Wiltshire she had admired Drew and felt his return to the pursuit of La Solitaire was somehow a betrayal of her judgment. As he crossed the Aubusson carpet to join the group around the gold satin sofa on which she sat, she tried to forget her anger at him for her role as Lady Yates.

"What ho, Farrington," Reggie Torrance called, giving a casual salute to the newcomer. The dandy eyed Drew's elegant turnout and made a mental note to find out the name of his tailor. "What brings you out in the light of the day? Always said you had a tin ear for musicales."

"It was surely the pleasure of your company," Drew responded, earning a chorus of laughter from the others in the group. "Besides, if you will notice, I took great care to arrive after the musical portion of this charming affair. Miss Meriweather. Robbie." He nodded his greetings and then turned to the figure on the sofa. "Lady Yates. I hope I find you well."

"Exceedingly," Blaine answered crisply. She ignored the eyebrow raised in surprise at her tone. "And you, Lord Farrington. I trust all of London was suitably appreciative of your return."

"Only in some quarters, ma'am." He lowered himself into a vacant chair, his eyes still intent on Lady Yates. "Have you been enjoying your visit to London?"

"Most assuredly, thank you." She wished he would not stare so at her. She knew her makeup and costume were excellent but she was always uneasy that somehow he would see through her disguise. However, as she searched his face she could discover no signs of recognition and she relaxed against the pillows of the sofa. "I do not get out as much as I would like but I fear I tire much too easily to keep late hours."

"You should have joined our party last night, Lady Yates," Reggie said, his pallid face lit for once with enthusiasm. "We went to Covent Garden to see Kemble in *Othello*. The man is a genius."

"Oh, yes, Lord Farrington," Fleur said, her face rosy with excitement. "It was ever so magical."

"I cannot agree," Robbie said, ignoring the pout of his lady love at his contradictory words. "The man's a poseur. He plays his parts as if above the common touch. It is all external and artificial elegance."

"And what would you have, Robbie?" Blaine asked, much interested in his assessment of Kemble, whom she knew well. He was Sarah Siddons's brother and Blaine had acted onstage with him often during her time at Covent Garden. "Do you find something lacking in his performance?"

"That's it exactly, Lady Yates," Robbie answered, his eyes narrowed in thought. "I do always feel there is something missing. I am not sure what exactly."

"Passion," Drew interjected. "The man has

majesty but one never gets the sense of a living, breathing character beneath the role."

"How very interesting, Lord Farrington," Blaine said, surprised at Drew's perception. "Yet with it all, he remains a very popular actor."

"Not so much since the riots at the Covent Garden five years ago," interjected Edward Baxter, another one of Fleur's flirts.

"Riots?" Fleur squealed, half in fear, half in excitement.

"Let me tell you, my dear," Reggie said, taking up the story. "It was after the fire and the opening of the New Covent Garden. The man was close to ruin and only a loan from the Duke of Northumberland allowed him to rebuild. He hoped to recoup his losses by raising the prices of the private boxes but where he made his mistake was raising the price in the pit by sixpence."

"That is not so very much," Fleur said artlessly.

"My dear child, the pit is a sacred arena and the English are not ones to take umbrage lightly," Edward said, eager to get back in the limelight. "I was privileged to be present on opening night. The bill was *Macbeth*, followed by a musical farce called *The Quaker*. From the moment Kemble set foot on the stage, pandemonium broke out. The audience had hand bells, clappers, and other noisemakers. I myself had come armed with a watchman's rattle."

"Oh, how exciting. Don't you wish you'd been there to see such a thing?" Fleur said to the listeners in general, who dutifully murmured similar thoughts.

Blaine said little as she remembered all too well sitting with a tearful Sarah Siddons as the woman told her of the appalling behavior of the audience. There were placards calling for a return of the old prices and the members of the pit began to chant "O.P." until the whole house had taken it up.

"Kemble showed himself a true thespian," Reggie said, picking up the threads of the tale and earning himself a black look from Edward. "He and the other actors continued with the play even though the lines they recited were practically inaudible. Every night was the same. Sometimes Bow Street runners would be called in to eject the worst of the ringleaders but still at every performance there was a hubbub. Finally after sixty days Kemble restored the old prices to the pit although he kept the new prices for the boxes."

"It all sounds quite exciting, but I feel rather sorry for the actors," Fleur said in a soft voice.

"Bravo, child," Blaine said, wanting to hug

177

her sister for her kind heart. "I cannot condone such rudeness. It has always surprised me that such a rough element is permitted to take over in a situation such as this."

"Truly, Lady Yates," Reggie said, "you cannot imagine the sort of manners that hold sway in the upper galleries. I have seen gentlemen hang coats and even waistcoats over the galleries and sit in their" — he lowered his voice in horror — "in their shirtsleeves."

"I'll admit in some theaters, the audience can be an unruly lot," Drew said. He smiled at Lady Yates, whose mouth was pinched in a thin line of disapproval. "I have seen those in the upper galleries dropping orange peelings on the heads of those in the pit. Naturally the pit responds by throwing things into the boxes. For the most part, it is all in good fun. Only occasionally does it get out of hand."

"Common courtesy would dictate more respect for the actors onstage." Blaine spoke briskly, annoyed that the group should find such behavior acceptable.

"Sometimes those onstage are so dreadful, it is a service to the audience to interrupt them." Reggie broke into laughter at his joke and the others smiled in agreement.

"If the players are talented, the audience is usually well behaved," Drew said. "I was recently at a performance that was astounding.

It was a small provincial troupe but their lead player was quite above the ordinary. His name is Edmund Kean and I found his acting totally electrifying. Mark you well his name, as I feel he has the talent to quite put Kemble in the shade."

Blaine had seen Kean act and she, too, had felt overwhelmed at his performance. She leaned forward eagerly, anxious to hear Drew's critique of the man. "I believe I have heard of the man, Lord Farrington. Short, odious person, I was told."

"That may be, Lady Yates," Drew answered gravely. "But as an actor he is unforgettable. When first he comes onstage there is invariably a rustle and some sniggers in the audience. He is short with narrow shoulders and a lithe body. I have heard he learned equestrian tricks in Saunder's circus and studied ballet and fencing, which perhaps accounts for his agile movements. He has a slender face, topped by wildly curling black hair. He is not imposing as is Kemble but his dark eyes glow with a fiery passion that is evident even to the one-shilling gallery."

"I have some acquaintance with Sarah Siddons, Lord Farrington," Blaine said, caught up in the interesting subject. "She did not think much of him. She remarked that he would never be a great actor because of his height."

"Do you really know Sarah Siddons, Bl — "
At her mistake, Fleur covered her mouth with her hands, eyes wide in horror as she stared at her sister.

"Words such as *blast* or *blimey* are considered very bad ton, my girl!" Blaine snapped to cover the gaffe. "Please apologize to the company or you will be thought of as fast."

"I am sorry," Fleur said, staring around in an agony of embarrassment. "I quite forgot myself in my excitement."

"Prettily said, my dear." Blaine caught her sister's eye and gave her a smile of encouragement. Fleur had done so well playing her part that she was entitled to the mistake. Heaven forbid there were others. "Now, to answer your question. Yes, I do know Sarah Siddons and she is a charming woman."

"But she's an actress," the irrepressible girl blurted out.

All charity she felt for her sister disappeared in the face of such a comment. "Despite what you might think, Fleur, the theater is not fraught with vice and immorality. There is a certain amount of it to be sure but then look around at society and you will find many who are quite beyond the pale of respectability."

"Oh, I say, Lady Yates," Reggie said with a gasp. "One can hardly compare the two."

"Do you feel society would be the poorer for the comparison?" Blaine dismissed the dandy with a cold look. "Sarah Siddons has done much to improve the performance of the actors. Many emulate her style, to the eternal gratitude of audiences."

"I have seen her many times, Lady Yates, and I agree with you," Robbie said. "Two years ago I came to town for her farewell performance as Lady Macbeth. I have never seen the part played so chillingly."

"She is wonderful, is she not?" Blaine smiled warmly in remembrance of her friend's many kindnesses. "Sometimes she could be quite outrageous. She once refused to go on until the attendants changed the carpet even though the performance was already in progress. It was her opinion that tragedies could only be played on a green carpet."

Under cover of the general laughter, Blaine watched Drew. When amused, his eyes crinkled at the corners and his generous mouth stretched in a broad grin. She had to admit, the man truly was a handsome devil.

"Do tell us more, Lady Yates," Reggie begged. "It is not often we have one among us who can tell us secrets of the famous Mrs. Siddons."

"I never tell secrets, Mr. Torrance," Blaine said, smiling to take the sting out of her set-down. "It was all a long time ago and many are privy to similar information so I shall not be considered a tattlemonger."

At this, the others burst into a chorus of denials that this would ever be the case.

"Do tell us more, Aunt Haydie," Fleur said, earning a nod of approval from her sister.

"Perhaps you have noticed the draperies that many of the actresses have taken to wearing." Receiving several nods, Blaine continued. "Some still stick to wearing the fashions currently in vogue but others have chosen to don the lovely flowing fabrics that Mrs. Siddons has made her trademark. Sarah always considered that the head and shoulders should be free to move naturally rather than to be restricted by the inventiveness of the milliner and hairdresser. She also felt that the shifting fashions did little to enhance an actress's performance since formal gowns were over-decorated with ribbons, lace, and other fripperies."

"Her wardrobe has a very classical look to it. Was she influenced by the Greek theater?" Drew asked.

"In a way," Blaine said, pleased that he had noticed. "Her very good friend, Mrs. Damer, was a sculptress and it was through her interest in Greek statues that Sarah thought of the soft effect of the flowing draperies. But of course when she played tragedy, she wore heavier materials to lend dignity to the role."

"How sad that she is retired now," Fleur said. "From what you tell me I feel I have missed someone very special."

"She is that, child," Blaine answered. "But never fear. Sarah is an old war-horse. Occasionally she makes brief appearances and, true to the lady she is, it is invariably to benefit some other actor. Now enough of this chatter. You young people should be circulating instead of letting an old lady rattle on about her memories."

Despite their vociferous objections, Blaine shooed them away with the excuse she was tired and would just as soon sit quietly for a time. Robbie, Fleur, and Reggie ambled away but to her dismay, Drew remained lounging in a chair beside the sofa. Her eyes met his in a question and he smiled.

"I, too, relish the quiet," he said. "Besides, I wanted to speak to you to assure myself that all goes well with you. You have not been much in evidence."

"Just because I do not keep the unseemly hours of a rakehell is no reason to surmise that I am poorly," Blaine said. Despite her feeling that she ought not encourage him, she was unable to keep a spark of mischief from her eyes.

"In truth, milord, everything is working out reasonably well. Your aunt's house and staff could not be more to our liking. I am quite sunk to all conscience at being so pampered."

"And Fleur?" he asked. He noted the quick dart of her eyes across the room and the quick worried look as she watched the little blond girl.

"I try to tell myself she is very young," she said with a sigh. "But I confess to a strong urge to shake the girl until her teeth rattle. I would hate to see her throw away her chance for such a fine husband as Robbie because she is too bird-witted to appreciate the fine qualities of your brother."

"It is heady indeed to have such a bevy of admirers," Drew said. "I trust she will come around before Robbie loses his temper. Perhaps we are too hard on her."

"Perhaps," Blaine said, biting her lip. "I realize I was never as young as Fleur and it is difficult for me to understand such a trusting nature. She sees no evil in the world so how can she be expected to make good judgments?"

"When did her parents die?"

"Fleur was eleven and Val was only five. It was a difficult time."

"Robbie mentioned there was another sister."

Blaine could not help the start of surprise at Drew's question. She carefully schooled her face to show nothing but politeness. "Blaine is away much of the time, caring for an elderly relative. The children see little of her." Eager to change the subject, she leaned forward, tapping him lightly on the sleeve with her walking stick. "Val tells me you have kept him well entertained. I can only hope the child has not nagged you to death with his questions."

"I quite dote on the lad," Drew said. "It is refreshing to hear Val's views on the, I believe he called them 'sordid, vice-ridden streets.' I have put him in the way of several boys so he will have fellows of his own age to create havoc with."

"So it was you who introduced him to Master Jamie Wildebrand." Blaine sniffed and glared daggers at the smiling Lord Farrington. "A loathsome child with a penchant for things that crawl. He presented Val with a delightful collection of mice, which your aunt may well mention to you if her staff is able to locate them."

Drew's deep chuckle rumbled in his chest. "Jamie has always been a particular favorite of mine," he said. "His father and I went to school together and we were sent down regularly for some highly imaginative prank that our headmaster viewed with opprobrium. I was sure that Jamie would find favor in Val's eyes."

"Wretched man!" Blaine cried. She joined in his laughter, the meanwhile chastising herself for once more falling victim to the man's charm. Suddenly her eyes shifted and she urgently nudged Drew with her cane. "Something is very much amiss between your brother and my niece. Would you have the goodness to inform the girl that I wish to go home before she disgraces herself completely?"

Drew was quick to present Lady Yates's message to Fleur and returned with the girl on his arm. As Blaine rose creakily to her feet, she noted the high color on her sister's cheeks. She took a firm hold of Fleur's arm as she made their excuses to Lady Forsythe while Drew went ahead to call their carriage. When her sister would have spoken, she hastily hushed her and moved regally down the stairs. She smiled thinly when Drew squeezed her hand in encouragement as he assisted them into the carriage.

"Not a word, until we are safely in our rooms," Blaine warned, afraid of what the girl might say in her anger. She was all too aware of servants' gossip and knew that the Portman Square staff would not protect the family secrets as would the retainers at Weathers. The ride home seemed endless to Blaine but

186

eventually they arrived and went immediately upstairs to Fleur's room.

"I cannot believe that you were close to creating a scene. Your voice was raised to such a degree that all were aware you were having a disagreement with Robbie." Blaine tried to keep her voice calm but she felt annoyance rise at the petulant look on her sister's face.

"Oh, Blaine, Robbie is such an old bore. He was prosing on endlessly, and I just couldn't stand another word."

Fleur flounced down on the edge of the bed, setting the bed hangings aquiver as if in further reflection of her discontent.

"You mean he was lecturing you?"

"Exactly," Fleur said, biting her lip to hold back tears. "He treats me like a child. He told me that I was puffed up by the attention that I was receiving."

"And are you?" Blaine asked quietly.

Fleur looked startled at the question but shrugged off any feeling of guilt. "I like the attention and it is no business of Robbie's what I do. And so I told him." Her smile of triumph faltered a little under Blaine's steady gaze. "Perhaps I was a beast but I am having such a wonderful time. All of the men I have met are such fun. And Robbie goes around with a Friday face just because I wish to enjoy myself."

"I will not lecture you, Fleur, for I fear it would set your feet on a more destructive path." Blaine rose to her feet, crossing the room to kiss her sister on the cheek. "You are very young but I hope you will discover Robbie's worth before you throw him over for one of your flirts. There are many men who will seek you out for a bit of fun, as you call it. That is an excitement of the moment and fades quickly. Be sure you do not overlook a man who would give you joy and happiness for a lifetime."

Without another word, Blaine left the room. For the remainder of the day she thought of her sister, knowing full well that much of her annoyance with Fleur was a result of her own situation. What she would not give to find a man who could love and respect her! She had seen so many men who only wanted La Solitaire for a "bit of fun" that she recognized Robbie's interest in Fleur as a genuine love. She carried her doleful thoughts onto the stage that evening and there was a particular poignancy to her performance as she played the cast-off mistress of an Arabian prince.

nine

Drew stood on the sidewalk in front of White's, oblivious to the pedestrian traffic that circulated around his immobile figure. His face was a study in boredom while his mind was focused inward as he puzzled out the origin of his discontent. He had attempted to while the day away with a game of cards. His concentration had been divided but, despite this fact, he had won, taking little pleasure in the windfall. He had always been a man of action, addressing a problem until he was able to work through a solution. And now he was ready to find answers to the questions that plagued him.

He nodded his head at the course of action he had mapped out and tipped his beaver hat back on his head with the knob of his walking stick. Looking around to get his bearings, he started off on a brisk walk through the city until he arrived at the offices of Upton and Sons. He presented his card to the solicitor's assistant, who scurried away with great importance. Drew rocked back and forth on the soles of his boots, humming softly under his breath. There was a slight smile on his generous mouth and his green eyes sparkled with mischief at his plan. When the assistant returned, holding the gate open for him to enter the inner sanctum of the Upton domain, Drew flipped him a coin for his trouble.

"Come in, Lord Farrington. Come in." Wesley Upton fluttered around his visitor with the anxiety of a mother hen. "Try this chair. I think you will find it quite comfortable."

With an arch nod of approval, Drew sat down in the comfortable leather chair Wesley pushed forward. The portly little man returned to the chair behind the desk, his fingers fumbling to neaten the pile of papers on the surface. Once he had established order, he beamed across at Drew, his bald head shining a cherubic pink and his spectacles winking in the light from the window.

"To what do I owe this pleasure, Lord Farrington?" Wesley asked. "Not that it is not always a welcome sight to have you visit."

Drew had done business with Mr. Upton on various occasions and he hoped to trade on the man's familiarity. "I have need of some information, Wesley, and I was assured that I might apply to you." He lowered his voice to a confiding tone, delighted when he saw the glint of interest in the solicitor's eyes. "My brother Robert is planning to marry. Lovely child just right for Robbie. Naturally this is *entre nous*, since there has been no formal announcement."

"I understand perfectly, Lord Farrington." Wesley placed a pudgy finger beside his nose and winked roguishly across the desk. "This room is very like a mausoleum. Sealed forever in silence."

Drew was not sure he liked the allusion but trudged ahead. "I have spoken to Lady Haydie Yates and she has given your discretion high praise. She mentioned you with great warmth." The little man preened, much to Drew's amusement as the scene he had interrupted in Lady Yates's drawing room flashed before his mind. "By the way, I understand I may wish you happy."

Drew hoped that this piece of information would clinch the fact of his intimate conversation with Lady Yates. A flush of pleasure suffused the solicitor's face and a lopsided smile added to the angelic countenance as he resettled his glasses.

"It is true, milord. I will be married in another month."

"I applaud your bravery, Wesley. It is a step I tremble to take although my brother is quite determined to step willingly into the parson's mousetrap." Drew paused, letting the curiosity return to Wesley's face. "In fact, it is for that reason that I have come. Lady Yates is reticent about the Meriweather family history. I assume she is far too modest to puff up the family just to make her niece appear a worthy addition to the Farringtons."

"Ah, I see," Wesley said, much impressed by the delicate way in which Lord Farrington was imparting the news of Robbie's soon-to-be-announced fiancée.

"Lady Yates indicated that you might be an excellent source of information." Drew chose his words carefully. He was unwilling to lie, but, if need be, he would, in order to get the little man to open his budget.

"A fine woman, Lady Yates." Wesley sighed in contemplation of the gracious old lady. Then he sat up, his manner totally professional. "What information did you have in mind, milord?"

"I have no wish for you to break a confidence. I wish only to protect my brother from a misalliance. To the best of my knowledge there has been nothing bandied about that would lead me to suspect any scandal within the Meriweather family. However, Wesley, as you know, I am a thorough man and where Robbie's happiness is concerned I wish no surprises."

"Your concern for your brother is laudable, Lord Farrington, and I will be as helpful as possible." Wesley leaned back in his chair, elbows on the arms as he contemplated his tented fingers. "Now, how may I help?"

"From Val, I have learned that his parents, Cedric and Juliette Meriweather, were killed in a carriage accident. Aside from a yearly allotment to Lady Yates, the money was left in trust until the boy is twenty-one. This, I gather, accounts for their current strapped financial condition." Drew stared at the solicitor's shiny head, bobbing in agreement, and then continued. "Further, I have been told that the estate is extremely sound so that once the trust is handed over, Val will be exceedingly well fixed. There was, however, some question as to the matter of dowries."

At these words a slight frown furrowed Wesley's forehead. He pursed his lips and stared at a spot on the wall behind Drew's head. Drew waited, his eyes gleaming with sudden interest. Eventually, the solicitor came to himself. He leaned forward and his glasses promptly slid to the end of his nose. In annoyance he took them off and laid them carefully on the corner of the desk.

"All that you have heard is basically true. They had a very rough time of it right after the parents' deaths. The older sister was forced to go out to work while Lady Yates stayed in Wiltshire to care for the children. She has done well by them, don't you think?"

"I agree with you fully, Wesley."

"Val is extremely responsible for such a young boy. According to his aunt, he has taken great interest in the estate. And of course Miss Fleur is a most taking little thing. I swear I have never seen such exquisite eyes. The color of violets. I am told her mother's eyes were the same."

"And the other sister, Blaine?" Drew asked.

"I have never met the girl. I have heard that she is quite different in looks. Only a half sister, don't you know," Wesley said, as if that explained everything. "Her mother died when she was eight. I have never heard that there was any bad blood between Miss Blaine and her stepmother. Naturally one never knows."

Drew was intrigued by the definite feeling that Wesley Upton did not approve of Blaine Meriweather. Perhaps the girl had been difficult over the suddenness of her father's remarriage. She may have taken a sharp dislike to the children who replaced her in her father's affection. But that was nonsense. Both Val and Fleur seemed to have a great love for their sister so there must be something else that stuck in Wesley's craw.

"Are the girls' dowries affected by the

trust?" Drew asked.

"Only Miss Fleur has a dowry."

"Devil you say!" Drew said in surprise. "Was Blaine written out of the will?"

"No. No. Nothing so dramatic," Wesley hastened to reassure him. "It was just that no dowry was ever set up for Miss Blaine."

"How unusual."

"These are rather unusual circumstances." He lifted a hand at Drew's sudden frown. "Never fear that there are any irregularities concerning Miss Fleur's dowry, Lord Farrington. I would never permit anything of the kind. The girl will not come penniless to this marriage. It has been growing steadily over the last three years and is now a very tidy sum."

"Growing, Wesley?"

"It is difficult to tell you a great deal about this since it is slightly unusual. I cannot give you any figures unless specifically applied to by Lady Yates." The solicitor took out a snowy handkerchief, wiping his forehead and his scalp, which were dotted with perspiration. "Perhaps if I gave you some background it might be helpful."

"I am all eagerness," Drew replied. His words were drawled, making the solicitor squirm under his steady gaze.

"At the time of the Meriweathers' accident,

there were no dowries for either girl. My father, who handled things prior to his death, spoke to Lady Yates about this, but the woman's allowance was not enough to give the young ladies any assistance. It was after I took over that I began to receive money to be deposited in Miss Fleur's name. The estate manager, a Mr. Visible . . . " Wesley looked up in surprise when Lord Farrington snorted.

"Your pardon, Upton," Drew said, smothering his amusement behind a hastily raised handkerchief. "Just a particle of dust. Pray continue."

"As I was saying, in the estate manager's correspondence, he explained that the older sister, Miss Blaine, had taken employment and wished to set up a dowry for her sister. The deposits have been sporadic but now I am happy to say Miss Fleur will come to the marriage with a satisfactory sum." Wesley folded his hands complacently at the conclusion of his explanation.

"What an enterprising young lady," Drew said. "A laudable deed to take such measures to ensure her sister's future. She has put nothing aside for herself?"

"Nothing, milord." The solicitor's face clearly showed his disapproval of such a thing.

"You have never met Miss Meriweather?"

"I have had the pleasure of Miss Fleur's acquaintance but Miss Blaine has been away from home during my visits."

"If you could hazard a guess, sir, what kind of a person would you suspect Miss Blaine Meriweather to be?" Drew's eyes were intent on Wesley's face and he did not miss the slight flush of embarrassment that tinged the little man's scalp.

"I don't know, Lord Farrington," he answered, his eyes shifting around the room.

"Give over, Wesley," Drew snapped. "Is the chit involved in some havey-cavey business? Do I need concern myself that we might find ourselves involved in some messy scandal broth?"

It was evident to Drew that the solicitor was more than uncomfortable with the topic of discussion. He kept his face expressionless but there was a hardness around the eyes that bespoke his determination to have an answer. Finally Wesley Upton loosed a tired sigh.

"To be perfectly honest, Lord Farrington, I know absolutely nothing to Miss Blaine's discredit." He pinched the bridge of his nose between thumb and forefinger, reaching out for his spectacles. He was silent while he polished the lenses, then returned them to his face and carefully arranged the earpieces. "However, sir, we are both men of the world and if I were to venture an opinion, I would say that the young lady in question may be leading a less than virtuous existence."

"Good Lord, man!"

"I know that may seem a harsh accusation but I cannot account otherwise for the sums of money placed in my hands. You know the kind of employment to be secured by a young gentlewoman. The salary is barely enough to survive on. Yet according to Lady Yates, Miss Blaine uses her own money to clothe, feed, and house herself. And beyond that, she contributes money to her sister's dowry. I am not able to contact the girl directly; all correspondence is handled through the estate manager. With the amount of her deposits and the secrecy surrounding her, is it any wonder, Lord Farrington, that I have serious doubts as to her employment? In my mind, it does not add up to honest labor."

Nor did it in Drew's mind. He waited but there was no other information forthcoming. After thanking the solicitor for his help and promising to mention nothing of the latter part of their discussion to Lady Yates, he left the stuffy office. Outside, he walked slowly, unconscious of the direction he was taking. His mind was busy with all that he had heard.

In his wildest imaginings he had never suspected that he would turn up such a bewildering piece of information. He admitted now that under the guise of investigating Fleur's background he had really been trying to satisfy his own curiosity about the mysterious Blaine Meriweather. Good Lord, he muttered. What a nest of snakes he had uncovered. Was it possible that Blaine was a woman of easy virtue, plying the oldest trade in the world? A kept woman or merely a self-employed entrepreneur?

A frown etched his forehead and at a shout, he stepped back, narrowly missing a collision with a carter. He concentrated on wending his way across the crowded streets. He ignored the shouts of the carriage drivers and dodged a curricle as he reached the gates of a small park. Walking along the quiet lanes, Drew once more focused on his thoughts.

He found it hard to get a picture of Blaine Meriweather. According to Wesley Upton, she was most probably involved in the muslin trade, a woman of few morals, supplementing her family's income with ill-gotten gains. He remembered how Val's face lit up whenever he spoke of his sister. By his description, Blaine was all that was wonderful. She was competent in managing the estate. She was teaching the boy good values and sound judgment. Even Fleur and Lady Yates mentioned Blaine with smiles and twinkling in their eyes.

Lady Yates would never mention the girl, if she were involved in some less-than-virtuous enterprise. Drew had seen in the old woman a lady of principles with a strong moral code. Perhaps she did not know? Impossible. Drew snorted. It would not be easy to fool Lady Yates with some Banbury Tale. She had a surprisingly jaded view of the world and would spot any moral weakness in her niece.

How then to account for the money? He supposed that he would just have to assume she was earning her way in some legitimate venture. Perhaps the mystery about her had nothing to do with her employment but, as he had already considered, with some physical deformity.

Drew slashed his walking cane, efficiently beheading several flowers along the pathway. It annoyed him that in seeking information about the elusive Miss Meriweather, he had turned up only more questions. He should have left well enough alone. Short of asking Lady Yates outright, Drew could see no immediate satisfaction to his curiosity.

He immediately brightened at the thought that he might approach Lady Yates but then a sudden thought made the brows bunch over his eyes in consternation. What was wrong with him lately? He was beginning to wonder if something had happened to age him prematurely. His brain must surely be softening since the only time he seemed to get any enjoyment out of life was when he was with a sharp-tongued sexagenarian.

The truth was, he really was fond of Lady Yates. He enjoyed her company and was intrigued by her conversation. The old woman never bored him and delighted in giving him ferocious set-downs. When he was with her, he never considered her age but treated her like one of his contemporaries. She had a straightforwardness he admired. He was perceptive enough to realize that one of the appeals of the woman was the absence of sexual tensions. He could never speak to a woman his own age with the same freedom he had with Lady Yates. Young ladies were always busy trying to affix his interest and he needed to have a care that they did not assume he might eventually he brought up to scratch. He must be getting old. Perhaps he should just adjourn to his library with a good book and a lap robe. Drew dug his walking stick into the packed earth of the pathway. *Too early to stick your spoon in the wall, my lad.*

His green eyes lost their look of confusion and sparkled in the late-afternoon sunlight. He would go home and change for an evening at the theater. Even if the object of his desires would have nothing to do with him, he would still have the joy of feasting his eyes on her. A note to Miss Mason might be acceptable. She had spoken kindly to him when he'd rescued her from that blackguard Stoddard. Perhaps she might look more kindly on his suit, especially if he couched it in respectful terms. Drew's steps were brisk as he walked toward the gates of the park.

Blaine opened her hand and dropped the crumpled note on the top of her dressing table. With shaking fingers, she smoothed the wrinkled paper, staring down at the beautifully formed pen strokes. Hearing Tate's movements behind her, she hastily folded the note and thrust it into the pocket of her dress.

It was impossible, she told the reflection in the mirror but her eyes stared back rebelliously. Her gaze dropped to the surface of the dressing table and she rearranged the glass bottles of scents in an effort to organize her thoughts.

Drew Farrington had invited her to meet him at a private inn the following night, when the theater would be dark. He said he only desired the pleasure of her company at dinner; she could come and go as she pleased. He gave her directions and told her he would wait for her there. One evening was all that he asked. It was these words that replayed over and over in Blaine's mind.

Her hand curled over the letter in her pocket and for a moment she debated whether she should rip it up or burn it. One evening. It was not so much to ask, her traitorous mind declared. Slowly her fingers relaxed and she stroked the material of her dress, smiling at the crackle of parchment beneath the silk.

It was such a temptation. She was so tired of her solitary life. For six years her social life had been less exciting than that of a cloistered religious. It would be wonderful to dine with a man, for once not playing a role but being herself. She had envisioned such an evening in her dreams and now the mere thought was delicious, despite the danger. And it would be dangerous.

Drew Farrington was a gentleman. She was sure that she could trust him not to go beyond the boundaries he had set for the evening. He was not the danger. She was.

The thing that frightened Blaine was that she was actually considering accepting an invitation from a gentleman. From the moment she had stepped on the stage, she had been besieged with offers from amorous suitors whose one objective was to bed her. She knew that Drew wanted to make her his mistress and, despite that fact, she still wanted to spend the evening with him. Ever since she had gotten to know him in Wiltshire, he had constantly been on her mind. If they were together she was aware of his every glance and movement. When she did not see him, she wove endless fantasies about him.

Any lasting relationship with Drew was a fantasy, she reminded herself bitterly. No matter her background or breeding. In the world that he inhabited, an actress was no better than a woman of the streets. He desired her, wanted her only for a brief tumble, and then, when she bored him, he would leave her. How could she even consider spending an evening with such a man?

"It's time," Tate said, her face suddenly appearing in the mirror behind Blaine's. "Come along, do. What have you been about, miss, that you're not ready? Have you got your fan? Your reticule?"

She let the nattering words of the dresser wash over her as she made her way to the wings. Her hand gripped the velvet curtain as she listened to the lines of the actors. She took a deep breath, held it for a moment, then expelled it slowly to relax herself. She closed her eyes and let her mind block out the sounds around her as she concentrated on the role she would be playing. When she opened her eyes, she was calm, moving onstage at the sound of her cue.

For the evening's bill, John Tibbles had chosen a comic opera, blatantly pirated from a commedia del l'arte offering at the Drury Lane. Blaine was Colombine and her entrance was met by a tumultuous roar of approval from the pit. Moving forward to the center of the apron, she sang her song, her eyes lifted to the upper gallery. Her movements were graceful and she kept a sweet smile on her face as befitted her part. It took all of her concentration to keep from looking at Drew's private box but she had made up her mind and was determined to ignore the man.

Teddy Mortimer, one of her favorites in the company, was Pantaloon. She smiled as he tugged at the absurdly long points of his short white beard. Teddy had a fine sense of comic timing and his rich deep voice rolled out over the audience as he raised his brown mask with the hooked nose into the air.

She knew Drew's eyes were on her. She could feel them almost as a physical pressure, weighting her down. Lethargy invaded her body and yet her heart felt light, as though she were floating. It took all her control not to raise her eyes but she fought the urge, keeping her gaze firmly on the actors onstage.

Harlequin capered across the boards and led her forward. Whitiker Chalmers was new to the company but he had shown well in rehearsal. He had a lean, wiry body that looked well in the costume of red, blue, and green diamonds. As he waved his sword-bat, he stroked his mustaches and slyly grinned, displaying a gap-toothed smile that made Blaine giggle. While he sang, she fixed her eyes on his face in wide-eyed admiration, although her mind was far away.

The play moved at a sprightly pace and, through it all, Blaine avoided glancing at the private boxes. She was proud of her determination but there was a bleakness to her spirits that she found hard to define. Her final song spoke of a love that could never be and her voice trembled with emotion as she completed the final trilling run. There was absolute silence in the audience when she finished and tears sheened her eyes, giving a rainbow effect in the light from the argand lamps.

Suddenly the roar of the crowd broke over her in a wild cacophony. For a moment she was disoriented. Without thought she looked up at Drew's box and was immediately transfixed by the blaze of emotion she read in his eyes. It was as though they were alone in the theater; two minds attached over a great distance. Nothing mattered to Blaine except to bask forever in the light of approval she found there. She knew he had been waiting all evening to discover her response to his invitation. For once his austere features were hesitant, almost as if he were afraid of her answer. Holding his glance, she dropped into a graceful curtsy. As she rose, she nodded her head in a simple sign of acceptance.

ten

"You have surely lost the wits you were born with," Tate snapped. "What will happen if he recognizes you?"

She stared at the figure on the window seat that faced out onto Portman Square. Seeing the set jaw of her mistress and the fiery determination in the gold-hazel eyes, the dresser sighed. It was never easy dealing with Blaine when she had already set her feet on a path. She shrugged, determined to fight against such a dangerous undertaking.

"I know the risks involved, Tate. Lord knows I have thought long and hard about this. With all my heart, I want this one night. For one night I want to pretend that my life is different. I want to be Blaine Margaret Meriweather, a young gentlewoman having dinner with a handsome gentleman."

The wizened little dresser heard the cry in her mistress's voice and could not harden her heart against the plea. For six years she had watched over Blaine, loving her much as if she were her own child. She had seen the girl combat loneliness and despair. She had been isolated from all of her own kind, living in a world renowned for its loose morals and debauchery. It was a wonderment that the girl had survived at all, let alone maintained the purity and innocence that lay just beneath the veneer of sophistication.

"Aye, lamby, I know it has been lonely for you," Tate said, an unaccustomed tear in her eye. "But it is almighty dangerous. Lord Farrington, of all people!"

"It is just for that reason that I can risk accepting his offer. He is the only man I know well enough to know that I will be safe. Despite his pursuit of La Solitaire, he is a gentleman, not prone to violence or drink. He would never force his attentions on me," Blaine argued.

"Some men needn't use force," Tate opined darkly.

The dresser was aware of something that made her extremely uneasy about the assignation. She had guessed the identity of the man who had sent the white roses and she had watched the expression in Blaine's eyes soften when she had received Lord Farrington's flowers. She did not know if Blaine realized her own feelings for the young lord, but Tate knew. Blaine was in love with Drew Farrington.

The thought of the pain that Blaine would endure when she came to terms with her own emotions was frightening for Tate. There was no possibility that anything other than a brief liaison could come out of this relationship. Men of Drew Farrington's background did not marry actresses and Blaine believed in the sanctity of marriage. Any other arrangement would destroy her since she never would be able to live with the realization that she had compromised all of her values.

"Please, Tate, won't you help me?"

Love made you weak, the dresser muttered under her breath as she stared at the eyes of her mistress. "All right," she said with a sigh. "I have a feeling in my bones that this is the greatest of follies, but I will do what I can."

"Oh, thank you. Thank you," Blaine said, hugging the glowering woman. "You shan't regret it, I promise. It will only be for one night and then I shall go back to being Maggie Mason without a grumble."

Tate was far too old to believe such rubbish. "I doubt that, my girl." She snorted. "All right, miss. What do you want me to do?"

Blaine was silent as she stared bleakly out the window onto the square. She wondered for a moment if one evening was worth so much trouble. Then Drew's face, as she had seen it last, appeared before her eyes. He had been smiling then, in recognition of her acceptance of his invitation. His eyes had sparkled with happiness and his face bore a curiously touching look of joy. She would not fail him. Blaine bit her lip, knowing the hardest part was tackling Tate. She could just imagine the expression on the dresser's face when she announced that she wanted help to dye her hair.

When she had decided to accept Drew's invitation to dinner, her only qualm was that he might recognize similarities between La Solitaire and Lady Yates. The makeup she used for her role as Aunt Haydie covered her skin completely and gave the impression of a lined and wrinkled face beneath the white paste. Tate had even changed the curve of her eyebrows for the part. Since she could do nothing to eradicate the telltale color of her eyes, Blaine had made it a practice to squint or use her lorgnette when in Drew's company.

Her white-blond hair was the problem. She was afraid that it might remind him of Lady Yates's white ringlets and even this small oversight might cause him to become suspicious. Too much rested on the continuation of her masquerade as Aunt Haydie, to leave things to chance. As an actress, Blaine had learned that many times it was the small inconsistencies in a role that made the character unbelievable in the eyes of the audience. With a heavy heart, she determined that dyeing her hair would be the only possible way to prevent any possible comparisons.

Blaine turned away from the window and braced herself. Taking a deep breath, she told Tate her plan and, true to form, the woman was not silent in her disapproval. Much to Blaine's relief, the catalogue of dire predictions, pointed barbs, and general disapproval did not last long. Once the woman had decided to help Blaine, she set to work with a vengeance.

They spent the afternoon dyeing her hair and fitting a dress Tate had borrowed from the wardrobe mistress at the theater. They were uninterrupted since Fleur, with the indefatigable Puff in tow, was happily engaged for a day of shopping with one of the girls she had met in London. Timing things to a nicety, the dyeing was completed and Blaine's damp hair covered with a turban before Fleur knocked on her door and flew into the room with an armload of packages.

"Is there anything left in the shops after your adventurous day?" Blaine asked from the comfort of her chaise longue.

"It was ever so much fun. Constance Flannery is such fun to be with. She knows everyone and is quite generous in her introductions." Fleur ignored Tate's sour expression as she dumped her packages on the floor. "No need to frown. Ellen will come to take these to my room."

"Since Ellen has become your abigail your habit of neatness has become far too lax," Blaine chided. "I trust when you return to Wiltshire, you will not expect the servants to pick up after you."

"I won't," the girl assured her, coming over to sit on the foot of the chaise. "I am just taking full advantage of being pampered. Now, no more lectures. Just wait until you see what I bought you. I know you shall love it."

"Let me guess," Blaine said, entering into the light mood. "A new lace shawl and some caps for my role as Aunt Haydie. No? I have it. A tapestry reticule to hold my tatting supplies."

Fleur giggled and shook her head, and even Tate's face turned up in a smile at their nonsense.

"A new cane? Or perhaps some more bombazine in a bright cherry-red," Blaine continued.

"You may tease me all you like but I know you will love this." The girl pouted but her violet eyes sparkled with mischief. "You are right that it is for your role as Aunt Haydie but I think I have found something that will find approval with even your most exacting standards. It is a hat."

"Oh," Blaine said, torn between annoyance and laughter. It was true that she needed new things for her wardrobe but it was a most lowering thought.

"Give a look, Blaine, do." Fleur opened a bandbox, pulling at the paper that covered her present. "I know how you keep to your room so that you do not have to wear that horrid rig of a costume. Well, I have found just the thing so that we can go jauntering around and at least you won't have to wear that pasty white makeup and yet you will be perfectly safe."

Fleur pulled a black hat out of the depths of the bandbox, flourishing it before Blaine's bemused glance. It was black straw with a wide circular brim. The top of the hat was covered with yards of satin in puffy great bows. However, the thing that made it so singular was the black veil that descended all around the brim of the hat to about shoulder height.

"The saleswoman called it a *chapeau de morte*. At least I think that's what she said. Constance was giggling so loudly I could hardly take in the woman's words." With a flourish, Fleur placed the hat on her head and flipped the veil down across her face. "Now, this piece of satin is to be tied at the neck so that the veiling won't blow about in the wind."

Tate could not resist being involved in the project and took the band of black satin that the girl was waving about. She tied it around Fleur's neck then pulled and prodded the veiling until satisfied with the effect. She stepped back and Fleur danced over to the chaise so that Blaine could see the genius of her idea.

"I can see perfectly well, but no one can see my face."

Blaine's eyes crinkled with laughter as she took in the truth of the girl's statement. The veiling was not very transparent so that there was only a vague suggestion of the figure behind. It was as concealing as a mask, without being confining.

"Darling child, you have surely given me the best present of all," Blaine said. "I hate wearing all that greasepaint and now I will be free to go out without fear of giving the show away. Take that off and come give me a kiss."

Fleur obeyed enthusiastically and then settled beside her sister to tell her about her plans for the evening.

"Constance told me that the Mayhews are all the thing and that the ball this evening will be a terrible squeeze. I thought, if you ap-

215

proved, I would wear the peach silk. I found some flowers just that shade while we were shopping and Ellen promised to weave them into my hair."

"Sounds just the thing, Fleur. Will Puff be up to the lateness of the evening after a day of gadding about? The good frau is not quite as young and I would not want her to exhaust herself taking you about."

"Constance's mother has volunteered to take me under her eye. She is almost as strict as Puff" was Fleur's irrepressible reply. "I wish you could go but I know how you relish your time alone on your day off. I do wonder at times if Cousin Lavinia is not working you too hard. Will I be able to meet her soon?"

For a moment a bubble of hysteria rose in Blaine's throat at the possibility of impersonating another old woman for her sister's benefit. She brushed the thought aside with a shudder of distaste. "If only dear Lavinia was well enough for visits. Sometimes she is fair moped, cooped up in the house."

Eventually, after showing Blaine the rest of her purchases, Fleur was sent off to her own room. They had agreed to have trays sent up but Blaine assured her sister that she preferred to eat later and then to go immediately to bed. Fleur agreed to join her for breakfast and tell her all the details of the ball. Blaine dozed on the chaise until it was time to prepare for her own evening.

"Just look at your lovely hair! It's surely a nasty color," Tate wailed as she settled the last hairpin in place.

"It's not so dreadful. It's different," Blaine said as she stared into the mirror. "I hope you're right, that this will wash out. I much prefer my own hair."

In place of her white-blond color, Blaine's hair was brown. It had the look of old oak but not nearly the deep tones. At least the hair had a sheen of sorts, and Tate had arranged it in a bundle of curls pulled high on her head and cascading down to her shoulders. Ignoring the frowning dresser, Blaine got up from the vanity bench and crossed the room to the cheval glass.

Her gown, a cool column of heavy ivory satin, was magnificent. Tate had purloined it from the theater's wardrobe where it had been placed after she had played Mary Queen of Scots the previous season. The lines were simple and it was unadorned, with the exception of a band of lace along the low décolletage and at the edge of the puffed sleeves. A sash of softer satin caught the material beneath her breasts and was tied in the back in a shimmering pouf. She wore no jewelry at her neck, only a wide band of ivory satin. Pearls dangled from her ears and swung gently against the side of her neck.

"You needn't look so satisfied, miss." Tate sniffed. "It's true you're a beauty but remember most gentlemen are beasts at heart."

Blaine laughed at the vision of Drew as a drooling, snarling animal but she sobered quickly, reminded that her assignation that evening was dangerous and most probably a dreadful mistake. She raised her chin in defiance. She had promised herself one magical evening and now was not the time to cry craven.

"That's enough, Tate. My mind is quite made up so there's no point in nattering at me. I shall be perfectly safe under Sarge's protection. I do not consider Lord Farrington a raving lunatic. I am sure he will conduct himself as a gentleman."

"I suppose you know best. My lips are sealed, miss," Tate said but could not resist one last reminder. "Keep your hood well forward and watch your step."

Sarge assisted her into the carriage, glowering darkly over what he considered the greatest folly. When she told him their destination he balked, and it was only after she ordered him that he slammed the door and stomped around to take the reins. As the carriage got under way, Blaine smoothed out her skirts and leaned back against the squabs, exhausted by her preparations and the nagging of the servants. She had a strong feeling of ill usage until she reminded herself that both Sarge and Tate were only trying to protect her. When she thought about the evening ahead, she found it was difficult to breathe naturally. Her chest felt constricted and she found herself nearly panting. Her heart was pounding in a most exaggerated fashion. Overcome by nervousness, she pressed her hands together in her lap to keep them from trembling.

She had to admit she felt frightened. Having never been involved in such a venture before, she was worried that something would go wrong. Drew's instructions had been explicit, to assure her of secrecy, and for that very reason she could not ignore the feeling of shame at the clandestine nature of their meeting. Once more she was caught up in a series of lies.

The servants at Portman Square knew her only as Lady Yates. In order to explain her absence in the evenings, she had told the housekeeper that she would be staying most nights with an old friend who was unwell. At the times when she had no performance at the theater, she stayed at Portman Square, keeping to her room with the explanation that she was overtired. Tonight after she was dressed, Tate had

had to smuggle her out of the house and would be waiting to admit her on her return.

The coach arrived much too quickly at the Rose and Trellis. From the name, Blaine had expected a charming wayside inn but the place was tucked into a copse of trees, looking timeworn and rather disreputable. She shuddered as she stepped to the ground and pulled her hood more securely around her face. Before she could lose courage, she walked quickly across the yard to the side door, leaving a sullen and disgruntled Sarge beside the carriage.

The door closed with a sharp rattle of the latch and Blaine was plunged into darkness. Through the walls she could hear the sounds of revelry from the public rooms of the inn, which did little to encourage her. Her heart tripped with fear in the darkened stairwell and she clamped her teeth together to keep them from chattering. She fumbled around in the darkness for the railing. When her hand touched the rough wood, she clung to it.

She smiled grimly in the darkness, telling herself not to be such a ninny, and took a deep steadying breath. Her heart still pounded in an erratic manner but she grasped the railing firmly and began to climb the stairs. At the first door on the right, she raised her hand, scratching lightly on the panel. The door swung open and firm fingers grasped her arm and swung her inside the room. Her hood fell forward, blinding her, and she struggled to pull herself from the binding fingers, gasping as the door closed with a sharp click of the latch.

"Forgive me, my dear, for giving you such a fright."

Drew's deep voice reassured her and as he released her wrist, she pushed her hood back. She smiled in relief at his elegant attire until she looked beyond him to the room.

In the light from the candles in the wall sconce, she could see that the room was not large and more nearly a bedchamber than a sitting room. Although there were two easy chairs in a windowed alcove, a large four-poster bed, covered by a brightly patterned quilt, dominated. There were more candles on the table beside the bed, surrounding it in a harsh glow. She pressed her back against the panels of the door, appalled that she had so mistaken Drew Farrington. It was painfully obvious that the room had been furnished as the backdrop for a scene of seduction.

The sight of the disillusionment on the beautiful woman's face struck Drew like a blow. "Please forgive me, Miss Mason," he said. "I had no intention of insulting you."

At his words, she raised accusing eyes and studied his face. He held perfectly still beneath her scrutiny and then opened his arms. With only a momentary hesitation, she trustingly stepped into his embrace as if to seek reassurance from her frightening conclusions. He could feel the trembling of the body pressed close to his and he was washed with a wave of shame that he had ever contrived such a shoddy arrangement. He could not believe that he could have been so thoughtless as to give her even a moment of discomfort.

Slowly she raised her face. His breath caught in his throat at the ivory perfection of her skin and the golden luminescence of her eyes. His eyes caressed her shining curls and he loosened the clasp at her neck, swinging the cape from her shoulders in a single movement. Standing back, he admired the elegance of her gown and the radiance of her lovely features. In the tawdry surroundings, La Solitaire shone like a lily among weeds.

Blaine had recovered a little of her courage and stepped away from Drew, giggling softly at the stunned expression on his face. There was no sign of recognition in his face, only a look of admiration that sent her pulse racing.

"I am sorry for displaying such missish airs, Lord Farrington," she said. "The stairwell was dark and I became confused."

"You need never apologize, Miss Mason. I am at fault. I should never have invited you to such a place." Drew folded her cloak and placed it on the seat of a chair against the wall.

"I do not normally accept invitations of any kind," Blaine said. "I am not really sure why I came."

Without commenting, Drew took her hand, leading her around the bed and over to one of the chairs that overlooked the inn yard. It comforted her to see a corner of her carriage and to know that Sarge was so close at hand. She eyed the ancient chair with misgivings, then gingerly seated herself. Much to her surprise it was quite comfortable.

"Do you come here often, Lord Farrington?" she asked as he pulled up the other equally disreputable chair.

Drew laughed, the sound harsh in the little room. "My apologies again, Miss Mason. I have behaved like a callow youth in arranging this evening. Until tonight I had never been to this dreadful place. I asked an acquaintance to suggest an inn close to town where we might be private. It appears that he misunderstood my intentions."

"Did he, milord?" Blaine asked quietly.

Even in the dim candlelight, she could see the rush of color to Drew's face. He looked much like an awkward schoolboy, and seeing the guilt written clearly on his countenance, she could not hold back a chuckle of amusement.

"Devil take it!" Drew leapt to his feet, glaring down at the smiling woman. "He did not mistake me. I will tell you truly, ma'am. It was my intention to invite you here for the sole purpose of seducing you and making you my mistress."

Blaine recognized immediately that the anger in his voice was directed at himself, not at her. She accepted his words but wondered what had made him change his mind. "Were you not even going to feed me?"

"Good God, woman!" Drew exploded.

When Blaine dissolved into giggles at the sight of his outraged expression, he threw himself back into his chair, his face black with fury. This action raised a cloud of dust and she was convulsed anew. Finally Drew caught the total idiocy of his anger and he joined in her hysteria, laughing until tears stood in his eyes.

"You are surely a most exasperating woman," Drew announced when he could pull himself together enough to speak.

"But I am hungry," she explained. "Since you are not going to dishonor me, the very least you could do is not let me starve."

"You obviously have few sensibilities to think of food at a time like this," Drew grumbled.

Muttering under his breath, he pushed himself to his feet and crossed the floor to a table against the wall. He dragged it closer to the alcove until it was within easy reach of their chairs. Then with an exaggerated flourish, he raised the covers to display the sumptuous feast.

"I apologize for the paltry selection," he said as he surveyed the sparseness of the fare. "The ham does smell delectable and I believe there is also the unavoidable roast beef. I can offer no personal recommendations but if you would care to sample, I will endeavor to pour wine."

Drew grinned as Blaine heaped a thick slice of bread with the thin-sliced ham. Before he was seated, she had taken a bite of the improvised sandwich. "It's a gourmet delight, Lord Farrington," she announced, accepting the glass of wine he extended.

She sipped the wine in silence as he helped himself to some food. He was still chewing when she made her next comment.

"It would seem to me, sir, that if your intentions were dishonorable, you might have made some push for a more lavish spread."

When he broke into a coughing fit, she tried not to laugh, but could not hold back a grin as he glared at her. "Sorry, Lord Farrington," she apologized, not the least bit contrite. "I thought you might appreciate a small suggestion for the next time."

"There will be no next time, you cheeky wench," he rasped out. "I have decided to give up women entirely."

"What a shame." She clicked her tongue in dismay. "I trust my plain speaking hasn't put you off your feed as well."

Drew snorted good-humoredly at this latest sally. "Baggage!" he said, smiling happily across at her.

They ate slowly, talking easily throughout the meal. They spoke in the way of old friends, comfortable in each other's company. It was only as the meal was drawing to a close that Blaine was aware of a sudden tension in the air. It had been a magical evening but there was an air of intimacy to their situation that suddenly made her uneasy.

Blaine had considered the possibility that Drew might ask her to become his mistress. She knew if she said no, he would never force her. He wanted her, but he was basically a principled man. In thinking of the evening, she had focused on his feelings and his behavior. She had not taken into account her own response and when she looked into her own heart, she was appalled at what she saw.

She was in love with Drew Farrington. She had already begun to like the man in Wiltshire but over the succeeding weeks she had let down her guard and somehow had fallen in love. The revelation of her feelings was truly frightening as she realized that her love had made her vulnerable; it had weakened her defenses and left her open to any advance he might choose to make. Without volition her eyes moved to his face and she found she could only focus on his lips. Her heart pounded in her throat and she knew she must leave immediately.

"Thank you for dinner, Lord Farrington," she said, pushing herself out of her chair.

At her abrupt movement, Drew leapt to his feet, moving quickly to block her path. She could feel a trembling weakness in her knees and she willed herself not to reach out for him.

"Must you leave so soon?" Drew asked, his eyes moving across her face as if he were memorizing it.

Blaine licked her lips and tried to speak but only a small cry burst from her lips.

At the sound, Drew took her in his arms, stroking the curve of her cheek with the back of his hand. She caught her breath at the contact and her eyelids fluttered in the rush of excitement that flowed through her body. She could feel the heat rising between them, a fire that she knew would consume her. He bent his head until his lips were only a breath away, as if waiting for her permission. She rose to meet him and he took possession of her mouth with a tenderness that she had not known existed.

The kiss seemed to last forever but eventually Blaine's senses cleared. She had known all along that she could have no relationship with Drew. She was an actress and as such he would never offer her marriage. If she remained, she would deny him nothing. Once she became his mistress, he would lose all respect for her and she could not bear that thought. With the last remaining strength in her body, Blaine pushed against his chest and he immediately released her.

"I must go," she whispered.

"When can I see you again?" Drew's voice was hoarse with emotion and he grasped her shoulders when she shook her head. "I will not ask you to stay. This is no place for you and I would not insult you so. But I must see you again, my dearest love."

Blaine bit her lip, knowing she must leave quickly before she gave in to the temptation of his nearness. "I will send you a note," she said. Then before he could question her further, she ran across the room and swept up her cloak. She swung it around her shoulders and opened the door into the hallway before Drew could stop her.

Blinded by tears, she stumbled as she closed the door into the hall. She grasped the stair rail and steadied herself, flipping the hood up over her hair. Then carefully she went down the stairs and opened the door into the cool night air. She crossed the inn yard, ignoring the horseman who had to rein in to keep from trampling her. Without a backward glance, she raced to the side of the carriage where Sarge was waiting. He thrust her inside and then leapt to his seat and gave the horses the office to start.

Talbott Stoddard sucked in his breath when he recognized the figure in the flowing cloak. La Solitaire! He would recognize her face anywhere. Beneath lowered brows, he watched the carriage as it turned out of the yard, then his eyes shifted and he glared up at the lighted window of the inn. It took him no time at all to check the stable and identify Drew Farrington's familiar black stallion. Cursing under his breath, he once more crossed the yard and vaulted into his saddle, roughly kicking his horse back toward London.

Although the carriage was traveling at a brisk clip, Stoddard's horse easily caught up with it. He stayed well back until it moved into the more populated areas of town. For months he had been attempting to discover where Maggie Mason lived but Sarge, her wily bodyguard and coachman, never took the same route from the theater. Tonight he was determined to follow the actress to the ends of the earth.

Curiosity was rampant as the carriage moved into the more fashionable neighborhoods of London. He could not believe that any nobleman would dare keep his light o' love under the very noses of the starchy tattlemongers of the ton. But what else could this mean?

Stoddard kept his horse close to the wall, moving cautiously as the carriage navigated the narrow side streets. When it finally turned into the mews behind Portman Square, his teeth gleamed in the darkness in a grim smile of triumph. He pressed his horse forward and was just in time to see the slender ivory figure slip inside the wrought-iron gates of an imposing town house. Patiently he waited and was eventually rewarded by the flicker of candlelight in an upstairs room. La Solitaire had come home.

Turning his horse out of the mews, Stoddard's face reflected the anger of his thoughts. He had sworn to possess La Solitaire. Damn Drew Farrington! The bastard might have breached the actress's defenses but by the look on the woman's face when she left the inn, Stoddard suspected that the seduction had not gone as planned. There was still hope that he would succeed before his rival. For years he had hated Drew and the thought that Farrington desired La Solitaire was impetus enough to pursue the woman. Besides, he had a score to settle with the celebrated Maggie Mason.

Stoddard stormed into his rooms and immediately poured himself a large brandy. He threw back his head and gulped the fiery liquor and then refilled his glass. Moving to the mantel he stared up at the portrait of himself, as always delighted by the artist's rendering. He had always been proud of his physique and the handsome face and Adonis-like curls that had won him so many females. The silly chits were easily wooed and even more easily won. All except La Solitaire.

With a snarl, Stoddard threw his snifter into the empty fireplace, smiling at the tinkling shower of glass on the tile surround. Now that he knew where La Solitaire lived it would be a simple matter to find out all about her. His brow furrowed in thought and he dropped into a chair, his fingers steepled under his chin.

There was something very confusing about the whole affair. He had recognized the house on Portman Square. It was owned by Aurelia Breckenridge, Drew Farrington's aunt, who was away on a visit in Scotland. If the man already had the actress in keeping then why had he arranged to meet her at the Rose and Trellis Inn? Besides, the Meriweathers were staying at Portman Square and even Drew would never dare to house an innocent debutante like Fleur Meriweather under the same roof as a notorious actress. Society would ostracize him for such an outrage.

Could there be some connection between the Meriweathers and Maggie Mason? A servant? A relative? The latter was clearly impossible. No woman of good family would ever become an actress. It was surely a puzzle and the more he thought about it, the more curious he became. Perhaps he might learn something if he called on the Meriweathers. He had not called on Fleur sooner because he had felt she was not worth the effort. There was little sport in the deflowering of such a simple child. But the petite blonde had been awed by his attentions in Wiltshire and surely he could use that to his advantage to find out what he most needed to know.

Did Drew know that La Solitaire was living at Portman Square? Stoddard doubted it and that thought did much to raise his spirits. How rich to be able to tell him that the wench had been right under his aristocratic nose. Despite the fact he had been meeting Maggie Mason at the inn, Stoddard was convinced that Drew had not been successful in bedding the actress. What sweet revenge to succeed with La Solitaire and flaunt her before the arrogant Lord Farrington!

His eyes kindled at the thought of possessing the beautiful actress. She would pay for rejecting his offer. He would have been gentle with her then, but now he would make her regret her insolence. Once he had her in his hands, he would see to it that no man would ever want her again.

eleven

"Why on earth did I ever consent to accompany you, Fleur?" Blaine said as she eyed the gilt chairs set out in neat rows in front of the stage. "Surely Puff would have done as well."

"She has a ferocious cold and is forever wheezing or snuffling into an enormous handkerchief," Fleur said with the uncompromising honesty of a child. "Besides, I prefer your company. When things get dull, I can count on you to whisper some sharp comment that makes me giggle."

"Pretty words, you naughty puss, surely meant to get around me," she said, her throaty voice sharp with sarcasm. Blaine sighed at the fresh-cheeked cheerfulness of her sister. "Sometimes, Fleur, I do feel as old as Aunt Haydie."

"Piffle, Bl — uh, ma'am." Fleur's eyes fluttered in horror at the slip. "Sorry, Aunt Haydie."

"If you wouldn't look so conscious when you make such a mistake, no one would notice," Blaine hissed in aggravation. At the

234

sight of the girl's crestfallen expression, she quickly softened her tone. "You are doing prodigiously well, Fleur. You just do not happen to be a very good liar. I would suggest you not consider making your fortune as a government spy."

Fleur immediately giggled at the ridiculous idea and as the smile returned to the girl's face, Blaine relaxed slightly. It would not do to have her upset. It had been amazing so far that she hadn't blurted out the truth of their bold masquerade in the midst of Hyde Park.

"How is Cousin Lavinia?" Fleur asked.

For a moment Blaine's mind was a total blank and then she remembered to look concerned for the woman whose companion she was supposed to be. "I have heard nothing from the doctor so I can only assume that my presence is still not required."

"I think it's the outside of enough that I still have not met our father's cousin."

"Her health has never been good, dear. Having a flighty chit fluttering through her rooms would give her a fit of the vapors at the best of times. Now, of course, she is far too unwell." Blaine winced at the continuous stream of lies she was forced to tell in order to allay her sister's curiosity.

"Despite your words to the contrary, I can tell you are fond of Cousin Lavinia. Since she became so ill, you have looked quite blue-deviled and several times I have seen a redness about your eyes that indicates your distress. I know you are far more attached to her than you let on. It is only natural since you have been with the woman for six years now." Fleur patted her hand as if to console her for her imagined unhappiness.

Guilt at her deception pricked Blaine's conscience and she was delighted when Robbie Farrington arrived to lure Fleur away to a quieter spot. She fanned herself briskly after the two young people left and closed her eyes as if she were dozing, but her thoughts returned to the night at the inn.

Immediately her mind whirled with her latest round of deception. After her escape from the inn, Blaine had realized she did not have the strength to see Drew immediately. She knew he would return to the theater to pursue her. Although she hated to lie to John Tibbles, she sent him a note saying that she was ill and would not be returning to the theater for several days. In order to explain her presence in the house at Portman Square, she had told Fleur that the fictitious Cousin Lavinia had taken a turn for the worse and was now under a doctor's care, relieving Blaine of her duties until her health returned.

She was surprised that Fleur had noticed

her distress. When they first arrived in London, the girl had been so caught up in her own concerns that she had little awareness of the feelings of those around her. Lately, Blaine had seen signs that indicated her sister was taking a more thoughtful turn. She seemed less lighthearted and flighty, and her eyes had a more contemplative look. Perhaps the irresponsible girl finally was changing into a sensitive young lady.

Another sign to be applauded was the fact that the girl was treating Robbie with more favor. After her last talk with her sister, Blaine had noticed a softening in Fleur's attitude toward him. It still was not a loverlike relationship but at least there was some reason to hope. She opened her eyes, smiling contentedly as her sister and Robbie returned.

"We've brought you some punch, Aunt Haydie," Fleur said as she offered Blaine a delicate cut-glass cup. "Robbie said it would be just the thing."

"Much you know, young man," Blaine muttered as she raised the cup to her lips and sipped the bland liquid. "Tastes like bathwater."

"Aunt Haydie!" Fleur gasped, looking around in embarrassment that the comment might have been overheard. In annoyance, she nudged Robbie, who had gone off into smothered fits. "Don't you encourage her, Robert Farrington. She'll only become more outrageous."

"Don't glower so, girl," Blaine said archly. "It will put permanent wrinkles in your skin. Old ladies are permitted a certain latitude in their speech. It's to compensate them for the infirmities brought on by advanced age."

"Surely you're bamming us, Lady Yates," Robbie said, struggling to compose himself. "You have always struck me as a particularly youthful woman. You can give your contemporaries at least twenty years."

Blaine flashed a look of warning as Fleur bit her lip in dismay and smiled sweetly up at the charming young man. "A fine speech, Robbie. You show yourself to be truly a gentleman. And as your reward for such gallantry, I will permit you to retrieve another cup of this loathsome punch. I must fortify myself for the coming musical recital. If it follows Lady Amberley's usual pattern, we are destined to be most suitably bored."

With another hearty laugh, Robbie goodnaturedly took her cup and moved off through the crowd. Blaine's eyes flickered past Fleur's shoulder and she braced herself as she saw Talbott Stoddard approaching. She could not hold back a shudder of distaste as the pale blue eyes targeted her sister. There had been rumors circulating for years and she could credit many of them as she noted the coldness of his glance. The man was definitely dangerous. For a moment she wanted to pull Fleur to her side and lash out at Stoddard with her walking stick. She shrugged away such nonsense but her fingers instinctively tightened on the cane.

"Greetings, Lady Yates," Stoddard said, bowing before her.

"Lord Stoddard." She nodded her head in brief acknowledgment.

"You are looking exceptionally well. It would seem that the hectic pace of London is a restorative to one of your age."

Blaine narrowed her eyes at his words, longing to give the man a firm set-down. Before she could open her mouth, he had turned to greet Fleur.

"Are you enjoying your stay in London, Miss Meriweather?" Stoddard said as the girl rose from her curtsy.

"Ever so much, milord," Fleur said, blushing at his pointed attention.

The girl did look well, if one's taste ran to such simple innocence, he thought. His eyes surveyed the youthful body beneath the white muslin dress. Give her a few years and he might reconsider but he suspected she was not worth the effort. For now it was information

239

he was after and he would stay his hand at the actual seduction of the chit. He would flatter her with attention and treat her with the courtesy of an older brother.

"With your aunt's kind permission, perhaps you would care to take a turn around the room. I would be more than pleased to introduce you to some of the people with whom you may not already be acquainted." The gaze that he bent on her was one of bright interest and he was amused to note her relief at his lack of amorous intent.

"I would like that very much, Lord Stoddard," Fleur answered breathlessly. "Aunt Haydie?"

"Watch your manners," Blaine said in warning, and waved her hand in dismissal.

Her eyes followed the progress of the blond nobleman and her sister as they moved around the room. She had noted the passionless scrutiny of the man. There was something havey-cavey going on for Stoddard to take an interest in the girl that was not physical. A vague uneasiness invaded her and she jumped as Robbie returned with the punch.

"Sorry, Lady Yates," he apologized. His mouth tightened as he followed the direction of her gaze. "Damn and blast!" he muttered under his breath, totally unconscious of his words until he noticed the start of surprise

240

from his companion. "My apologies again, madam."

"No need, Robbie," Blaine said. "The words were on the tip of my tongue already."

"I cannot like the fact that Fleur spends any time with Stoddard. She is much too innocent to recognize the kind of man he is." He shook his head in frustration but as he followed the couple with his eyes, a frown of puzzlement rode between his brows. "That's strange. I have watched Stoddard over the years and he appears to be treating Fleur with the attention of an older brother. Perhaps, for once in his life, he is being kind. A token gesture for the hospitality he received in Wiltshire."

"And pigs may fly" was Blaine's retort. Startled by her words, Robbie made as if to go after the pair, but she caught him before he could move away. "She is safe enough in this squeeze."

"I do love her, you know," Robbie said, pulling awkwardly at the lobe of his ear.

"You have been the soul of patience, sir. It has been difficult for you, I know. Fleur is a good girl at heart which is the only thing that has stayed my hand. I can tell you though, I have been strongly tempted to violence by her flighty behavior." She smiled to take the edge of anger from her words. "I have spoiled her and overprotected her and this is the result."

241

"It is easy to spoil her, Lady Yates," he admitted. "I find myself torn between wanting her to enjoy herself in London and wanting to shut her away from the eyes of others. Drew says it is like that when you are in love. He says she has good values and will eventually tire of this social scene."

"There are times your brother amazes me with his insight," Blaine said.

"He has his moments," Robbie agreed. "He is not at his best today and I am sorry for the brusqueness of his greeting."

Blaine had been so happy to see Drew that she had not minded the black look he had worn when he and Robbie arrived to escort them. She had not seen him since the night at the inn and she chastised herself for the pounding of her heart at the very sight of him.

"No need for apologies, Robbie. Your brother is probably annoyed that he is stuck in the company of a flighty chit, a lovesick swain, and a doddering old lady," Blaine said. "Run along and fetch Fleur. I do believe the festivities are about to begin."

Drew sat on the small gilt chair at the side of the room, his arms folded across his chest. Several people approached him but one look at the grim set of his features sent them scurrying away to seek more congenial company.

He did not want to be present in the Amberleys' ballroom and the fact he had promised to accompany Robbie, Fleur, and Lady Yates was the only reason for his attendance. He had kept to his word but he saw no need to pretend he was enjoying himself.

Felicia Amberley was the sort of hostess he most detested. She was decidedly long in the tooth and yet she persisted in thinking herself a young deb. She wore clothes at least twenty years too young and moved with the fluttery gestures of a schoolgirl. There was something sad about the large woman with the well-lined face and droopy-lidded, mournful eyes. Drew might have been able to abide an evening of boredom but to make matters worse Felicia was convinced that she was a patron of the arts and delighted in holding recitals for her latest protégés, all of whom were male with the oily manners of cicisbei.

Beneath his half-lowered lids, Drew watched as Felicia, dressed as usual in maidenly pink, introduced Gaylord Ledger, a young man with deep-set brown eyes that were trained on his patroness in soulful admiration. She simpered as he kissed her hand, while flapping a long scrap of pink chiffon with the other. Drew had to admit that the woman's gown was a triumph of the dressmaker's art. Made up of thick swatches of chiffon that billowed and writhed at every movement of her large body, it reminded him strongly of some sort of window hanging gone berserk. As the young man began to sing of the agonies of lost love, Drew closed his eyes and leaned his head against the wall behind his chair.

Immediately La Solitaire's face filled his vision. The apparition was so real that he jerked his eyes open, in the hope that she was not merely a figment of his imagination. Disappointed, he returned to his daydream.

For the past few days he had been consumed by thoughts of La Solitaire. Returning to the theater the night after their meeting at the inn, he had been informed that Maggie Mason was ill and had taken leave to recover her health.

He was convinced that her absence was only an extreme measure to avoid him. When she had run out of the room at the Rose and Trellis, he had forced himself not to pursue her. She had told him she would send him a note and he would have to trust that she would. After three days, he suspected she had merely used the excuse to make her escape.

He winced when he remembered the evening at the Rose and Trellis. From the moment Miss Mason entered the shabby room, Drew knew he had made a mistake. It was apparent that she had come to the inn for no other reason than to have dinner. He had seen the disillusionment in her eyes as she looked around the room and, for the first time in his life, he cringed in shame. At that moment he had wanted nothing more than to take her in his arms to apologize. When he did, the trusting eyes she raised to his face sent a jolt of pain through his very vitals. There was something in her face and in the defensive way she held her body that told him she was an innocent. Her beauty had a radiance that took his breath away and in a sudden flash of intelligence he recognized the character of the woman all of London called La Solitaire.

From such a sorry start, the evening had progressed to one of sheer magic. She had teased him for trying to seduce her, putting him at ease with a mischievous touch of humor. They had talked through supper with the ease of old friends and Drew had been amazed that he could enjoy the company of a woman for her own sake. He had found pleasure in her quick mind and caustic wit. He had delighted in challenging her and discovered she was not only well read but highly intelligent.

Her abrupt announcement of her departure had thrown him off-stride for he was so enjoying the evening that he had little desire for it to end. The moment he touched her, he realized the strength of his feelings. The sweet freshness of her scent rose like an aphrodisiac to fill his senses. The sensuous feel of the satin beneath his hands ignited a fire in the very core of him. He wanted to plunge his fingers into her shining tresses and taste the delights of her soft mouth, raised in a moue of surprise. He could no more have kept from kissing her than he could have kept from drawing breath.

Thinking of it now, he shifted in his chair as his body responded to the remembrance of her. He opened his eyes, concentrating on the excruciating voice of the young artist. The man's voice quavered in an orgy of lamentation and his enormous eyes sheened with tears of emotion. Drew groaned in disgust. Thankfully his mind had gained control of his wayward body and he could return to his thoughts.

The evening with Maggie Mason had turned out totally different from what he had imagined. He had planned seduction but gained instead a charming dinner with an intelligent young lady. Where he expected brittle sophistication, he found a fresh naïveté. By God, La Solitaire had kissed him like an untried virgin. It had not been an act. Drew had kissed enough women in his time that he was well able to recognize an imposture of purity.

At the sound of applause, Drew sat up straight with the faint hope that the recital might be at an end. As the beaming Felicia fluttered her way to the front of the room, he knew he was doomed to further torture. His eyes roamed the room, encountering Robbie, who rolled his eyes in sympathy.

Drew shifted his attention to the girl at his brother's side. Seeing the tiredness around Fleur's eyes, he wondered if she might not be beginning to have her fill of the joys of society. He had noticed her last night in the company of Talbott Stoddard and the way she had shied away from his effusive attentions. In Wiltshire, when the rake had flirted with her, the chit had been all smiles and airs, but now she did not seem as pleased as she ought in the presence of the blond gentleman. Drew had seen an occasional flash of bewilderment in her eyes, and hoped that she had begun to come out of the haze of euphoria brought on by the excitement of her presentation to society. There might be hope for Robbie yet.

Beyond the lovebirds, Drew spotted Lady Yates. Her white face with the outrageous rouge spots seemed thinner than he recalled. He hoped she wasn't tiring herself out with jauntering around London with her niece. As if she sensed his glance, she looked up and smiled grimly. She plied her fan briskly as if to encourage Felicia Amberley to speed up the proceedings.

Felicia introduced another young man, Louis Destarte, who was definitely not in the same mold as the woman's other protégés. Beneath an unruly tumble of dark curls, he had smoldering black eyes and wore a sullen, moody expression. His clothes were ill fitting, almost shabby. He had the look of a laborer and the muscles beneath his jacket threatened to burst the already strained seams. Monsieur Destarte glowered at his patroness, brushing her away with a look of supreme disinterest as he approached the piano.

Drew could not resist a look at Lady Yates and was pleased to note that she was already glancing his way to catch his reaction. He raised a questioning eyebrow and she shrugged as if to say she was withholding her opinion. He returned his attention to the stage and, surrounded by the expectant rustling of the audience, waited for the man to begin.

At the first notes, Drew realized his coming to the Amberleys' was well worth the aggravation. For all Monsieur Destarte's musculature, there was a surprising lightness to his touch. Drew had not heard Mozart played so well. When the Frenchman moved to a heavier piece, he brought a passion to the melody that filled the room. Drew leaned back to let the music flow over him, washing his mind free of the troubling thoughts that had been plaguing him. Serenity seeped into his body as he listened and he was able to picture La Solitaire with a clarity that pleased him. Her gold-hazel eyes gleamed with enthusiasm for the music.

Drew jerked upright, staring across the room. His attention was fixed on Lady Yates and he realized with a start that, behind her lorgnette, the old woman had eyes identical to Maggie Mason's. At first he was afraid that he was losing his mind, so obsessed had he become with the actress. He focused on Lady Yates and studied her through half-shuttered lids. Now that he looked more closely at the woman he could see other similarities between the old woman and the actress.

Drew pressed his temples with the tips of his fingers as his thoughts whirled in confusion. He supposed the similarity he was seeing, between the old woman and the actress, could be a family resemblance. Suddenly he thought he had stumbled on the truth and nearly fell off his chair. By God! Was it possible that La Solitaire was Lady Yates's niece, the mysterious Blaine Meriweather?

Only waiting for the applause to start as the music ended, Drew rose to his feet. He had to get away. The air in the ballroom was suddenly stifling and he needed someplace quiet to think. He was barely civil to Lady Amberley as he pushed his way out of the room and down the stairs.

Walking was Drew's answer when he needed to work out a problem. The brisk physical movement and the rhythm of his pace had a hypnotic effect that freed his mind. He gave quick instructions to his tiger to return his curricle and then set off on foot for Hyde Park. The tree-enclosed pathways would have a soothing effect on his feverish brain.

He searched his mind for every detail concerning Blaine Meriweather and La Solitaire. He replayed his interview with Wesley Upton and the snippets of information he had gleaned in his talks with Val. Slowly the pieces came together and the jigsaw puzzle began to take shape. Although he still found it impossible to believe, he truly believed that Blaine Meriweather was Maggie Mason.

It would explain so much that had confused him. He could see where the money for Fleur's dowry had come from. In the last four years, La Solitaire had been a star, able to command a salary well above that earned by a governess or companion. It would also explain why she was never seen in Wiltshire and why the Meriweathers were reluctant to talk about her, for fear of giving something away.

He had heard that Fleur and Blaine were only half sisters, but he had assumed Blaine was an older version of the little blonde. Val more closely resembled Fleur and it was now apparent that Blaine took after her father's side of the family. Lady Yates was the sister of Blaine's father, which would explain the similarity of eyes and facial structure. If it hadn't been for the lucky chance that he had spotted the family resemblance between Lady Yates and La Solitaire, he might never have discovered her identity.

"Devil take it, what a coil!" Drew said aloud.

His words startled two little old ladies who had been sitting on one of the benches that lined the path. When the glassy-eyed man threw himself down on the bench opposite, they quickly gathered their things and scurried away but the young man did not even notice their desertion.

"Poor Fleur," Drew said, brushing his hand over his hair. If word of this ever leaked out, the girl's reputation would suffer. The scandal would be the *on dits* of the century. Drew could just hear the old tabbies and how they would delight in the shame of a woman of good family who had so debased herself as to trod the boards. Would Robbie still want to marry a girl whose family tree had an actress swinging from the branches?

Awareness of the injustice of it all filled

Drew with fury. From what he had gathered from Val and Wesley Upton, the death of Blaine's parents had left the family nearly destitute. How devastating it must have been to know that the money was there but untouchable. Blaine would have been twenty at the time and he could not even imagine the desperation she must have felt. He had nothing but admiration for the girl to have chosen to sacrifice her own life for the sake of Val and Fleur.

Did Fleur and Val know about Blaine? He doubted it. They had been too young at the time of their parents' deaths to be trusted with such a secret. It was doubtful, even now, if the countrified girl would be able to view the career of an actress as a fit livelihood for her sister.

La Solitaire. Maggie Mason. Blaine Margaret Meriweather. So many names, Drew thought. Blaine suited the woman he knew, more surely than the other names. Blaine. He rolled the name over and over in his mind, then said it aloud to savor the taste of it on his tongue. How did he feel about her? A fatuous smile creased the lines of his face as he thought of the beautiful actress.

He loved her.

The thought came to him simply, with little fanfare. He did not know why it did not surprise him that he had fallen in love with Blaine. He freely admitted that he had planned to make her his mistress when he first saw her onstage. No other relationship had occurred to him. Men of his class did not marry actresses. It was only when she came to the inn that he discovered he could never offer her such a relationship. He wanted more of her than just her body. He wanted to be with her and share thoughts and laughter. He wanted her to bear his children and live beside him until they were old and crotchety.

Drew looked around him and the world seemed a better place. The colors of the flowers were more vibrant. The trees were more imposing. The air was fresh and carried the scent of herbs and other growing things. He chuckled at the lyrical quality of his thoughts, amazed that love, an emotion he believed he would never find, not only existed but had taken over his life completely.

In his eyes, Blaine's life on the stage did not make her any less a person. He respected her for taking the risk that would ostracize her from the society into which she was born. He suspected she had been very lonely in the last six years because he knew without question that she had lived a solitary existence indeed. Her innocence was far more amazing since it was not from lack of temptation. As an actress, she must have been inundated with offers but she had not taken the easy route to financial security. She had shown herself to be highly principled and there was nothing in her life that she need ever be ashamed of.

Would she marry him? Drew wished he knew the answer to that question. He knew she had felt attraction for him and when he kissed her, she had not pulled away in disgust. Their minds were attuned and they could converse easily, almost as if they had known each other for years. He was not unaware of his attributes in the marriage mart but Drew knew that the woman he loved would judge him on much higher standards.

Perhaps Lady Yates would help him. Drew wondered if the old woman knew what her niece had been doing for the last six years. Even knowing Lady Yates so little, he suspected she did know and approved. She had mentioned that she knew Sarah Siddons, and Blaine had come to the notice of the public while working in the same company as Mrs. Siddons.

The thought of Lady Yates cheered him immeasurably. The feisty lady liked him and enjoyed his company. Surely she would approve of his pursuit of her niece and do what she could to push forward the match. Although Lady Yates did not normally attend evening functions, he knew that she would be at the Earl of Larchmont's affair since she had expressed interest in seeing his much-talked-about ballroom. He would talk to her there and enlist her help.

It came to him suddenly that there was a great deal to be done if he intended to marry Blaine. For one thing he needed to remove her from London before her identity could be discovered. For himself, he was proud of her talents, but he knew there were others who would take great delight in giving Blaine the cut direct, if it was known she was the celebrated La Solitaire. He would not permit such hypocrites to hurt Blaine. She had suffered enough already.

Even with the help of Lady Yates, he was not assured of Blaine's agreement to his suit. He would love to woo her with the patterned rituals of courtship but he had a feeling of urgency that he could not gainsay. She had been lucky so far in avoiding detection but it was a risky business. He must move quickly in order to safeguard her, for he had a feeling in his bones that she was in danger.

twelve

"It certainly is a monument to poor taste," Blaine said, in a whispered aside to Fleur as she stared around the ballroom in amazement. "If you ask me, it looks like a cross between a Greek temple and a Moorish seraglio."

Fleur gasped at the comment, then dissolved into a fit of the giggles at the expression on Robbie's face. He was so stunned as his eyes took in the profusion of naked cherubs on the ceiling that he almost walked into a pillar.

"Larchmont must be cork-brained to have decorated it thus," Robbie said.

"More likely his new wife." Blaine nodded in the direction of the young girl who clung to the arm of the ancient earl. "He was quite miffed when Lord Northcote complimented him on the beauty of his daughter."

"Aunt Haydie!" Fleur squealed.

"Stop saying that, girl, or I shall fall into a decline. I have little enough fun tramping after you while you dazzle an army of cow-eyed dandies," Blaine muttered, eyeing her sister with disfavor. "My feet hurt and this wretched dress is much too hot for this unusually warm weather."

"I noticed your dress, Lady Yates," Robbie said, jumping into the conversation at the woebegone look on Fleur's face, "Is it new? I swear I haven't seen it before and you look a treat."

"You're a sweet boy but a terrible liar." Blaine grinned, back in charity after his gallant rescue. "It is called dowager purple and is the newest rage of the white-haired set. I thought it might make a change from my usual blacks and browns. However, if my suspicion is correct, my profile most resembles a ship of the line, decked out in mourning sails."

Robbie smothered his laughter and continued leading Fleur and her aunt around the room. "Look to your left, ladies. If I'm not mistaken that figure in the alcove is Poseidon. I recognize the trident, although the costume has a faintly Roman air."

Fleur blushed at the lifelike statue, but couldn't prevent herself from taking a thorough peek. "Oh, my," she uttered in dismay at the nakedness of the figure.

"One wonders where the sculptor found his models." Blaine cocked her head to one side, eyeing the statue with some amusement.

"Demmed figure is malformed, Robbie, if you catch my drift. Although I am far too much of a lady to mention it, I seriously doubt any human has such a bulging of chest muscles. Besides, I thought Poseidon was supposed to be an old man."

"Old but apparently quite virile," Robbie declared. Aware of Fleur's interest in the bodily development of the figure, he quickly moved them around to the next alcove.

"Now, children, this must surely be the masterpiece," Blaine announced, coming to a stop before the enormous tableau. "If I were to venture a guess, I would say Hera, Goddess of Marriage. For once, the dimensions are approximately right, although she appears to be a dash wide in the hips. I don't think this sculpture will do much to encourage viewers to wed. The lady looks none too pleased. Perhaps she is slightly apprehensive seated on the back of the cow."

"You'll have to admit, Lady Yates, that the peacock is a charming touch," Robbie whispered close to Blaine's ear. "See how our talented sculptor has caught the wide spread of the tail. Proportions are a bit off. Looks rather more like a partridge than that noblest of birds but then I am not much of a judge of this sort of thing."

Both Blaine's and Fleur's eyes had begun to

tear with suppressed laughter so that Robbie hurried them through the room to the buffet. Giggling madly, they filled their plates and, despite the heat in the room, enjoyed themselves immensely. When the dancing began, Blaine moved to the section reserved for the dowagers and was thoroughly entertained by the passing parade.

Her eyes found Fleur and she watched her sister, her heart swelling in pride. The girl had done exceptionally well. Not only had she handled the newness of her social debut but she had had to contend with the worry that Blaine might at some time be unmasked. Fleur was not much of a dissembler but had made only a few mistakes. Perhaps the fantasy of Aunt Haydie was easier for her to deal with if she pretended it were true. Blaine had been amused at how often, even when they were alone, Fleur leapt to her feet to help her aged aunt to get out of a chair or to cross the room.

Robbie had seemed happier in the last few days so perhaps he was beginning to make some headway with Fleur. In the beginning of the London visit, her sister had been almost frenzied in her efforts to embrace every entertainment and to meet every available male. Now it seemed she was content to go about with a few close friends, a crowd that pleased Blaine for it was not the fast set.

"Have you seen the Pallas Athena?" a voice whispered in her ear.

Drew's sudden appearance sent Blaine's heart racing and she pressed her fingers to her chest in an instinctive gesture. Seeing the frown of concern on Drew's face, she immediately forced herself to relax and smile archly.

"Is it worth my getting up, young man?" she barked, safe in the role of Aunt Haydie.

"All I can tell you is that her suit of armor is most impressive. The sword is covered with jewels; however, it is my considered opinion they are paste." Drew held out his hand to assist her to her feet.

"If she's in the same vein as the rest of these monstrosities, I presume she has muscular limbs the size of tree trunks." Blaine placed her mittened hand in his, unable to hold back a slight tremor at the contact with his warm flesh.

"Not only tree trunks, my dear madam, but very old trees."

Drew smiled when the old lady snorted, but his face immediately sobered at how shaky she seemed. Perhaps he should have let her remain seated. Although he had seen little sign of it until now, he had been told her health was not good. He had seen how quickly she had placed her hands over her heart and he worried that the London pace was too much for her. Shortening his stride, he led her slowly around the rooms to the doors that led out into the garden, hoping the fresh air would act as a restorative. Spring had arrived at last and the evening was warm, with little risk to the old girl's health.

"The earl may have little taste in ballrooms but at least he's a competent gardener." Lady Yates sniffed appreciatively of the lightly perfumed air.

"I will take you for a stroll among the plantings, if you feel you will not be compromised in the eyes of society," Drew said, leading her down the shallow marble steps.

"It's your reputation that will be in shreds, Farrington. If you're seen tramping through the brush with an antique on your arm, word will get about that you are dotty in the head," she retorted.

They meandered along the paths, leaning down occasionally to sniff a particularly pungent specimen. For the most part, their conversation was general, covering the news of the campaign against Napoleon and the latest troubles in Parliament, among other topics. Finally Drew became concerned at the length of their walk and found a stone bench, which he dusted off for Lady Yates.

"I had no intention of leading a pilgrimage, ma'am," he apologized.

"Fustian! I am not so infirm that I cannot enjoy myself," she answered, her throaty voice sounding strong to his ears.

Drew wondered how to broach the subject of Blaine to Lady Yates. He realized that the old lady would be shocked that he had somehow ferreted out the secret of her niece. Concerned for her health, he didn't know if she was up to such a jolt to her constitution. Perhaps he ought to wait for a few days until he could ascertain for himself that his news would not send her into a fit of the vapors.

The thought of putting off his discussion depressed him thoroughly. He was impatient to see Blaine again and eager to push forward his suit. He was sure that she could not be comfortable with Fleur and Lady Yates in London where, if her identity was discovered, they would be subjected to great humiliation. If he could spare Blaine even a day of worrying, it was worth the risk of upsetting Lady Yates.

"Might I bring you something to drink?" he suggested, thinking a restorative might be in order shortly.

"It would seem, Lord Farrington, that you have done more than enough to entertain me. You should be inside doing the pretty."

"I can truly say, madam, there is no one in the ballroom I would rather be with," Drew said with sincerity. "You know I enjoy your company."

Blaine was silent for a moment, then nudged him mischievously with her walking stick. "I'd hate to put you to such trouble, but a drink sounds most tempting." As Drew started back toward the ballroom, she called after him. "None of that namby-pamby punch, Farrington. Champagne would be preferred."

As his footsteps faded on the flagstones, Blaine sagged wearily against the back of the bench.

From the moment Drew had appeared at her side she had been torn between joy and sadness. She never should have accepted his invitation to walk about. It was painful to have him so close and have to treat him impersonally. She knew that soon she would only see him across the footlights if he continued to come to the Green Mews. As La Solitaire, she would never agree to see him again. She was far too weak to risk such a thing. He would quickly lose interest in the actress who rejected all communication. Eventually he would stop coming to the theater.

She had told Tate that she asked for only one magical evening and then she would return to her life as Maggie Mason without grumbling. Now she realized the folly of such a statement. Perhaps she wouldn't grumble but her life would never be the same. Her heart had been given for all time and the thought of the loneliness of the rest of her years was enough to make her cry out in pain.

Since the night in the inn with Drew, Blaine had known she must plan to return her life to some order. The romance between Robbie and Fleur seemed to be progressing quite well. If the boy declared himself, she felt confident that her sister would accept. Blaine would push for a brief engagement and at the wedding she would give her final performance as Aunt Haydie. After that, Lady Yates would leave, ostensibly for a visit to the north of England, never to return. Robbie could be trusted to care for Fleur and to look after Val.

When she left Weathers to become an actress, Blaine knew that her reputation would be forfeit but it had meant little at the time. Since Fleur had come to London, she sensed that the girl would be ashamed if the truth of her identity were known and this brought home to Blaine a harsh reality. She could not stand the thought that her actions would cause her sister any embarrassment.

Val would be affected by any revelation that Blaine was La Solitaire. He was only eleven now but eventually he would be a young man going about in society and if someone slandered his sister, he would be forced to defend her. Most insults were defended on the dueling field and Blaine would never forgive herself if he were wounded or killed. Only her disappearance from Fleur's and Val's lives would protect them from possible harm. If she loved her family, Blaine knew she must cut herself off from them.

The thought of leaving her family forever was almost more than Blaine could bear. It was enough that she had given up Drew but now she would have nothing. She raised her face to the night sky, her eyes blind to the beauty of the silvered moon. How she wished that she were a young girl in her first season, waiting in the garden for the gentleman of her dreams. She was dreaming, and wishing never made dreams come true. Blinking her eyes to hold back tears, she swallowed painfully over the lump in her throat.

Drew stood at the edge of the path, transfixed by the sight of the woman on the stone bench. Moonlight bathed the scene like the footlights in a theater and with the insight of love he recognized what he should have known all along. Blaine was not only Maggie Mason but also she was Lady Yates.

He had been stunned at the earlier revelation but this new discovery literally took his breath away. He couldn't believe that, after noticing the family resemblance, he hadn't looked beneath the white makeup of the wasp-tongued Lady Yates. In his defense, Blaine was an accomplished actress but he should have suspected a double masquerade.

For a moment he was furious that she had so easily duped him. He ground his teeth as he remembered leading the sharp-tongued old lady around the garden while his mind had been busy with thoughts of her niece. He had fretted over the state of her health and was concerned that his news might distress her. While he mooned over La Solitaire in a darkened theater every night, every day the contrary wench was seated in the drawing room of his aunt's house on Portman Square.

He stepped back into the shadows and leaned against a stone wall, knowing he was too upset to face her. With an indignant gesture, he threw the champagne glasses to the ground, stamping on them for good measure. The pulse at his temple throbbed with his rancor and his hands tightened as he contemplated wringing Blaine's neck.

Suddenly the humor of the situation struck him. He flopped down on the wall and put his head in his hands. By God, Blaine Margaret Meriweather would lead him a lively dance!

The final piece of the puzzle slipped into place. Now he understood why he had fallen in love with La Solitaire after only the one evening at the Rose and Trellis. He was already acquainted with her in the guise of Lady Yates, so when he met her at the inn they had actually met as old friends. He could also see why she had so readily trusted him. He was not a stranger to her. She already knew a great deal about him.

What had possessed her to take on the role of Lady Yates? The yearly allowance! Drew suspected that the old lady must have died and Blaine had impersonated her in order to keep the desperately needed allowance. And Robbie's courting of Fleur had forced her to make an additional appearance.

The knowledge of this further charade did not change anything for Drew except to intensify his need to remove the Meriweathers from London before disaster struck. He broke out in a cold sweat just thinking about the risks of discovery Blaine had run. No wonder she looked tired. The cheeky girl had been forced to change characters with increasing frequency.

It annoyed him that he could not confront her immediately but the thought of unmasking her in the midst of a party was not to be considered. Brushing his hair back impatiently, he muttered at the embarrassing situations Blaine could fall into with her masquerades. He chuckled as he remembered the scene he had interrupted with the reluctant Wesley Upton. The deceitful chit deserved a severe tongue-lashing at the very least. He wondered what punishment he might exact for her outrageous behavior. Suddenly his eyes lit with mischief and he rose to his feet. It was time Blaine Margaret Meriweather learned a valuable lesson.

He hurried back to the ballroom, searching the rooms quickly until he discovered the whereabouts of General Bartholomew Treadwell. The man was a septuagenarian who, luckily for Blaine, had more lecherous ideas than speed. It took little time at all to suggest to the general that he take Lady Yates some champagne in the garden. Drew hoped he hadn't been gone long enough for Blaine to feel abandoned and return to the ballroom. He supposed he ought to stay near enough, to come to the rescue in case the old lecher should be fleeter of foot than reported.

After helping himself to a full bottle of champagne, Drew once more exited the ballroom, whistling softly under his breath. He strolled through the paths in a leisurely fashion, following the old general, but stopped at a shadowed bench on the path behind the arbor that enclosed his lady love. After establishing himself comfortably, he raised the bottle of champagne to his lips and awaited his moment of revenge.

"What ho, my little flower." The general's cry rang out clearly in the night air as he spotted his prey.

"Good heavens," Blaine muttered as she recognized the figure tottering toward her. She started to rise, but realized the futility of trying to escape. With a groan, she subsided on the bench.

"I have brought you ambrosia, the nectar of the gods, Lady Yates," he said as he extended the champagne glass.

"How sweet of you, General Treadwell." She accepted the glass and raised it to her lips. "I will admit that I was growing quite parched."

"I shall drink to the glory of your eyes," he said, leering at her across the rim of his glass.

"Couldn't we drink instead to your illustrious campaigns?"

Blaine hoped her question might discourage General Treadwell from anything more energetic than a discussion of war. His wife had died several years earlier and since then he had become a terror in the drawing rooms of London. She knew his reputation and had been careful to steer clear of his gleaming eye and pinching fingers.

"What a delightful woman you are to speak of my battles. It is well known that many of my tactics have been studied in this present campaign against that upstart Corsican."

Blaine's eyes widened in apprehension as the general finished the champagne in one gulp and threw his glass over his shoulder. Quickly she burst into speech. "In what arena have you won the most victories, General?"

"In the bedroom, my little sweetheart," he said as he lunged for her.

With a squeal of dismay, Blaine jumped to her feet, hurling her champagne, glass and all, into the nearest bush. She ignored the old man as he scrambled to keep his balance, debating what she should do. Although she knew she could outrun him, she could not race off and risk having someone see the slow-moving Lady Yates galloping through the garden. If she couldn't fend off his attack with her wits, she would have no other recourse than to trounce the man.

The general, wheezing from his unaccustomed exertion, dropped down on the stone bench and patted the area beside him. "Come and sit down, my dear."

"I dare not, sir, while you are thus overheated. Give a care for your health and at the same time for my reputation," she said, voice icy with hauteur.

"At our age, sweet lady, one need no longer be bound by society's conventions. As long as the body is intact one should grasp all the pleasure one can," he said.

Ye gods! Blaine muttered. Aloud she said, "Hush, General Treadwell. I heard something and I am sure it is Lord Farrington returning."

"Never fear, little lady, we shall not be interrupted. Lord Farrington received an urgent message and asked me if I would do the honors."

Blaine promised herself that she would somehow do bodily injury to Drew for placing her in such a predicament. Her hands closed around the knob of her stick and she considered the damage it would do on Lord Farrington's very thick skull. She was brought out of her reverie by a sharp pinch on her backside and she screeched as she slapped away the general's hand.

"Behave yourself, General Treadwell, or I shall be forced to more painful actions," Blaine snapped.

"You are such a little armful that I cannot keep my hands to myself. We might as well enjoy ourselves. There is little enough else to do for amusement," he finished unflatteringly.

Blaine cocked her head as she noted the querulous tone in his voice and squinted her eyes in the darkness at the drooping figure on the bench. The old general might not be a lecherous old fool. If her suspicions were correct, the poor man was lonesome. She could see he was preparing for another assault he quickly thought of a new approach. She called on her acting skills to deter him before he made a perfect cake of himself.

"Oh, please, forgive me, sir, but I cannot encourage you, knowing that it would break the heart of a bosom bow of mine."

"What's that?" the old man asked raspily.

"What a talebearer I would be, if I told you. Now don't be cross. I can only tell you that there is one who looks on you with great fondness." Blaine fluttered her eyelashes coyly as she thought of such a romantic situation.

"Fondness, you say?"

"Well, perhaps fondness is not quite a warm enough word to describe this lady's feelings. Oh, but I mustn't go on, General Treadwell. After all, I was told in strictest confidence." Blaine bowed her head and wrung her hands in agitation.

"Come, come, Lady Yates. There is no need to upset yourself." He patted the seat once more. "We shall sit quietly and talk. Just like old friends."

Examining his face, Blaine knew it was safe and, with a slight simper, she sat down beside the old man. "I hope, General Treadwell, that you do not think any less of me for letting my little secret slip out."

"Of course not, my dear." The general's

laugh was affable but she could tell he was consumed by curiosity. His watery eyes took on the crafty glint of an old campaigner. "I would never ask you to break a confidence. Besides, I already know of whom you speak."

"Has Felicia spoken of her feelings?" Blaine gasped and quickly covered her mouth with her hands, peeking at the general over the tips of her fingers.

"Felicia Amberley?" he asked in surprise.

"Oh, you are a sly one," she said, giggling into her mittened fingers. "Is it any wonder that you were so successful in battle? You have quite torn the secret from me when I had given my word that I would never breathe a word to a soul."

"Did the woman actually say that she has a care for me?"

Since her whole life was a pack of lies, Blaine did not know why she caviled at one more but she was unable to build up the man's hopes too strongly. She sighed and then admitted, "She did not tell me in so many words. It was more that I sensed her feelings."

"I cannot believe Felicia holds any fondness for me since she spends so much time with those young artists," he snapped.

"I think it is because she is pining for attention," Blaine said, wondering if in fact that might not be the case. The few times she had met the woman she had noted a look of unhappiness in her mournful eyes. "Her husband died about four years ago and it was then that she became interested in supporting the arts."

"She is not a bad-looking woman, I suppose," the old man grumbled, much to Blaine's amusement. "Ought to dress her age. A woman of maturity, when gowned correctly, has a serenity that is pleasing to the eye."

"I never met your wife, General Treadwell. Did she have the calm look of a dowager?"

"Elizabeth was a most amiable woman, Lady Yates. We used to sit for hours and discuss my campaign strategies and the strange customs of other lands. She dressed in a fashion that was most becoming. She favored purple, madam." In the moonlight, Blaine could see the twinkle in his eyes as he glanced at her dress. "Perhaps that is why I was most anxious to become better acquainted with you. I understand your husband was a soldier."

Carefully choosing her words, she said, "Neddy Yates was a fine man. I think you would have approved of him."

There was silence in the arbor for several moments but it was a comfortable time for both Blaine and the general. Finally he struggled to his feet and turned to face his companion.

"Perhaps I ought to call on Lady Amberley tomorrow," he said.

"An excellent plan, sir. I think she would enjoy your company. It might take some little time to get to know her but I think the effort will be worthwhile. Perhaps she is not fully aware of her feelings."

After a long considering look, the old man saluted her smartly.

"You are an exceptional woman, Lady Yates," he said as he shuffled down the path toward the ballroom.

From his hiding place deep in the shadows, Drew Farrington had to agree with the old man's assessment. She had treated the man with a finesse and kindness that was most impressive. He felt rather ashamed that he had seen only the foolish side of the general, not looking beyond for the loneliness that Blaine had so clearly discerned. She had handled the affair with no embarrassment to the old man and had possibly hit on a solution to combat two people's loneliness. Drew could learn much from her about dealing with people.

In a short time he heard the rustle of Blaine's skirts and he stepped off the path as she came nearer. She was deep in her role of Lady Yates and leaned heavily on her stick on her return to the ballroom.

Watching her with new knowledge, it was hard to believe there was a youthful body inside the slow-moving figure. She was perfect in her role as Lady Yates. There was such assurance in the movements and gestures of an old woman that he did not feel quite so stupid for not recognizing her. She played Lady Yates with the same skill that she brought to her stage performances. He wanted to applaud but contented himself with a smile of pleasure as he followed her with his eyes.

Tomorrow he would call on the lady and, after he had unmasked her, he would ask her to marry him. He could not even consider the fact that she might turn him down. He loved her desperately and he suspected that she loved him too. In any case, he would accept no refusal. He knew that they belonged together.

thirteen

"I swear by me sainted mother that nobody in the 'ole bleedin' place knows anythin', guv." Jasper Pickles hung his head at the shame of it all.

Talbott Stoddard glared at the ragtag creature who shifted from foot to foot as if uncomfortable in the handsomely paneled library. He had to keep himself in hand not to shout at the shuffling figure but his patience was sorely tried.

It was three days since he had seen La Solitaire at the Rose and Trellis but in all that time he had not been able to discover the present location of the beautiful actress. She had not returned to the Green Mews Theater and according to John Tibbles, she had sent a note saying she was ill. The only bright spot in all of this was the fact that he had seen Drew Farrington and, by the surly look of the man, he did not know where La Solitaire was either.

"What about the little abigail that you said offered such promise?" Stoddard snarled across the desk at Pickles.

"She was ripe for a tumble, is all," he said.

Shuddering at the gap-toothed smile of the man, Stoddard prodded, "Did you even question the slut?"

" 'Course I did. And she tol' me that aside from the little blonde, the brat, and the ol' lady, there was no one else in the 'ouse than there oughta be."

Pickles's voice had the nasal whine that Stoddard associated with the more deplorable members of the servant class. He was sorry now that he'd paid the little weasel to get information, but the rogue had demanded payment before he would take on the task. Despite that, or maybe because of it, the man had produced practically nothing.

"And you are quite positive that you have told me everything?"

"On me word, guv." Pickles raised his hand as though testifying before a magistrate. "Nobody saw nobody in the 'ouse what shouldn't have been there. At first, I thought it might've been the sister but me fluff tol' me she ain't ever been there."

"Sister? Whose sister?" Stoddard asked irritably. He hated to prolong the interview with the odious man but he couldn't believe that his three-day watch of the Portman Square house hadn't turned up a single clue to

278

La Solitaire's whereabouts.

"The little blonde's sister," Pickles said. By the sudden tension in the figure across the desk, he suspected that he finally had reported something the nobleman didn't know. He smiled triumphantly as he announced, "The sister's name is Blaine Meriweather."

"Where does she live?" Stoddard asked, sitting forward in his chair.

"Dunno," Pickles answered. At the flash of anger in the nobleman's eye, he hurriedly continued. "Ellen said no one knew where this Blaine was. She'd only 'eard the little blonde talking about 'er. Do you want me to go back and see if I can pick up anything else?"

"No thank you, Mr. Pickles," Stoddard said. "You've been of inestimable help."

After Stoddard had waved the man out of the library, he leaned back in his chair and considered the nuggets of information he had. He had seen La Solitaire entering the Portman Square house. Obviously she had slipped out sometime that night or the following morning before Jasper Pickles had arrived to watch the place. The only significant piece of information his informant had come up with was the fact that Fleur Meriweather had a sister.

Was it possible that Fleur's sister was La Solitaire?

On the face of it, the idea was clearly ridiculous. The more he thought of it, however, the more the ridiculous theory seemed to fit. For one thing, it would explain the lack of information on Maggie Mason's background. He had never considered the fact that the actress might be from a respectable family. If true, he could understand why no one knew where she had come from nor where she lived. It was, at the least, worth pursuing because as it stood he had absolutely no other avenues to follow.

A smile touched Stoddard's face but it did not reach his eyes. Perhaps he ought to have a little chat with Fleur Meriweather. He suspected once he pointed out to her the magnitude of the scandal if the identity of her sister became known, the girl would cooperate. For the price of La Solitaire's address, she could purchase his silence.

"Give over, Fleur. You know Timour the Tartar was far more fearsome than Bluebeard," Val cried as he burst in the room behind his sister.

"I hated both of them!" she declared. She shuddered for emphasis as she blew Blaine a kiss and untied her bonnet.

"Softly, children, softly." Blaine put down the book she had been reading. "Kindly close the door, Val, and then come tell me all about

280

Astley's. I take it that the outing was a success."

"Rather!" the boy said, drawing out the syllables of the word. He quickly closed the door then raced to the chaise longue so he could fill his sister in on all of the details. Fleur pulled up a chair, sharing a smile with Blaine at Val's enthusiasm.

"It was absolutely wizard! I can't wait until tomorrow when I meet with Jamie. I have ever so much to tell him. He'll be positively green!" His eyes sparkled in anticipation of having such a choice morsel to pass on. "There were hundreds of horses, and the tricks they could perform quite put my Fatima in the shade."

"Please remember when you return home, dear, that your pony is moving into her gracious matronly years," Blaine cautioned. "You would not wish to do her an injury."

"Oh, Blaine!" His tone was aggrieved. "I would not be so buffleheaded."

"Besides, Robbie already lectured him," Fleur finished in sisterly smugness.

"It was very generous of Robbie to take you both for such a treat," Blaine added at the thunderous look of the boy. "Did Puff enjoy the show?"

"She certainly did," Fleur answered. "She has gone upstairs for a rest. As she would say,

'I have had a day of the greatest exhaustion.' "

"You should have seen her, Blaine. I think there is Tartar blood in Puff's family." Val crowed. "We were seated on the very edge of the equestrian ring and she got caught up in the excitement of it all. During the scene at the Tartar camp, the Baghwan chief was a particularly expert rider. When he leapt on the back of a galloping stallion, Puff quite forgot herself and sprang to her feet cheering loudly."

"Everyone around us just stared at her," Fleur said. "I was too embarrassed for words."

"Oh, stubble it!" he cried. "You were just as bad. Screeching like a cock being slaughtered whenever things were exciting."

"I did not!"

"Did too! What about when they stormed Bluebeard's castle?" he said scoffingly. "It wasn't me what was caterwauling. Clinging to Robbie like the veriest ninnyhammer when Timour and Bluebeard were slain."

To keep the discussion from dissolving into the usual name-calling, Blaine said, "It sounds as if it was quite a wonder-filled production."

"Oh, Blaine, I wish you might have been there," Val cried. "It was super!"

"Now that I know what a lively event it was, I am sorry I missed it," she admitted. "It seemed such a perfect opportunity to be lazy with everyone out of the house. Ever since you left, I have been reading, which is something I never get a chance to do."

"I must say, Blaine," the boy said, his face suddenly serious. "Ever since you came home from Cousin Lavinia's, you have not been looking quite yourself. I know the old girl is unwell, though I do not know what disease she has. Jamie thought it was most probably influenza. He had been holding out for the French sickness but I told him that was the pox."

"Great heavens!" Blaine gasped, trying to hold back her laughter. "I begin to wonder if Jamie Wildebrand is a very good influence on you."

"He's top of the trees!" Val considered this encomium his highest compliment. "I suppose I am not supposed to say 'pox' in front of ladies but you and Fleur are just sisters and that doesn't count. What I wanted to ask was, since you've been looking so peaky, is there any possibility that you were coming down with the same thing that Cousin Lavinia has?"

"Oh, Blaine!" Fleur cried, eyeing her sister with dismay.

At the expression of worry on the two young faces, Blaine could no longer contain her laughter. She was happy to see that the sight of her amusement relieved some of their concern and she quickly got up from the chaise to give each of them a hug.

"Such a farrago of nonsense, my dears," she said. "I have just been sunk in the doldrums, not sickening. No need to get out the black crepe yet. I promise you I have several good years left."

"What is the matter with Cousin Lavinia? Does she have fits?" Val asked with ghoulish relish.

"What a vulgar thought," Fleur said with a shudder of distaste. "Use your noodle, Val. She is just a very old lady."

"Although I might have put it more tactfully, Fleur is right, my dear. I fear Cousin Lavinia has only a little more time left until she is only memory."

The sadness in their sister's voice dampened the enthusiasm of the youngsters' mood, so it was a welcome relief when Tate arrived with the tea tray. Fleur brightened considerably when the dresser presented her with a gaily wrapped box.

"Ellen was just about to take this to your room. Your abigail looked decidedly flustered when I took it over. Said it came by messenger, but the butler knew nothing about it. I trust, Miss Fleur, you have not been encouraging any unacceptable gentlemen," Tate finished with a minatory glance.

284

"Of course I haven't," the girl snapped.

She accepted the box, and gingerly opened it to reveal a delicate bouquet of spring flowers. She smiled in relief at the unexceptional bijou, handing it regally to the dresser to be put in water. A frown of curiosity creased her brow as she opened the card. After reading only a few lines, her face whitened and for a moment it looked as though she were about to swoon.

"What is it, Fleur?" Blaine asked, her voice sharpening in concern.

"We are surely undone!" the girl cried. "We shall be the laughingstock of London and it is all my fault!"

"What does the note say?" Blaine snapped.

Fleur's violet eyes clouded with tears and they overflowed, running unheeded down her cheeks as she continued to sob. "All I wanted was to have a little fun, and now I have brought ruin to our name and Robbie will never propose. I shall turn into an old, crotchety spinster like Cousin Lavinia!" she wailed.

With a look of supreme disgust, Val snatched the note from his weeping sister and, after blotting the tearstains on the sleeve of his jacket, he smoothed out the crumpled parchment. He looked questioningly at Blaine, who nodded her permission for him to read it aloud.

" 'Please accept these flowers as a token of my good faith. If you wish to keep all of London from talking about your sister's masquerade, I would ask you to meet me tomorrow in Hyde Park. Due to the necessity for discretion, I would suggest you contrive some excuse to come alone.' At the bottom, there are directions and a time. The note is signed by Lord Stoddard," the boy concluded, looking thoroughly confused.

There was a heavy silence in the room when Val finished reading. Blaine's eyes leapt to Tate's and she saw the same question on her dresser's face as she had in her own mind. What exactly did Stoddard know? Since neither Fleur nor Val knew of the double masquerade, they assumed the letter referred to Blaine's pretense as Aunt Haydie. Blaine was not convinced of that. With a sinking feeling in her heart, she suspected that the infamous man had somehow stumbled on the far more damaging intelligence that she was La Solitaire.

"Oh, Blaine, whatever are we going to do?" Fleur wept. "I shall absolutely die, if everyone is sniggering at us behind our backs."

"Stow it, you hen-wit," Val snapped, losing patience with her wailing. "How can anyone think with all your squawking?"

Despite his sharp words, Blaine could tell

the boy was also troubled. He could not like the fact that his family might be held up to ridicule. He would be appalled, she knew, if he realized the full implications of this situation. Quickly she took a hand before things could get further out of hand.

"Sit up and dry your tears, Fleur. Nothing will be served by such behavior." Blaine bit her lip as she tried to organize her thoughts. "While this appears to be the end of the world, I assure you it is nothing of the kind. If we can manage to keep calm, I suspect we may be able to brush through without a scratch."

She crossed her fingers behind her back, hoping she was not just giving the children empty promises. Their expressions were a mixture of hope and fear, overlaid by a belief in their sister that for her was considerably daunting.

"What will I tell Lord Stoddard?" Fleur whispered.

"You will have absolutely nothing to do with such a villainous person. I myself will deal with Lord Stoddard," Blaine announced to the girl's obvious relief. "For this evening, you will cancel any plans and remain quietly in your room. This has been a shock for you. Although you have done exceptionally well so far, you are not a good enough actress to pretend nothing is the matter. Until this business is settled, you will not be home to anyone."

"Not even Robbie?" she asked in a very small voice.

"Not Prinny himself!" Blaine answered. "Now run along with Tate and she'll tuck you up for a rest before dinner. We will carry on exactly as usual. Be warned though, Fleur," she cautioned as the girl sniffled her way toward the door. "If you tell any of this to Ellen, I shall wash my hands of you completely. Tate will tell Puff what is afoot but not one word of this is to go beyond these walls."

Once Fleur was dispatched, Blaine turned her attention to Val. The boy had watched wide-eyed as his older sister had taken charge but now there was a stiffness to his shoulders that told her he would not be content to be summarily sent to his room. Reseating herself on the chaise, she patted the cushions beside her.

"Well, laddie, we've gotten ourselves in the soup once again," she said as she placed a comforting arm around his narrow shoulders.

"I did not much like the tone of that man's letter, Blaine," he said.

"Nor I."

"It sounded very much like one I read about in one of those Gothic novels that Fleur reads. The wicked count was planning to do something dishonorable and he sent just such a letter to the heroine of the piece. She was all fluttery like Fleur, but not half so nice." The boy tilted his head to look up at his sister. "Did it sound to you as if Lord Stoddard was planning to do something not quite cricket?"

Looking down at the grave little face, Blaine's first instinct was to shield the boy. For one so young, he had dealt with enough tragedy and she hated to add to his already heavy load. It was the thought that he looked to her for guidance that convinced her she must treat him with honesty. She always had stressed that he must face the truth before he would be able to work through a problem.

"His letter did sound that way to me too." She hugged him tightly before she pushed him slightly away so that she could look down into his face. "I am afraid that Lord Stoddard is not a very good man. He has tumbled to our secret and is planning to use it to his own advantage."

"If I were older, I would call him out."

"Oh, no!" Blaine cried. "When you are older, sweetheart, try to remember that a duel is never the answer to a problem. The death or injury of another is a terrible thing and just creates further complications."

"Will you meet Lord Stoddard in the park?"

"Yes." She tried to appear disinterested,

grateful that her brother could not feel the pounding of her heart at the very thought. "I shall have words with him and that will be the end of that."

"I could go with you" was his hopeful response.

Blaine hugged him again. "Though I would like nothing better than to have a brave champion at my side, I must go alone, according to the instructions of the note. No need to look so worried. Lord Stoddard knows how bird-witted your sister is and that is why he sent her the note. In me, laddie, the man has met his match."

Perhaps the confidence of her voice and the humor of her last words convinced Val that the nature of the discovery was not quite as serious as he had first imagined. Blaine was relieved when a smile stretched his mouth and his eyes twinkled with merriment.

"I begin to feel rather sorry for Lord Stoddard," he said. He chuckled, then his face sobered once again. "You are not going to confine me to my room like Fleur? I was to meet Jamie tomorrow and we have enormous plans for the rest of the day. Sarge was going to drive us down to the docks to see the ships."

Blaine surveyed the pleading in her brother's eyes and knew it would be easier to have him busy, under Sarge's watchful eye, than moping about the house.

"I will agree to your meeting with the irascible Jamie if you give me your solemn word you will tell him nothing of this matter."

"Word of honor," he said without hesitation. Then he jumped to his feet and solemnly placed one hand over his heart and the other over his eyes. "If I break my word, may the animals of the forest eat my heart and the bats of hell pick out my eyes." Then he dropped his hands and spit on the carpet.

"Good God, child!" Blaine screeched. "Where on earth did you learn such a thing?" Before he could speak, she held up her hand for silence. "Don't tell me. Let me guess. Jamie, perhaps?"

"Righto, Blaine. Smashing, isn't it?"

"Give me a kiss, you loathsome child, and then run along."

The grinning boy did as directed and left Blaine with a smile on her lips. She tried to hold on to her amusement but it was difficult to get through the rest of the day. Her thoughts whirled round and round in her head but she could come up with no viable way to avoid the meeting with Stoddard. In the evening, she consulted with Tate and Puff but neither woman had any ideas to offer. She would meet with him and then decide on a further course of action. So much depended on what Lord Stoddard knew and what he wanted for his information.

The next morning dawned gray and cloudy. There was a chill dampness to the air that did little to cheer Blaine. Val, more quiet than usual, had stopped by on his way to meet Jamie to wish her good luck in her meeting with Stoddard. She was able to give him a confident smile that remained, stiffening on her face, until the door closed behind the boy.

Fleur was also subdued when Blaine invited her to join her in her room for breakfast. The girl's eyes were red-rimmed, as if she had cried half the night. Her voice had a lackluster quality in answer to Blaine's questions. After breakfast she left, promising to remain in the house until her sister's return.

Once more Blaine donned the costume of Lady Haydie Yates. She had the feeling that it would be the last time the old woman would make an appearance. The dress she chose was funereal black to suit her mood of depression. She eschewed the white makeup, preferring instead to wear the black hat with the veil Fleur had bought her at a happier time. She grasped her cane and her reticule in her mittened hands and then turned toward Tate.

"Thank you for your help," she said. "Your loyalty has been one of the mainstays of my life in the last six years, you know."

"Get along with your nonsense, my girl." For all her ferocity of manner, there was an unaccustomed softness in her voice as she continued. "I wish you would let me go with you, lamby."

"It is something I must handle alone." Blaine's tone permitted no argument. "I do not think there is anything to fear. If I read Stoddard's note correctly, he means to intimidate Fleur by his threat to bandy his great discovery about town. I would assume he is contemplating blackmail. All I need do is determine the price of his silence. Besides, Tate, I need you here to keep an eye on Fleur."

"I do not like your taking a hackney," the dresser said as she tied the satin band around the veiling at Blaine's throat. "I would feel far more comfortable if Sarge were driving you."

"He is much better occupied keeping Val and that scamp Jamie out of trouble." As she started out the door, she tried to reassure the older woman. "I will be meeting Stoddard at noon in a public park. There can be little danger in that."

Blaine repeated those words over and over as the hackney jolted through the streets. She hoped that Stoddard already would be at the meeting place because she wasn't sure he would make contact with her instead of Fleur. The blood pounded at her temples in the beginnings of a headache and she stared bleakly through the veiling of her hat at the passing buildings. She would offer the man money, but she doubted that he was out for money. If she was correct in her conclusions, Lord Stoddard's price was La Solitaire.

The hackney driver set her down just inside the park. He was already out of sight before she got her bearings and pulled out Stoddard's note to confirm the meeting place. With a quick glance at the watch pinned inside her pelisse, to see that she still had ten minutes to spare, Blaine readied herself for her performance.

She shook out the heavy folds of her black dress and adjusted the padding of her matronly bosom more securely. Looking around, she was pleased to note she was able to see remarkably well through the veiling even though the sunshine, even at noon, was almost nonexistent. She pulled the netting away from her mouth and nose to ensure that the features of her face would remain invisible. She slipped the strings of her jet-beaded reticule around her wrist and then, taking a breath, she leaned heavily on her stick as she walked stiffly along the path.

If she was right, Stoddard had guessed that the real name of La Solitaire was Blaine Meriweather. She was counting on the fact that he might not have discovered that she was also playing the part of Lady Yates. If not, he would be under the impression that he had only an old woman, a young girl, and a child to deal with. In underestimating his adversaries, Stoddard would give her an advantage.

The already gloomy day appeared more threatening as Blaine approached the rendezvous. When she discovered the spot and realized its isolation, she was grateful that Fleur had not come. An iron bench with wooden slats was tucked into a shadowed bend of the walking path. The path was dark, covered over by heavily leaved, massive oaks. An army could hide in those hedges, she thought. She surveyed the area but could not see anyone other than the wretched Stoddard, who leaned arrogantly against the trunk of a tree beside the bench.

For a moment, she experienced the same fright she felt prior to a performance. Her throat was dry and her heart was pounding erratically. In point of fact, she was involved in a play, one with more tragic consequences if she did not act her part well. Thus reminded of her theatrical experience, she took a deep breath and stormed onto the scene.

"Well, young man," she rasped in Lady Yates's throaty voice.

With the speed of a scalded cat, Stoddard pulled away from the tree against which he had been leaning. He stared in confusion at the veiled woman in black who was confronting him. Blaine pushed her advantage.

"What is the meaning of all this rubbish?" she snapped.

"Lady Yates!" He could not keep back his start of surprise.

"Don't Lady Yates me, you disreputable rake! How dare you send secret notes and flowers to my niece! What kind of a girl do you think she is that she would be privy to such hugger-mugger goings-on?"

"W-where is Fleur?"

It was obvious that Stoddard had not twigged to her imposture of Lady Yates. His face was a picture of confusion at the appearance of the old woman and his stammered words clearly showed that he was stunned. Blaine pressed her advantage, hoping to rout the man.

"Such underhanded dealings, Lord Stoddard, indicate a certain want of moral rectitude." Blaine rapped out her words in stentorian tones and was pleased to see the flush of color that stained his cheeks at her insult. "My niece will not be here today and as far as I am concerned you are never to seek to converse with her again."

Stoddard blinked when she finished, then his face changed from the tint of embarrassment to the deep red tones of fury.

"I am not so easily gulled, madam," he said through gritted teeth. "If you are here, you have read my note and are well aware of the reason for this meeting. I was hoping to deal with Fleur but you will do equally as well."

Since her berating of the man had failed to make him turn tail, she decided it was time to come to business. She planted her walking stick firmly in front of her feet and leaned on it with both hands, while holding the rest of her body stiff with offended dignity. "What do you want, Lord Stoddard?"

"I want your niece, Lady Yates."

"Fleur?"

"Don't be stupid." He snarled. "I want La Solitaire!"

At his unrestrained anger, Blaine swallowed a lump of fear and tried to keep her voice bitingly cold. "Quite impossible, young man. Do you really think I would turn the girl over to you?"

"If you do not want your reputation, and that of your innocent little niece, to be dragged into the muck of scandal, you will tell me what I want to know. Where is La Solitaire?"

"I don't know." Blaine was shaking so much, she had little need to fabricate the querulous tones of an old woman. "I sent her away. It was too dangerous for Fleur to have the actress in London. I have told her, we will never receive her again. She is a disgrace to the Meriweather name!"

There was silence after her angry speech. She prayed that Stoddard would believe her and look elsewhere for answers. Her body felt chilled with fear at his words, which confirmed that he was not out after gain. He wanted La Solitaire. Through the veiling, Blaine could see that he was wavering. Suddenly, his expression changed and her heart plummeted.

"I do not believe you, Lady Yates," he said, his voice gloating. "If you had meant to cut the actress, you would have done it long ago. I am sure you and the little Fleur have worked out ways to contact her."

"Fleur knows nothing," Blaine snapped in fear and anger. "She can tell you nothing."

"Perhaps not, Lady Yates. We shall just have to see."

"Leave her alone!" Blaine was not sure if her cry was for her sister or for herself. She clenched her hand on the knob of her walking stick, the urge to strike out at the man almost overpowering.

"I had the feeling you Meriweathers would be difficult to deal with. I had made my plans for Fleur but I suppose you will have to do," he said.

Before Blaine could take in his meaning, he raised his hand and two men appeared on either side of her. The size and generally disreputable appearance of the men did not encourage her to struggle. She knew that in her encumbering skirts she could not hope to outrun them. Worst of all, any intimate contact with her body might reveal the falseness of her padded figure. She would be in far less danger if Stoddard and his bullies continued to think of her as the aged Lady Yates.

"I would say you have the advantage, milord," she said.

"If you would be good enough to follow me, Lady Yates."

Without another word, Lord Stoddard moved off the path into the bushes. She spared a brief glance for the walkway, empty of strollers on this gloomy day. A call for help would be useless. Her eyes flickered to her escort and their very immobility was daunting. She gritted her teeth, forcing away her fear.

"Your arm, sirrah!" she demanded.

She was surprised at how quickly one of the brutes thrust out his arm in a courtly gesture. She placed her shaking hand on the stained woolen sleeve and leaned heavily on her walking stick as she moved after Lord Stoddard. A short distance away, a coach waited with curtains already drawn. Stoddard sneered as she approached, his lip curled as she graciously accepted the help of the two ruffians to enter the carriage. The door closed behind her and the men moved to the head of the horses, out of her earshot.

The carriage was luxuriously appointed, apparently Stoddard's own. She quickly rummaged through the interior but could discover no pistols or anything else she might use as a weapon. Since she could hear nothing except vague creakings and groanings from the carriage, she was afraid to prolong her search for fear Stoddard would return. She shuddered at the thought of having to share a seat with the frightening man. She moved to the center of the seat and placed her walking stick across her knees as a barrier.

With a sharp snap, the door was snatched open and Talbott Stoddard entered. He gave a snort of annoyance as he glanced at the cane, but without further comment, he threw himself on the opposite seat with his back to the horses. One of the ruffians shouted and the carriage took off with a jerk.

"Once society hears of your outrageous conduct, Lord Stoddard, you will no longer be received," Blaine announced.

"No one will care what happens to the Meriweathers. The family of an actress is of little import to the members of the ton," he replied.

"I find it hard to believe, sir, that your parents were ever joined in lawful wedlock. You have the distinct odor of *le bar sinistre.*"

A wave of fury crossed Stoddard's face at her words. "Shut up, you vicious old biddy!"

Afraid he would strike her, Blaine shrank against the squabs. His unleashed anger was terrifying. She tried to control her breathing, knowing she could not let him see her fear. She took courage from her role as the indomitable Lady Yates.

"What do you hope to accomplish by this idiocy, young man?"

"A simple trade, madam. I will return you to Portman Square, the moment you tell me where I can find La Solitaire."

"Quite impossible," she said in bored tones. "I have already told you that the actress is gone. Not only is she beyond your reach, milord, but she has always been above your touch."

"Bitch!" Stoddard snarled. "Have a care, Lady Yates. I could just as easily abandon you far from civilized London. At your age, the vultures would be picking your bones before anyone could find you."

"Their company would be a decided improvement," she retorted.

"Damn your blistering tongue!"

At his latest outburst, Blaine subsided. She

could sense that he was on the ragged edge of violence and it was no plan of hers to incur injury as well as abuse at his hands. She could see little hope of bettering her situation but she was at heart an optimist and far too stubborn to give up in despair. She kept her body in the stiff posture of an angry dowager but tried to relax. She knew later on she would have need of her strength.

It was difficult to control the fear that sent her thoughts spinning in endless mind pictures. She did not know what would happen when she did not return to the house on Portman Square. Tate would be frantic and Fleur, once she heard, would go into the usual hysterics. When they returned from their tour of the docks, Val and Sarge would be told, but there was little that a servant and a child could do against the strength of a titled lord.

Even if she managed to escape on her own, she knew that, in his fury, Stoddard would blacken the name of the Meriweathers. He would take great delight in spreading the tale of how Blaine Meriweather had taken the name of Maggie Mason, the notorious La Solitaire. The thought of Val and Fleur's humiliation at such a scandal was too painful to bear.

For the love of her family, could she bargain with Stoddard? She knew his price. If she agreed to his terms, could she trust him?

She truly didn't know. And if she could trust him to keep his half of the bargain, could she bring herself to become his mistress?

The thought of Talbott Stoddard's hands touching her made the bile rise in her throat. From the candid speech of the chorus girls in her early years in the theater, Blaine was aware of the details of lovemaking. The only actual experience she had had was the kiss she had shared with Drew Farrington. Without question, Stoddard's embrace would not give her the joy she had found in Drew's arms. She knew by the coldness and the fury she had seen in his eyes that he would not be gentle with her. He would make her pay for her insults and rejections. Stoddard would degrade her and defile her, destroying her very soul.

She had only herself to count on, Blaine thought as she fought back tears of self-pity. There was little hope of rescue. There was no one with curly brown hair and flashing green eyes who could save her from this nightmare. No one at all.

fourteen

Drew raised an eyebrow as he handed his cape to his aunt's butler. Even without Robbie's note, which had brought him to Portman Square, he would have known there was something amiss. Timmons had the look servants reserved solely for houses of mourning. Behind the closed door of the drawing room, he could hear a high keening wail and he quickened his steps across the marble foyer and opened the doors.

Robbie sat on the sofa, his arm around a crumpled Fleur, who was weeping desperately onto his waistcoat. He recognized Tate, La Solitaire's dresser, in low-voiced colloquy with Frau Puffentraub, Fleur's governess. Sarge, La Solitaire's bodyguard, wore a black expression that boded ill for someone. Drew's eyes searched the room but he did not see Val and, most ominous of all, there was no sign of the imperious Lady Yates.

"Thank God you've come, Drew!" Robbie cried.

Suspecting that whatever the calamity, there

was little need to broadcast it beyond the drawing room, Drew quickly closed the doors and moved into the room. Robbie attempted to climb to his feet, but Fleur clung to him convulsively. The servants stared at him, their eyes clearly weighing him.

Drew tried to control the fear that invaded him at the presence of both Tate and Sarge in the room. He had never seen them outside of the theater and he supposed that since their arrival at the Portman Square house they had played least seen. From their sharpened glances at his entrance, he had little doubt of their complicity in Blaine's masquerade. She could not have succeeded in such a deception without their help. He was proud of their loyalty to her but he could not refrain from giving them an accusatory glare; then ignoring them, he pulled a chair up to the sofa and addressed Robbie.

"I gather there's been some disaster," he said.

"It's all my fault!" Fleur wailed.

"Stop that bleatin', girl," Sarge snapped before anyone could say a word.

Instantly, Fleur stopped her crying, sniffling into a soggy handkerchief Robbie must have given her. Drew was much impressed and saluted the enormous bodyguard before he turned back to his brother.

"I just got here myself, Drew, but as near as I can figure it, Val, Jamie Wildebrand and Lady Yates are missing, Robbie blurted out.

"All of them?" Drew asked in amazement. "Where did they go?"

"The lads was with me, your lordship." Sarge ground out. "I had taken Val and his friend Jamie out for the day. We were on our way to the docks. To see the ships."

"How long were you there before the boys disappeared?"

"We never arrived." Sarge's brows met over his nose in a line of thunder. "We had just started off and the traffic was heavy. The boys was ridin' up top with me. All of a sudden Val shrieks that he feels mortal sick. Then Jamie says he'll help the lad back to the house since there's not enough room to turn around. Afore I can make a move, the little bleeders are off, racing back toward 'ome."

"They weren't here when you got back," Drew finished, before the man could spit out the words. "It sounds to me like it was planned. Did the boys mention anything like a fair or a cockfight?"

"All they talked about was the ships." Besides being worried about the boys, Sarge was clearly furious that he had been so easily tricked.

"It would seem to me that the boys are

clearly off on a lark. There is little we can do, without at least some idea of where they have gone," Drew concluded.

"Should we alert Jamie's father?" Robbie asked.

"We will hold for the moment. Val is a responsible child and I cannot believe he is unaware of the upset he is causing. I would hope the boys will return shortly with a very good explanation for their conduct. And it had better be good," he said grimly. "Now, then. Where did Lady Yates go?"

In the midst of the silence, Drew's eyes roamed the room, settling at last on the figure pressed to his brother's chest. There was a stillness to the blond girl that did not fool him.

"Sit up, Fleur." Drew's voice indicated he would brook no nonsense. When she complied, her violet eyes began to overflow and he fought back the desire to shake her. "Stop that immediately and tell me where Lady Yates went."

"To the park," she whispered.

"What?" Drew shouted, expecting anything but that.

"I say, Drew, there's no need to shout at the girl," Robbie said as Fleur cowered in the circle of his arm.

"There is every reason to shout at her. They are all playing a May game." Drew waved his hand at the still figures of the servants, hovering behind the sofa. He fought down his temper and leaned toward his brother, his voice calmer. "Listen to me, Robbie. It is time that you knew at least some of the truth. There is no Aunt Haydie. She doesn't exist. The woman you know as Lady Yates is Fleur's sister, Blaine."

"Devil, you say!" Robbie leapt as though he'd been stung, his face set in denial. At the low moan issuing from the blond girl at his side, his eyes widened in confusion. "Fleur, is this true?"

The girl continued to moan and finally even Robbie lost patience with her. "Look at me this instant, Fleur Meriweather!"

The note of sharp authority brought her head up. It was amazing that despite her tears the girl still was lovely. Her eyes shone like violets after a rain and there were rosy spots of color high on her cheeks. Robbie swallowed convulsively but continued to command her attention.

"Is Lady Yates your sister?" he asked.

"Yes" was the whispery reply.

"Why was she pretending to be your aunt?"

"For the moment it does not matter, Robbie," Drew said impatiently. "I am sure, later on, Fleur will be delighted to fill you in on the details. What is of immediate concern is the whereabouts of Lady Yates. Or Blaine. Whichever you prefer." Drew held Fleur's eyes as he asked, "Where is Blaine?"

Now that the terrible secret was out it appeared that Fleur was prepared to cooperate. She seemed to think she had no more to lose. Drew had seen the agonized glance she had given Robbie but he suspected she had little to worry about on that head. Despite the shock of the news, his brother was as much under her spell as he had ever been.

"There was a note," Fleur began. "It said that he was going to tell everyone in London about Blaine. He said we would all be ruined unless I met him. Even though I was frightened, I would have gone, but Blaine said I mustn't. She would go in my place and meet Lord Stoddard."

"Damn!"

Drew jumped to his feet, glaring furiously around the room. Out of the corner of his eye, he caught the uneasy glances between Tate, Frau Puffentraub, and Sarge. He started to speak but was checked by a slight shake of the little dresser's head. Unconsciously his eyes dropped to Fleur's youthful face.

It was obvious that Fleur did not know of her sister's life as an actress. Blaine had sacrificed much to protect her sister and brother and to keep this intelligence from them. Since

309

she had chosen not to tell them, could he break her confidence? He understood that Stoddard's letter referred to La Solitaire not Lady Yates, and he suspected that Blaine was in grave danger. He fought to control his impatience. He wanted to dash out of the house to her rescue but he couldn't until he got all the information.

"Robbie," Drew said. "I want you to take Fleur into the music room. It is quiet in there and she will have a chance to recover from all the upset. She can tell you all about Lady Yates while I remain here to discover what has become of her missing relatives. Not to mention the abominable Jamie."

Despite the lightness of his tone, Robbie stared at him sharply. He suspected there was more to this business than he was aware of and he disliked the fact his brother was obviously trying to get him out of the room. If the idea of soothing Fleur hadn't appealed to him, he might have put up more of a battle. As it was, the chance to be alone with his love and his curiosity over the impersonation of Lady Yates won out. He helped the girl to her feet and, with his arm around her, left the room. There was silence after the door closed, and Drew met the hostile stares of the three servants without flinching.

"I know Blaine is La Solitaire," he said, and

the tension in the room eased.

"He took her, Lord Farrington," Sarge said. "She went dressed up as Lady Yates and he took her anyway. When she didn't come back, I went to the park. There were no sign of her at the spot where they met. There was holes from her walking stick leadin' off into the brush and the wheel marks of a carriage. It were beside the path, what I found this."

Grimly, Drew reached out to take the reticule. He remembered seeing Blaine with it several times when he had escorted her in her role of Lady Yates. His fingers stroked the jet beads and they were cold to the touch. "Where was it?" he asked hoarsely.

"Underneath the hedge beside the bench where she met Stoddard. The strings ain't broke. Looks like she throwed it there."

"Good girl." He grinned at Sarge and there was an answering twinkle in the otherwise glum face. They both knew that it was a fair indication that although Blaine might be frightened, she was still thinking. Drew was filled with a wave of warmth for his brave lady. Then he returned to the business at hand. "Did you go to Stoddard's?"

"He were gone." Sarge's mouth hardened. "He took his carriage afore noon. There was two thugs on the box according to one of the grooms. Stoddard's expected back tonight."

Every muscle in Drew's body tightened at the realization of the danger Blaine was in. He was only slightly heartened that she was dressed as Lady Yates. It would give her some protection unless her impersonation was detected. One false note and she would give the game away. What would Stoddard do when he discovered that he had the woman he was obsessed with right in his hands? Drew knew and the thought terrified him.

Blaine had fought so hard and suffered enough lonely years that he would spare her if he could this final indignity. It would make no difference in his feelings for her. He loved her for herself, for the character he knew she possessed. If the worst happened, she would be devastated. Drew vowed he would spend the rest of his life making her happy again.

To do that, he had to find her and he hadn't a clue where to look. His grim thoughts were interrupted by a commotion in the hallway and the sound of a boy's high-pitched voice. Drew threw open the doors and strode into the foyer.

"Jamie!" he cried as he glanced at the disheveled boy.

"Lord Farrington. Good-o!" Jamie grinned and the flash of teeth was all the brighter for the streaks of dirt that lined his face.

"In here, lad." Without a word, he whisked

the boy into the parlor and closed the doors once more. "Before I call you to book, where's Val?"

"He's still following the bloke that nabbed his old auntie." Jamie grinned again at the thunderstruck expression on Lord Farrinton's face. He had never thought to hand the man such a facer and was thoroughly proud of himself.

"Spill it, Jamie."

"It was Val's idea, but I did help him out," he admitted as he sat before the spellbound audience. He avoided Sarge's eye, embarrassed that he had tricked the man. Focusing his eyes on Lord Farrington's face, he began. "Val wouldn't tell me much because he had sworn a blood oath and he would die a most grievous death if he broke his word. He did say as how his aunt was meeting a sly boots in the park and he was right worried about her. So we thought it would be good experience to be right on her trail. We're planning to join the Bow Street Runners, you know."

"I am sure they will be delighted that you will be expanding their ranks," Drew said dryly. He was relaxed for the first time since he had entered the house. If his suspicions were correct, they would soon have the solution to Blaine's whereabouts. He smiled fondly at the filthy child, who was looking uneasy at the tone of his voice. "Go on, lad."

"We got there early so we might get an idea of the setup. Val had copped a peek at some letter with directions so we knew where to go. I found a smashing climbing tree. We skinned up it and waited and sure enough along comes this bloke and, believe it or not, Lord Farrington, the man leaned right up against our tree."

"Good God!" By his triumphant smile, Drew knew that Jamie had little conception of the danger in which they had been. He hoped Val was more perceptive.

"Along comes Val's aunt. There was a lot of flapping back and forth and I can tell that the old lady's not best pleased. I didn't 'azactly' understand all that was said and when I look up at Val he's just as confused as me. There was a lot of talk about cards. The man wanted some card game and the old lady wouldn't give it to him."

"Solitaire?"

"Right-o, guv!" Jamie congratulated Drew for his guess. "Well, sir, they nattered awhile and then the fancy dress bloke whistles up two real mean types and they haul off the old lady. Val wanted to jump down right away but I couldn't see any sense in it. We waited a few minutes and then as soon as we could, we lit into the bushes. They were just stowing Val's aunt in the carriage."

"Did all three of them go with the carriage?"

"Yes, sir. The two bruisers on top and the fancy Dan inside."

At a growl from behind, Drew glanced back at Sarge, who was gripping the back of a chair with both hands. He had been so caught up in the boy's story that he had quite forgotten he was not alone. Tate's usual expression of disapproval was replaced by one of unvarnished fear, and Frau Puffentraub sat on a chair, her face pinched and white. Drew turned back to the child, anxious to hear the end of the story.

"When the rascals moved forward to talk, Val crept along the ground to the boot. I followed him, of course. We climbed in all right and tight just before the carriage took off. I can tell you, Lord Farrington, I'm never letting Momma put my turtles in the boot. It's a very nasty ride."

Drew hid a smile behind his hand at the disgust in Master Wildebrand's voice and marveled at the bravery of the boys.

"We bounced and jounced for ever such a long time until I felt like I had a touch of the quinsy. Then all of a sudden the ride seemed to smooth out, even though the horses were going at a fair clip. Val could see a bit of the road and he told me we were going out of London. He told me as how I would have to get

315

out so that I could tell someone where he had gone."

Here the boy's voice broke and there was a suggestion of dampness to his eyes. Drew leaned forward and clamped a comforting hand on the small shoulder.

"The ground was moving frightfully fast and I knew it wasn't going to be a great comfort when I smacked up on the flat. To my shame, sir, I didn't want to jump."

"Ah, Jamie. You would have been stupid to want to jump. War heroes know the danger but still do what they have to do," Drew said, as he squeezed the scrawny shoulder. He ruffled the boy's hair. "I think you've shown great courage all the way. And so I will tell your father."

"Wizard, sir!" An enormous smile erased the doleful expression and he wiped his eyes with the back of his sleeve, distributing the dirt into a more uniform design.

"The proof of your courage is that obviously you did jump," Drew said.

"Well, more or less. Val called me some names and then gave me my instructions. When he threatened to shove me out, I decided it was time for my move. We waited until we clattered into some woods and then I rolled out of the boot."

"Bravo, lad." Sarge interjected much to

everyone's surprise.

Jamie winked at the giant before he took up the tale. "I was rather winded at first. My ears were ringing something fierce but all in all I was in good shape. Val had told me to lay perfectly still until the carriage was out of sight. In actual fact, sir, I couldn't have moved at all. After I cast up my accounts, I walked as fast as I could until I finally was able to hitch up with a carter who was going to London. And here I am."

The low-key triumph at the end of the boy's tale was more touching than a shout of joy. Drew could well imagine what the child had been through, more from what was left unsaid than what he had mentioned. Beneath the dirt, there was a gray pallor to the boy's face that indicated his exhaustion.

"You've done an admirable job, Jamie. Tell me about Val and then we'll see about getting you washed up and fed. It's almost four and I can imagine with all your activities, you may have worked up quite an appetite."

"I'm bloody starving, Lord Farrington!" the boy howled, delighted when his audience broke into laughter.

The tension in the room had eased once they realized that the boys were not lost in London but hot in pursuit of Stoddard. Although Val and Blaine were still to be accounted for, at least the situation was not as hopeless as it had been earlier.

"Just a little bit longer. Jamie," Drew said as he noticed the droopy-lidded eyes of the boy. "What was Val's plan?"

"It was pretty difficult talking much for fear of being overheard. We were whispering and such but I think I got the drift. I gave him the pocketknife that my father gave me and a bit of the ready. I was flush today because Momma slipped me some coin for our trip to the docks. Val made me keep some in case of emergency but he's plump in the pocket, I can tell you. He was going to stay with the carriage until he was sure they had gotten to their hidey-hole and then he would hightail it back here."

"Excellent plan, lad."

Drew was more and more impressed with the boy's enterprise. The Bow Street Runners could not have produced any better detectives. He was silent for a moment as he considered his own plans. Once decided, he began issuing orders.

"Tate, take the boy up to Val's room for a wash. I'm sure you can find something for Jamie to wear until his own things arrive. Frau Puffentraub, you will arrange for a tray and the preparation of a room for the night." He turned to the boy, taking in the wide grin of delight. "I will send off a note to your father, asking permission for you to remain with us until tomorrow. You have played an important part in this drama so it is only fair that you remain for the denouement."

"Good show, sir. I'd rather like that," Jamie said.

Suddenly his expression changed and the eyes staring up held a haunted quality. Drew was painfully aware that for all his bravery Jamie was little more than a child.

"Lady Yates will be all right, won't she?" The boy swallowed several times before he could continue. "She's a grand old girl. Didn't take a bit of lip from the fancy Dan and when those two bullies come up on her, she snapped at them and they shuffled their feet like babes with their nanny. You will get her back all right, won't you, sir?"

"You have my promise," Drew said.

The boy's eyes flicked over his face, then he nodded in satisfaction. Drew was incredibly moved by the word picture Jamie had drawn of his courageous Blaine confronting the two thugs. He clenched the muscles in his jaw as he turned to Sarge.

"Alert the stables to ready my rig and tell them to keep a sharp eye out for Val. It would be best if you waited out front. He'll be in a hurry so he might not take time to go round to

319

the stables. Also, on your way out, send Timmons to me." Drew ground to a halt. He took in the motionless figures, then barked, "Jump to it."

Like well-drilled troops, they leapt into action. Sarge jerked open the doors for the bustling Frau Puffentraub as Tate swept down on the startled Jamie. Drew grinned as he strode across to his aunt's dainty desk. Uncaring of the chaos he was creating, he rummaged through the contents until he found some stationery. The cough behind his left shoulder alerted him to Timmons's presence and he spun around to address the unflappable butler. He noticed with amusement that, always the soul of tact, the man had closed the doors when he entered.

"Unless you're deaf and blind, Timmons, I suspect you have a fair idea of what's afoot," he said.

"Yes, Lord Farrington. Thankfully the boys were not lost but had only strayed. Master Val will soon be back in the fold, I gather, although Lady Yates is still unaccounted for." There was no break in the bland expression of his face as he reported these events.

"Must have been quite a scene before I got here."

"Miss Fleur was in spasms, milord." An ever so slight smile crinkled the corners of the butler's eyes. "I have kept the servants below stairs and cautioned them. You aunt's staff is trained to discretion."

Inventing quickly, Drew explained that Lady Yates had been trying to abort the kidnapping of Fleur by an overeager suitor when she herself had been taken. He reminded himself to talk to Robbie and Fleur when he returned. They would all have to tell the same story to avoid any possible scandal that might arise from the day's events. After thanking him for his support, Drew dismissed the butler and dashed off a note to Jamie's father. He chuckled as he wrote, contemplating the retelling of the story for his old schoolmate's delectation. Like father, like son, he thought as he blotted and sealed the note, then left the room to give it to Timmons.

"Have Cook prepare a basket of food, suitable for myself and Val. Send something out to Sarge so that he's ready to leave when the boy arrives."

"I've told them to prepare your aunt's coach. The new grays are dependable and built for speed," Timmons declared authoritatively. "If I might offer a suggestion, Lord Farrington, it might be a good plan to send Lady Yates's abigail. Lady Yates is not a young person and may be considerably overset by her experiences. It is always good to have another woman along in such circumstances."

Drew hardened his heart to the shaft of pain at the parade of ugly pictures that rose in his mind at Timmons's words. He turned, biting off his words as he headed for the door. "Have Tate ready to leave when I return."

After a quick word to Sarge, Drew leapt into his curricle and returned to his town house. He changed into buckskins and then went to his library and removed two pistols from the gun cabinet and quickly loaded them. After throwing down a rejuvenating glass of brandy, he returned to Portman Square.

The wait was agonizing. His mind was filled with the danger to Blaine and the helplessness of his own inaction. Although it seemed like centuries, it was only an hour before his patience was rewarded.

At the sounds in the foyer, Drew hurried into the hall to find Val, dirty but jubilant. The boy's face was gaunt and the expression in his eyes spoke volumes of his harrowing day. Unlike Jamie, who thought of Lady Yates as an old lady, it was obvious Val had considered the real dangers that were facing Blaine. Drew's eyes were reassuring as he squeezed the boy's hand.

"Well done, Val," he said, his voice deep with pride.

"I know where she is, sir, but I think we should hurry."

"Steady on, old thing." Drew felt the shaking of the boy's body as he pulled him against his side. "Your troops are ready to march. Just give me a direction and then you can tell me the rest on the way."

At the touch of humor, the fear eased in the boy's eyes. "The west road out of London. Just beyond Twickenham."

Without a word, Timmons opened the door and Drew strode outside, followed by Val with Tate bringing up the rear. In a twinkling they were on their way, the grays moving steadily through the early-evening traffic.

"I would guess the inside of my aunt's carriage is significantly more comfortable than the boot," Drew said as he noticed the stiff movements of the boy.

"Rather!" Val said. For the first time since his arrival, a natural grin creased his features. "I shall think twice before I travel that way again."

Drew nodded to Tate to open the basket of food. He was amused that the first thing she presented to the boy was a wet cloth to make his ablutions. He relaxed, eating sparingly as he waited for the first pangs of Val's hunger to be satisfied. The efficient Timmons had included a bottle of wine, and he savored the sharp bite on his tongue as the carriage sped through the twilight.

"It's a cottage, sir," Val said, talking behind a partially gnawed chicken leg. "Just outside of Twickenham. I just waited long enough to make sure they were set for the night."

There was a bleakness in the voice that was painful to hear. "It won't take us long now," Drew assured him. "One road out of town?"

"Two. The one we want is near an alehouse. I put a mark on the signpost so I would be sure of the right one."

"Very sound plan. Jamie told us he had lent you his knife."

"It came in dreadfully handy, sir. I used it to mark a trail from the cottage because I didn't know if I would be able to find the place in the dark." The boy wiped at his mouth with the back of his hand until Tate coughed sharply, and then he reached for his napkin. "I'm glad that Jamie got back all right. I was feeling pretty awful that I had got him into such a bramble patch. He was good to go along even though he didn't know what it was all about. I had promised Bl — my aunt that I wouldn't tell anyone what was going on."

"If it would ease your mind any, Val, I am fully aware that Lady Yates is your sister Blaine."

Wide eyes flew to Drew's face. "Oh."

"Quite" was the crisp reply.

"I suppose it was Fleur who cried rope," he said in disgust. "Girls have no sense."

"A sentiment with which I can wholeheartedly concur." Drew's voice was dry as he eyed the discomfited child. To smooth over the embarrassment of the moment, he returned to business. "What was the place like?"

"I only took the briefest of looks. I was anxious to return for help. It's a small cottage with a thatched roof. Several rooms below but I spotted a window above so I think there's an attic room. Set in a copse of trees and no other houses visible. If I hadn't been so worried, I wouldn't have half minded the place. Lots of flowers about, even this early in the year."

Drew could picture the quaint little cottage outside of Twickenham. It had all the sound of a rented love nest. Close enough to London for convenience, yet secluded enough for privacy. Stoddard would pay dearly, he vowed.

"Aside from Lord Stoddard and the two ruffians, was there anyone else around?"

"None that I could see. His lordship flung out of the carriage and shoved open the door of the cottage as if he were really in a temper. Blaine waited for the uglies to come around and then, believe it or not, they helped her down like she was their own mother."

Drew snorted at the mental picture. He had seen Blaine at her haughtiest, playing the part of Lady Yates. Thank God, her disguise was still intact. "Now, before we get to the village, suppose you tell me how you made your return in such timely fashion."

Val wiped his mouth carefully with his napkin, shooting a mischievous glance at the primly observant Tate. The little dresser nodded her head gravely but there was an answering smile in her eyes.

"Well, after I left the cottage, I marked the trees as I told you and just kept walking until I arrived in the village. I wasn't quite sure what to do then. I wanted to ask for help but I wasn't overly confident that a magistrate would be moved to action on my word alone. So after a bit, I decided the only thing to do was come back to town for help."

Drew could imagine the hopelessness that must have threatened to engulf the boy. He wondered exactly what Val had planned, since there was really only Fleur and Blaine's servants for the boy to apply to for help. Though the danger to Blaine would be uppermost in his mind, there also must have been a fierce need to protect his family from scandal. A heavy responsibility for a twelve-year-old.

"It was the correct decision, Val," Drew said. "We were at a stalemate until you arrived.

Incidentally, Sarge said to tell you he was quite impressed with your steed."

"Bloody fat cow, is more like." Drew laughed at the boy's obvious disgust. "It was all I could find, sir. It's a sad state of affairs when adults slum-guzzle a child."

"A sorry state indeed," Drew agreed, trying desperately to keep his expression serious.

"I went to the livery first and spun them a tale about Gypsies stealing me away. Jamie thought of that bouncer. Said country folk believe Gypsies kidnap children to sell into slavery. Unfortunately, they weren't having any." It was apparent Val was downcast at the suspicious nature of the citizens of Twickenham. "After wandering around, I finally bought a horse. The price the farmer quoted was much too dear so I jawed him down a bit. Then the bloody sod took all of my coin and gave me this great, ugly bag of bones that goes by the unlikely name of Chastity."

Drew choked on his wine at the outraged tones. For several minutes laughter filled the carriage, with even the taciturn dresser joining in. The amusement did a great deal to ease the tension that had been building as they approached their destination.

While Tate put away the remains of the meal, Drew and Val talked. After Drew had given him the latest news, he ordered the

327

exhausted boy to stretch out for a rest. He stared out at the darkened night, his eyes unfocused as he considered his plans. He was exhilarated by the thought of imminent action, although he was still filled with a sense of urgency.

He knew what lengths Blaine had gone to in order to protect her family. Knowing her as well as he did, he knew she would risk much to keep the secret of the notorious La Solitaire. Escaping Stoddard would offer no solution to her troubles. Only if she could strike a bargain with the man could she ensure his silence. For Val and Fleur she might be willing to risk all, even though the sacrifice would ultimately destroy her.

fifteen

"Would you like some more tea, mum?" Romulus held the teapot aloft.

If Blaine hadn't been so apprehensive over the coming of night, she would have laughed at the picture of the enormous ruffian holding the delicately painted teapot. The two brutes, incongruously named Romulus and Remus, might have been Stoddard's hirelings but they had been offended by his treatment of a little old lady. Touched in some deep corner of their black hearts, they had become Blaine's champions. Unfortunately, they drew the line at setting her free.

"Perhaps later, Romulus. It was very good tea," she said, careful not to overdo the quaver in her voice as he returned to the kitchen.

Romulus and Remus were twins who had been born in the back of a tavern and would most probably end their days at the end of a rope. She could tell them apart by the scars on their faces, blunt reminders of the violent lives they led. Romulus, the younger by ten minutes, bore a long slash from the tip of one eyebrow to the edge of his jawline. He had told Blaine quite proudly that the blade of the knife had broken clean off when it hit the jawbone. Romulus was her favorite, for he had a cheerful verbosity not exhibited by his more taciturn brother.

Remus, whose face was marked by myriad scars and abrasions, generally spoke in a single word or a grunt that one could interpret as one pleased. He had not been as forthcoming as his brother, but Romulus had explained that his reticence was due solely to shyness and not to dislike.

Blaine leaned her head back against the cushions of the chair as she debated how soon Stoddard would return. She had been lucky so far with her jailers and, despite her apprehension, she could view their arrival at the cottage earlier with some amusement.

Stoddard had waited until the men had brought her into the parlor of the cottage before he had ordered them to tie her. Blaine was terrified that, despite her costume, her identity would be discovered if the men handled her. She clutched her heart and staggered to the nearest chair, thankfully one well cushioned, where she gave her finest performance as a shocked and feeble old lady. Apparently her pitiable cries were sufficiently moving, because the two men refused to tie her up.

For a heart-stopping moment, Blaine thought Stoddard would tie her himself. She held motionless as he stood over her. His face was red with anger, and his hands were clenched at his sides. She had little need to pretend to have difficulty catching her breath, since it wheezed and rattled in her throat from fear. She must have looked pathetic enough to convince him she was harmless, for, with an oath, he stormed across the room and slammed out the door of the cottage.

She pretended to a slow recovery, giving herself time to examine the room. It was decorated in a very feminine style, slightly overdone, and had the definite look of a cottage used only infrequently. She assumed Stoddard either rented or owned the little love nest.

Her eyes roamed the room, but other than a very large Oriental vase, which she marked for possible use, it yielded up nothing by way of a weapon. Even the hearth was disappointingly barren of either a poker or shovel. It did, however, give her an idea. Behind her veil, her eyes narrowed as she surveyed the giants doing their best to press themselves into the woodwork.

"Boys," she called in her frailest voice. "Would it be possible to have a bit of a fire? My bones are quite chilled and I fear an inflammation of the lungs might set in."

She was decidedly cheered when, after a whispered conference, the two men agreed. She watched as they traveled back and forth from the kitchen, brought bundles of sticks, and then laid the fire. Although she was glad of the heat, they had cleaned up meticulously and she was no closer to the possession of a weapon than she had been before.

After a trip to the necessary, with her embarrassed guard of honor shuffling nearby, Romulus suggested tea and she accepted eagerly. They presented the tea in a none-too-clean mug, cautioned her to behave herself, and then retired to the kitchen. Keeping one eye on the kitchen and the other on the door Stoddard had used, she loosened her veil and drank down the reviving brew while warming her hands on the mug. She refastened her veil and smoothed out her skirts, feeling fortified for the coming events.

Stoddard did not return and Blaine used the opportunity to make friends with Romulus and Remus. After minimal success in discovering where she was, she did learn that the men did not work for "his bleedin' lordship" but had been hired for the day. Stoddard had told them he was planning to elope and, when they discovered he was actually kidnapping an old lady for blackmail, they were offended, clearly disgruntled at such an affront to their personal code of honor and truth. It was due to their dudgeon that they felt justified in entertaining her with the stories of their lives.

The kitchen door squeaked, bringing Blaine out of the contemplation of her disastrous day. Romulus entered with a lamp, followed by Remus carrying a small bundle of wood. She noted the shadowy corners of the room with a sinking feeling. It would be full dark soon and she knew Stoddard would return.

"Would you like me to build up the fire, mum?" Romulus asked as he placed the lamp on the table beside her chair. "My brother thought as how you might take a chill."

"You are both very thoughtful boys," she said. "I didn't mention it at the time but I am sure it was a sad day when your mother died."

Remus grunted as he handed his brother a bundle of wood.

"That it was." Romulus shook his unkempt head and hunkered down on the hearth. "We was glad to be with her though. They had sprung us from Newgate just two days 'fore she was took. It was the gin what got her. Just you have a care, mum, and stay away from Blue Ruin."

"I shall heed your words, young man."

"Ma were only a mug short o' the tavern record, when her eyes rolled back in her head and she fell over dead."

Remus grunted twice to indicate he was moved by the memory.

A silence fell over the room in respect for the much-lamented woman. Blaine closed her eyes and gingerly rested her head against the back of the chair, being careful not to disarrange her hat. She had tried not to think of the possible consequences should Romulus and Remus discover that she was not a little old lady. Their gentle treatment thus far did not fool her. She had heard enough to know that they were cruel and dangerous men. If they discovered she had tricked them into believing she was old and frail, they would be ruthless in their revenge.

The outside door slammed against the wall and Talbott Stoddard stormed into the room. Blaine sat up straight, placing her cane directly in front of her feet. Her pulse pounded in her throat and she swallowed convulsively as the blond nobleman glared at her.

"Get out, you two," he said with a snarl.

Romulus and Remus hesitated, then shrugged in resignation as they went out to the kitchen. Stoddard kicked the door shut and walked across the room. He threw himself in a chair across from the prim figure in black and eyed the fire with disfavor.

"All the comforts of home and hearth, eh?"

"Not quite, Lord Stoddard," she said.

"Have you come to your senses? Will you take me back to Portman Square?"

"Not, Lady Yates, until I have the information I want!"

"Surely, you do not think I will just hand my niece over to you?"

"That is exactly what I think. I have been walking around trying to figure just exactly what might induce you to listen to reason. I believe that I have discovered the answer."

Blaine tensed at the tone of his voice. There was a gloating quality that warned her that the man was done playing games. Through the veiling, she observed the casualness of his pose, which gave the same intimations of danger as a snake sunning on a rock. He was a handsome man, almost beautiful, with his golden curls and fine-featured face. She contrasted him to Drew, whose face was all angles and planes. There was little comparison.

Stoddard lacked the laugh lines in the corners of his eyes and the hint of a smile that always lurked on the edge of Drew's mouth. He was just as tall and lean but his body lacked the masculinity that radiated from Drew's body. But most of all, he did not possess the qualities that Blaine loved in Drew. Stoddard had neither heart nor soul.

"I grow weary of threats from a person of such insignificance and low morals." Her scornful voice was filled with contempt. She was pleased by the flush of color that rose to his face but she knew her victory would be short-lived.

"It is not a threat, old lady! It is a promise!" he shouted.

Stoddard slammed his fist on the arm of his chair, pleased when the woman flinched in fear. He had had enough of her viperous tongue. He had no need to lose his temper. Soon, he would have her begging him to take La Solitaire off her hands.

"Now, madam, this is my proposition." Leaning back in his chair, he crossed his legs and smoothed the material with his long fingers. "I am quite willing to take you back to Portman Square — or anywhere else, for that matter. I am convinced you will be more than willing to make me known to Blaine, once you have the opportunity to consider the alternatives."

"The alternatives?"

"Your niece Fleur is an enchanting child. If I cannot have La Solitaire then I will have to be content with second best. I believe I will take great pleasure in bedding the virginal Fleur."

"You devil!" Blaine snapped.

Tears of fright started in her eyes as she realized at what risk she had placed her sister.

Even knowing the foulness of Talbott Stoddard, she was still appalled at the depths to which he would sink.

A smile of derision crossed Stoddard's face. In the dim light he was able to see the slumped shoulders of the figure in black. He had won! "Well, madam?" he prodded.

Blaine knew when she was beaten. If she had only herself to consider, she would have fought to the death. She knew in her heart that she would never survive if anything happened to Fleur. The thought of the price she would pay meant little as compared to her sister's safety. The girl must be spared. Once her decision was made, Blaine pulled herself up in the chair. She might have lost the war but they still had to settle the terms of surrender.

"The game is yours, Lord Stoddard."

In the silence that followed her capitulation, the hinges of the door squeaked loudly as the outside door swung open. At the noise, Stoddard turned his head sharply and then leapt to his feet. For Blaine, no guardian angel or cherubic messenger could look as much like a vision of heaven as the figure in the doorway.

"Although I am reluctant to contradict a lady," Drew said, bowing gallantly, "I believe the game is mine."

"Damn your eyes, Farrington!"

"Don't make a move, Stoddard. I would take great pleasure in shooting you."

Seeing Drew's pistol, Stoddard froze but his eyes flashed toward the back of the house and Blaine gasped. She was just about to shout a warning when the kitchen door burst open and the giants emerged. The gun in Drew's hand seemed faint protection from the combined forces of Romulus and Remus.

Drew moved away from the doorway, and Sarge, his leathery face seamed with fury, took his place. His hamlike hands were bunched into fists, prepared for the coming battle. The odds were considerably better, Blaine thought in satisfaction. Grinning, she lifted her cane. Now it was three against three.

"Are you well, Blaine? Or should I say, Miss Mason?" Drew asked.

"Just fine, now that you're here, Lord Farrington. I approve of a man who will arrive in the wings in time for his cue."

Stoddard swung around to her, staring in disbelief at the figure in black. Even without Drew's words, he would have recognized the ringing tones of her voice. It was a voice he had listened to, night after night, in a darkened theater. A voice that had haunted his dreams and filled him with an obsession to possess her.

"La Solitaire," he whispered.

"Your servant, milord." Despite her bulky skirts, Blaine dropped into a graceful curtsy.

The thought that he had her in his hands all along sent a shaft of rage through Stoddard's body. He grimaced in fury and the muscles in his neck stood out in cords. "Take them, you idiots!" he shouted to the motionless ruffians.

With a guttural snarl, Romulus and Remus charged. Drew discharged his gun over the heads of the mountains of flesh roaring across the room but neither man checked. Romulus butted Sarge in the stomach with his head, slamming him against the wall with a bone-crushing crash. Remus was not as lucky. As the giant rushed him, Drew sidestepped the assault and hit him on the back of the head with the gun he still held in his hand.

Sparing a quick glance for Sarge, who was holding his own, Drew shoved the gun in his pocket, stepped over the recumbent Remus, and advanced on Stoddard.

As the two men squared off, Blaine hiked up her skirts and ran across the floor to assist the beleaguered Sarge. Owing to the fact that Romulus was considerably younger, the old soldier was having a difficult time of it. She skidded to a stop beside Remus, who was beginning to come around. He was on his hands and knees, shaking his head like a dog with fleas. Gripping her walking stick like a club, she brought it down, wincing at the dull thud as it crashed into the back of his head. The cane shattered and Remus dropped to the floor once again.

She heard a gasp and swung to face Romulus. The giant had Sarge in a neck lock but his eyes were on her. She grinned at the offended expression on his face as he surveyed the damage she had done to his brother. Clearly she had sunk in his estimation of the behavior proper for little old ladies. Perhaps it was the loss of attention, for in the next second, Sarge had extricated himself and elbowed Romulus in the stomach. As the man doubled over, Sarge clenched his hamlike hands together and slammed them down on his back. Romulus dropped as if he were poleaxed.

Blaine's hat had tilted to the side and the veiling inhibited her vision so she untied the band at her throat and threw the hat into the nearest corner. Now that Romulus and Remus had been taken care of, she could turn her attention to the other combatants. She snatched up the Oriental vase she had noted earlier, gripping it tightly with her mittened hands, and waited for the proper moment to hurl it into the melee.

Up until then, she had been enjoying the fight. She had been filled with excitement to be in the thick of action. Now, as she watched Drew and Stoddard, she was sickened and the vase slipped from her nerveless fingers to crash on the floor. Sarge moved to stand beside her. He put his arm around her but she could take little comfort from it.

While she had been fighting, she had thought little of injury. The sight of the blood on the face of the man she loved was agonizing and at every blow he took, she felt pain. She clutched at Sarge's sleeve, her nails biting through the woolen material. Even the fact that Drew was winning made no difference.

Drew punched Stoddard in the stomach and felt a sweet thrill at the shudder of the man's body. He ignored his own bruises, bent on doing as much damage as he could. A trickle of blood rolled into the corner of his eye and he wiped it away with his sleeve. Stoddard was tiring but Drew hoped he wouldn't surrender yet. He had a driving need to punish him and took satisfaction with every blow. A feint to his right caught him on the shoulder but he dodged away. As Stoddard fought to keep his balance, Drew brought his arm back and slammed his fist into his jaw. Stoddard stiffened and then slowly crumpled to the floor.

Lip curled in disgust, Drew turned his back on the unconscious figure, searching the room for Blaine. The sight of her worried face above the well-padded costume of Lady Yates gave Drew a moment of amusement. He blinked at the Psyche knot of silvery-blond hair that shimmered in the lamplight, a perfect complement to her lovely features. He much preferred it to the brown curls of the woman at the Rose and Trellis and hoped that this was her natural color.

Despite her ridiculous costume, she was beautiful. There was a look in her golden eyes that weakened his knees more surely than any of his injuries. Her lips were parted, red and swollen as if she had been biting them. Even in his battered condition, he could feel his body's response to her at the thought of kissing her rosy mouth. He started toward her but the sudden movement sent a searing pain through his ribs. He stopped in his tracks, narrowing his eyes until the agony passed.

Blaine caught her breath as the expression on Drew's face changed from joy to anger. She moved away from Sarge, crossing her arms over her padded chest as if she could warm the sudden chill of her body. Drew had wanted to come to her; she had seen that but she also had seen the moment he changed his mind. She should have expected such a reaction. She had kept her identity from him, knowing how he would feel about her, once he discovered her background.

In the world into which Blaine was born, an actress was no better than a courtesan. Perhaps she had not known that when she first trod the boards but eventually she had observed the way the gentlemen of the ton treated women of the theater world. Actresses were playthings, unacceptable in polite society and given little respect. Now, in Drew's eyes, she was no longer La Solitaire, an actress he desired. She was, instead, Blaine Margaret Meriweather, a respectable woman who had debased herself by going on the stage. Even the thought that he had wanted to come to her was poor consolation for the pain cutting through her. Even in the crowded room, she felt terribly alone.

"What a dustup!" Val shouted as he catapulted into the room, followed by Tate, who stared around the room in disgust.

"Val! Tate!" Blaine cried. "What on earth are you doing here?"

The boy's face lighted up at the sight of her and he ran across the room to hurl himself into her arms. She took comfort from his presence and tried to pull her mind from her personal agony to deal with her brother. She had taken in his dirt-streaked appearance, and she cast a questioning glance over his head at her dresser.

"Lord Farrington brought us," Tate said. Assured that Blaine was unharmed, she disappeared into the kitchen.

"Your brother is the hero of this piece, madam," he said. "He followed you here and then returned to London for help."

"What an amazing lad you are, Val," she said. She tipped his head back and smiled at the grubby face turned up to her.

"Jamie helped too."

"And after all of the terrible things I've said about the boy." Blaine laughed at the affronted expression on her brother's face. "Obviously I owe him an immediate apology. I shall never say another word against him."

"Even if he swaps me for his snake?" Val asked, peeping up at her through his mop of hair.

"Wretched child!"

At a groan from one of the bodies littering the floor, the attention of the party was returned to the devastation of the room. There was very little that had survived the fray. Chairs and tables were splintered, and what few knickknacks there were lay shattered on the floor. The only item standing was the table that held the lamp.

"Oh, I wish Jamie were here." Val sighed, his voice heavy with regret. Then his face brightened as he beamed up at Drew. "You certainly gave him a leveler, Lord Farrington. I saw it all through the window and it was the finest fight I ever saw. 'Course, it was also the only one I've seen," he admitted, wanting to be totally honest with his hero.

"I thought I told you to remain with Tate," Drew said.

"Well, I did at first, but then I considered the fact you had only taken one pistol and I thought you might need the other."

Val reached in his pocket and pulled out the pistol and Drew was torn between wanting to beat the child and wanting to thank him. He gingerly removed the loaded gun from the boy's grimy hand, unloaded it, and then threw it to Sarge. The big man grinned as he slipped it into his pocket.

"You definitely need a firm hand, brat," Drew snapped, but he clapped the boy on the shoulder to remove the sting from his words. Then looking around the room, he stroked his chin in thought. "I do not quite know what to do for the best."

"You can't turn them over to the magistrate," Blaine blurted out. As all eyes shifted to her face, she blushed. "In the first place, Romulus and Remus were good to me."

"I don't believe it," Drew said in amazement.

"Well, it's true," she said defensively. "They

made me tea and lit the fire and — "

"Oh, I believe that part," Drew said, interrupting. "Is that really their names?"

Blaine chuckled at the skepticism in his voice. "I swear to you. The one over there is Romulus and the other one is Remus. They're twins. I believe the names were courtesy of a mother with a penchant for Roman mythology and Blue Ruin."

"Devil, you say!" Drew laughed aloud as his eyes swung back and forth between the abominable giants. "Surely, madam, you're not pleading for clemency for these ruffians?"

"Yes, I am!" She stamped her foot impatiently. "I would have been in worse case had they not taken my part. When they are not trying to kill anyone, they are both rather sweet. They've had a very hard life and I am quite sure they will receive no pay for their work today. Besides, their mother has just died and I hate to make things any more difficult by turning them over to the constabulary."

By the end of this breathless defense, Drew's eyes had taken on a glazed look. Blaine ignored him totally and waved Val off to the kitchen in search of Tate. She fixed Sarge with a jaundiced eye and he shrugged in resignation.

"All right, Miss Blaine. There's a cart out back. I'll lug 'em out and put 'em in it. The nag will find her way home. More, I'm not prepared to do."

"Thank you, Sarge. And thank you for your aid in subduing the men. You acquitted yourself well."

"I would say, miss, you did a fair bit. Sorry about your cane," he said, chuckling as he set to work. He reached down with his enormous hands and grasped Romulus by the neck of his coat, dragged him across the floor and out the door.

"What about him?" Drew said, nodding at Stoddard, who was still unconscious.

"I don't know." Blaine stared bleakly at the crumpled figure on the floor. After his beating, Lord Stoddard would be twice as eager for revenge. He would take great delight in regaling the ton with the news of La Solitaire and the children would have to live with the dishonor of their name. She had become an actress to protect Val and Fleur from financial ruin, but by her actions, she had destroyed them. Suddenly she was overwhelmed with a wave of exhaustion. She swayed and Drew grasped her shoulders to steady her.

"Are you all right, madam?"

"Don't call me that," she snapped.

"I am uncertain of exactly which of your names to choose. Lady Yates? Blaine Margaret Meriweather? Maggie Mason? La Solitaire?"

"Hush! Val doesn't know." She threw an agonized glance at the door to the kitchen. Then she turned back and caught sight of Stoddard and her shoulders sagged in defeat. "I wanted to keep this from him but there is no way now to keep Lord Stoddard from making it known."

"Would you really have become his mistress?" Drew asked. His voice sounded politely curious but his green eyes were angry.

"Yes." Blaine held his gaze, refusing to feel ashamed.

"I wonder with what he threatened you? Scandal? Bodily injury? I think not. You never would have weakened under such a threat. Dear God, it was Fleur." In his fury, he shook her. "It was Fleur, wasn't it?"

"Yes," she whispered.

Blaine staggered when he released her and he stormed across the room. He grabbed Stoddard by his bloody cravat, dragging him to his feet. He shook him like a terrier with a rat. Stoddard's head bobbed like a rag doll's but he finally came to his senses. His eyes were glazed, staring groggily around the room, and Drew waited until Stoddard's eyes focused before he spoke.

"Listen well, you scum," he said in a voice far more chilling for its softness. "If you ever say one word about La Solitaire, Lady Yates, or any of the Meriweathers, you will rue the day you were born. If one hint, one rumor, comes to my ears, I will strip you of every penny you possess and make your name anathema in London. Then, Lord Stoddard, I will kill you."

Without another word, Drew pushed him toward the door. He shoved Stoddard outside and followed him, leaving Blaine alone in the empty room. She sniffed back a tear as she surveyed the wreckage of the room. She wondered how soon they could leave for she was weary to death of this pitiful place. After they returned to London, she, Val, and Fleur would pack up and return to Wiltshire. Perhaps there she could find some measure of peace, before she left them forever.

Sarge stamped into the room, giving her a sour smile before he reached down for Remus. Like his brother, the enormous giant was dragged across the floor and out the door.

"Tate made us all tea," Val chirped as he wobbled through the door with a tray of mugs.

Blaine looked around the scene of devastation, then raced across to the table and removed the lamp. "Set it here," she said as she placed the lamp on the mantel.

Manfully navigating through the piles of debris, Val plunked the tray down with a grin of triumph. Blaine removed her mittens and shoved them into the pocket of her skirt. Picking up a mug, she sipped slowly and reveled in the warmth that radiated through her body. She had her back to the door but she was aware of Drew's presence the moment he entered the room. She stiffened as he crossed the floor to join them but she could not resist one quick look to assure herself he had taken no terrible injury.

He had taken time to wash the worst of his injuries. There was a cut on his eyebrow but it was no longer bleeding. His cheek was red and swollen beneath one eye. Aside from a lump on his forehead, near his temple, he was blessedly free of marks. He moved stiffly as he picked up a mug and went to lean against the mantel. She caught her breath at sight of the cut and swollen knuckles of his hand as he raised the tea to his lips. She would have cried out, if Val hadn't spoken.

"Did Lord Farrington tell you about Fleur?"

"If you recall, halfling, I have been rather too occupied to make polite conversation," Drew said.

"Right, sir," Val said, then turned to his sister, smiling broadly. "Robbie came up to scratch!"

"That's a perfectly dreadful expression." It took her a moment to take in the significance of his words but when she did, she smiled warmly. "What incredibly splendid news. What did Fleur say?" she asked Drew.

"I do believe, madam, that your sister will be an extremely damp bride. After a substantial bout of tears, she went on a bit about what an idiot she had been not to have realized that she was in love with Robbie. It would seem that the visit to London was instructive. The frivolous dandy set did not come off well when compared to the solid worth of the landed gentry. She said, and I quote, 'Robbie is the kindest, sweetest, and best of friends.' Then she burst into tears. How can she possibly cry so much and still look so lovely?"

He looked totally bemused and, knowing their sister well, Val and Blaine laughed.

"Through it all, Robbie stared at her with a glazed look of adoration that will hopefully remain in place until after the honeymoon. They have decided to be married in Wiltshire and the date for the glorious event is set for next month after the banns have been called."

When he finished, there was silence as the threesome sipped their tea and considered the happy couple.

"How's your eye, sir?" Val asked over the rim of his mug.

Drew reached up to touch the puffiness under his eye. "A bit sore but otherwise fine."

"It's going to be very colorful. A regular painted peeper," Val said with relish.

"Go away, brat. I want to talk to your sister." Seeing the boy's speculative glance, Drew winked. "Sarge is out in the kitchen with Tate. Tell them to be ready to leave shortly."

"Aye, sir," Val said as he carried his cup toward the door.

"And don't come back until I call."

"Spot on!"

Blaine watched the disappearing figure with a feeling of abandonment. She curled her fingers around her mug and stared into the murky liquid. She was worn-out, both physically and mentally. She did not want to be alone with Drew, now that she knew how he felt. The thought that he might discover she was in love with him was too painful to contemplate. She dropped her head to avoid his eyes, swallowing back tears of self-pity. When Drew removed the mug from her hands, she stepped back in apprehension.

Drew observed the droop of Blaine's shoulders and wanted to rush to her and take her in his arms. But he was puzzled by her behavior. After the fight with Stoddard, he had been convinced that she returned his love. Could he have misunderstood the flash of emotion in her gold-hazel eyes? Was it possible that she did not share his feelings and would reject his suit? He stared at her in bewilderment.

"Can you not look at me?"

"No," she said lifelessly.

"Why not?"

"I cannot bear to see the contempt in your eyes."

Suddenly everything was clear and Drew was washed by a wave of relief that erased all his doubts. He grasped Blaine's shoulders and shook her until her head came up and she glared at him, her eyes flashing with their usual fire.

"You bird-wit!" he shouted. "Can you know me so little that you would think that I could ever look at you with contempt? I love you, you impossible woman! Do you hear me?"

"You love me?"

There was such a look of wonder on Blaine's face that a lump rose in Drew's throat. Her gold-hazel eyes blazed like twin suns and a flush of pink tinted her cheeks like the petals of a rose.

"First I desired you," he said. "I sought La Solitaire with the knowledge that together we would know passion unrestrained. Then I found a friend in Lady Yates. I sought her out with the awareness that we enjoyed each other's company. In the woman at the inn I found love, a combination of friendship and passion that will never grow tiresome or boring. I love you," Drew repeated simply, and there could be little doubt of his feelings by the worshipful quality of his voice.

Blaine stared up at his dear face. Her eyes locked with his green gaze and together they searched each other's hearts. Pain, loneliness, anger, and fear were shared and thus lost their ability to wound. Joy and happiness seeped into the dark places and erased the shadows of despair. Slowly, Blaine slid her arms around his neck, raising her face to accept the kiss that would bind them for all eternity.

Drew kissed her tenderly. His lips were soft, moving on her mouth with the subtle whisper of silk. His arms folded her against his chest where she could feel the beat of his heart echoing her own. She felt as if she had come home and she burrowed against him, seeking the security of dreams she had never believed would come true. When he released her, she was content for the moment. They would have years to taste the further joys that had been promised in his kiss.

"Will you accept my offer, Blaine Margaret Meriweather?"

"Are you offering me marriage, Lord Farrington?"

Drew caught his breath, hurt that she would

not trust him enough to know he could never offer her less. Brows bunched over narrowed eyes, he glared down at her, snorting as he caught the light of mischief in her golden eyes.

"Baggage!" he roared. He grabbed her around the waist and pulled her against him. At the feel of her body, he pushed her away. "What in God's name have you got in there?" he asked, poking at her padded bosom.

"Stop that!" she said, slapping his hand away. "In order to prevent any further attempts to satisfy your curiosity, I will tell you. For your information, sir, it is bed pillows."

"Surely, my dear, we can find a better use for them."

Drew kissed her as a furious blush suffused her cheeks. This time he was not gentle. His mouth took possession of hers with a passion that was all-consuming. She was breathless when he released her, holding him at bay with a hand on his chest.

"Obviously, Lord Farrington," she said, her voice disdainful, "I will have to marry you, now that you have taken such advantage of me." She spoiled the effect by giggling and there was such a magical quality to her laughter that Drew was totally entranced.

"If you look at me that way, my darling girl, we shall never leave this dreadful place," he growled. Then surveying the wreckage of room, he said, "Remember for next time, sweetheart, that we must leave at least one chair standing. I am something of an expert in the field of lovemaking but this devastation may be beyond even my much-vaunted skills."

"Drew!" Blaine quickly raised her hands to her reddening cheeks.

"Come along, girl," he said, tugging her across the room. "Get your hat. We shall round up our merry little band of conspirators for the denouement of our play of the infamous kidnapping of Lady Yates. I would advise you to employ all your acting skills for the benefit of the servants at Portman Square for, I swear to God, Blaine, it shall be your final performance."

"Won't Lady Yates have to appear at Fleur and Robbie's wedding?"

"I absolutely forbid it," he said. Now was definitely the time for firmness.

"But I had such a perfect dress picked out. It was a dark blue brocade with — "

Lord Andrew Farrington ended the argument by the simple expedient of kissing all of the women he loved. The talented and desirable La Solitaire, the sharp-tongued and companionable Lady Yates, and the adorable and exasperating Blaine Margaret Meriweather. And finally, for all time, his beloved Lady Farrington.

THORNDIKE PRESS hopes you have enjoyed this Large Print book. All our Large Print titles are designed for easy reading, and all our books are made to last. Other Thorndike Large Print books are available at your library, through selected bookstores, or directly from the publisher. For more information about current and upcoming titles, please call or mail your name and address to:

THORNDIKE PRESS
PO Box 159
Thorndike, Maine 04986
800/223-6121
207/948-2962